MW01134733

Savage Kind of Love

Prairie Devils MC Romance

Nicole Snow

Description

SAVAGE LOVE: FIERCE, SEDUCTIVE, AND LIMITLESS...

Shelly "Saffron" Reagan's life is in shambles, and it's about to get worse. Keeping up a broken home and a brother in the vicious Grizzlies MC is more than any woman can handle. Remembering the tough talking biker who nursed her after a savage attack is all she has, a bad boy who's impossibly out of reach.

Or so it seems.

When Saffron gets caught in biker's crossfire, there's only one man to lead her out. One man to protect her, one man to lay his claim, one man to make her burn forever with his kiss...

Michael "Blaze" Sturm swears he won't get tied down by any woman. Easier said than done when the babe with the body he can't forget keeps storming back into his life. When he answers her desperate call one dark morning, nothing will ever be the same.

As President of the new Prairie Devils Montana charter, Blaze always gets his way. Now, his sights are set on beautiful Saffron, and he won't stop until she's wearing his brand and surrendering her lips.

Will Saffron find outlaw love in his fire – or will Blaze's harsh world turn her heart to ashes?

Note: this is a dark and gritty MC romance with language, violence, and love scenes as hard and raw as they come. Outlaw love strikes without mercy!

· The Prairie Devils MC books are stand alone novels featuring unique lovers and happy endings. No cliffhangers allowed! This is Saffron and Blaze's story.

I: Three Nights (Saffron)

They say it only takes one night to change a woman's life. For me, it was three, each more savage than the last.

Deep in the darkness, forced to wrestle with dreams and desires and nightmares, a girl finds out what's really important really damned fast. And when it's all over, there's no more doubt.

Scars don't lie, and neither do hearts.

Three sunrises later, I knew I'd never know uncertainty again.

Three nights. Three vicious, unforgettable, pitch black collisions with life and death, love and hate. Three nights to mold me into what I was always meant to be.

I still think about the last one the most.

Starting with the way the sick, soulless bastard held the knife to my throat, digging in so deep he drew blood. His words echoed like a lion's growl in my ear. Distant and distorted by fear, but unmistakably dangerous.

"I see you've made your choice, baby doll. If you're not gonna tell us what we need to know about your boyfriend and his Prairie Pussies, then I guess we'll do things the hard way." He paused, his stained teeth shaping a smile. "Lucky for you I like it hard."

"Kill me now. You're a dead man either way," I growled.

The knife relaxed its deadly pressure on my throat. His other hand tangled itself deeper in my hair and jerked, twisting my face to his, just the right position for a grotesque kiss.

I'd bite his lips if I had to. Only one man's skin belonged on mine, and I wouldn't forget it, no matter how hopeless this battle was.

Evil excitement flickered in his dark eyes, mingling with surprise. He stopped just short of planting his kiss and getting my teeth ripping at his lip.

"Kill you? No, dolly, I'm in no rush. Not until I've torn you up and sent you home to Blaze with plenty to remember me by. Gotta fucking burn some sense into you, make you give up what you're holding behind that pretty little face. And then – maybe then – I'll put you and the rest of those Devil cocksuckers out of their misery…"

My mind usually blanks at the sound of my belt coming unbuckled in his dirty fingers. Then everything becomes a mess, a deafening chaos like the world itself ending.

The fire consumes everything. My pants drop, and he lowers his cigar, letting it linger so close to my skin I can feel the heat.

"What the fuck is this?" He rubs tenderly near my hip, tracing my tattoo. "My, my. Pretty flowers for a pretty lady. It's nice to have a target. Hold still, doll. Those flowers can't do much screaming, but you sure as hell can…"

Did I really live through it?

Hell yes. This night, and so many more.

Nobody ever said becoming an old lady to the biggest badass in Montana was easy…

Never in a million years did I expect to end up on the stage, shaking my twenty-four year old bare ass for grubby dollars.

At home in Missoula, I was Shelly Reagan, a college dropout who couldn't even get a damned job stocking shelves. Here in Python, I was Saffron, the most popular dirty dancer since June did her last act on the stage before taking on the manager's role.

Rolling my hips and wearing nothing but a fuckable smile paid the bills a lot better than shuffling around a grocery store. It wouldn't have been so bad, except for the fact that everybody I'd grown up with knew who I was and what I did.

Everybody except Mom, of course, and she was my only friend left since the others took flight. Same as it had been since my older brother Jordan went West after our family's last explosive fight.

A working class girl does desperate things in a recession with a disabled mother and a big brother missing in action. The dollars were all that mattered.

Dollars and drinks, maybe. At least Pink Unlimited's drinks were free to dancers, and the managers were nice.

My supervisor June was a stone cold bitch on the outside, but deep underneath, I could tell she cared. I stayed on her good side by doing my job and making money for the Prairie Devils' new strip joint.

I think she respected me for not whining and creating worthless drama like the other girls.

It was a good gig, until the night when I ran into a giant in leather out back.

I was trying to breathe in the fresh mountain air when the bike came roaring in. He rode an older Harley, and it snorted an oily, greasy stink into the narrow parking strip, mucking up my lungs.

So much for break time! I thought unhappily.

I tried to ignore him, but I couldn't when I saw him coming right for me. June always said to leave the guys sporting patches alone. I knew enough about MCs not to question her advice. Didn't have any trouble drawing the line between their club business and ours, just like the boss said.

"You work here?" he asked, eyeing me up and down.

Men ogling me wasn't anything new. Still, I wished I'd at least thrown on my pants before going out here instead of the flimsy robe we wore to cover up when we weren't dancing.

"Nope. I just like to stand out here half-naked."

I should've known. Sass never got me anywhere, and it wouldn't tonight.

The man pushed closer, corralling me against the wall with his gut. His huge leathery hands slapped the brick, poised on both sides of my head.

Jesus, can't you take a joke?

"Let's try this again, bitch. You give me a serious answer this time. This is strike two, and I don't do three."

He smelled drunk. This wasn't at all how the Prairie Devils who owned this place were supposed to be. Then I noticed his patches for the first time.

They're different. Is this a support club?

"Yeah, I'm on my break. How can I help you, sir?"

Stuffing the sarcasm wasn't easy. Unfortunately, not knowing who this stranger was or what he wanted didn't leave me much choice.

"Need to speak to your boss. Got some cash to pick up, and it better be ready. Take me backstage so I can get the hell out of this dump." He looked down and his eyes feasted on my cleavage while I wondered how to answer. "Fucking Devils. Fucking whore."

My eyes narrowed. I ignored the leering and studied him instead. I'd seen the Prairie Devils guys a few times, and their patches weren't like this. They definitely didn't have a strip going up the side of their jackets that said GRIZZLIES MC.

Uh-oh.

How could I be so damned dense to miss it? The Grizzlies had terrorized towns in the Flathead area for at least a generation.

The reeking alcohol rolling off him suddenly smelled like trouble. So did the greasy bandage tied tight across his head.

He pushed past me and grabbed for the back door. I caught up, gently tugging on his sleeve. He swore when the lock caught.

"Open this fucking thing. Right now!"

"You can't go in there! If you have a message, I'll pass it along. Manager's instructions. I'm sorry, we've all got our rules and it's what I've been told to –"

He spun, a nasty twitch in his lips pulling at his unkempt beard. His fist was like taking a brick to the face. Everything turned to giant red stars, exploding in a fiery ring around my socket, anchoring around my poor eyeball. I fell.

It took me several seconds to realize he'd punched me in the face. Then several more to look up, crying at the pain.

The same fist hovered in mid-air. I rolled into a ball, afraid he was about to beat me to death. He stuck out his finger instead.

"Pass this along: if we don't get our fucking money, the deal's off. You can tell that asshole Maverick and his whore that they've got twenty-four hours to cough up what's owed, or else our whole charter's gonna pay them a visit."

I tried to remember the threat, but the stars blossoming in my skull wouldn't let me. They swelled bigger, brighter, ten times more painful.

The roar of his bike was the last thing I heard before I blacked out.

I woke up chilled to the bone. Must've been out well past break time.

The sharp fire in my head was gone, replaced with a steady throb. I threw my hands against the wall and used it to help myself up, wincing when I touched my eye. New pain howled fiercely through the tender flesh around my socket, so sharp I thought I'd faint again.

"Shit…need help," I muttered to myself.

My brain was barely functioning. My legs switched onto auto-pilot and carried me inside, fumbling for the key card to the back entrance in my pocket. Never knew how I got it in and opened the door half-blind and consumed with agony, but I did.

June flipped out when she saw me. It was the first time I'd truly seen her surprised. Ironic, because that night was the last time I saw her.

I mumbled something about a stranger hitting me in the face, and she helped me over to a vending machine. For the next half hour I had a cold can of root bear on my face and Sandy at my side. Some other badass showed up and June had to step away, leaving me with the other girl to make sure I didn't have a seizure or something.

My boss and the beast in leather approached a little later. Jesus, I was scared, begging him for protection. I couldn't go home tonight. Not after this.

He granted my request to spend the night at the clubhouse. I had to wait it out until I could go home in the evening, just like normal. Mom wouldn't even notice if I was gone longer than usual, though I wasn't sure how I'd hide the bad eye.

Ice cold metal nipped at the pain in my skull. It wasn't a proper ice pack, but it did its job. Numb twilight buzzed around my brain when I felt a heavy hand on my shoulder.

I flew out of my chair and would've hit the floor if Sandy wasn't standing by to catch me.

"Jesus, Mister! Can't you see she's a little jumpy? A hello would be nice!" Sandy sounded pissed, ready to lay into him. But her words melted when she raised her head and took a good look at the man.

"Maverick sent me. See this patch?" He tapped the VP tag on one breast.

I felt Sandy nod.

"Means I'm here to help your friend stay safe from the assholes she really needs to worry about. Same patch that writes your check too," he growled. "Let me see it..."

A powerful hand tugged at my arm, quick but gentle. I struggled to my feet, opening my eyes for the first time in awhile.

I couldn't make out much more than a tall silhouette with broad shoulders, medium length hair, and some serious stubble on his face. He took both my hands, steadying my feet, drawing me into him.

"Fucking shit, my bro never said it was this bad." He shook his head with a snort. "Those fucking bears are gonna pay big time. Can you walk, baby?"

I groaned incoherently. Thought I could, anyway. Maybe I just wanted to be away from bikers so badly right now I convinced myself of the impossible.

"That's okay," he said, softening his voice. "Slow and easy. Come to papa. I'll get you home safe and put some real ice on that shit."

His powerful arms went to the small of my back, and then the whole world turned upside down. My stomach lurched at first, adjusting to the movement. I realized I was floating.

He was carrying me outside, careful to avoid jostling me too much. I let my head slump to his leather clad shoulder, wondering what I'd gotten myself into.

Should've just asked to be taken home. Do I really want to be at their clubhouse if something's going down between two clubs full of men like this?

A resounding NO rattled in my head. Too late, though, because we were already out in the darkness.

Going home wasn't much easier. Mom was sure to lay into me if she saw my eye, and then I'd have to explain how I'd gotten nailed at a strip joint she didn't know I was working at. All while I had the brutal headache throbbing behind my eyes too...

Big mistake. Everything.

Every part of me screamed I'd made a mistake ever taking this job. Beneath the cool and sexy mask I wore to make money, I wasn't cut out for this life, not for the violence and crime, and probably not even for shaking my tail.

God damned bikers! If their drugs and scuffles hadn't trashed this town in the first place, maybe there'd be more real jobs.

Anger pulsed through me. I had a feeling an MC had something to do with Jordan up and disappearing too. He'd talked about going West and joining up to ride since he was eighteen. Three years later, all signs said he'd actually done it.

It was easy to hate the men on bikes who roared around like they owned the fucking planet.

Except for right now, when the tough guy carried me so sweetly to his truck, tucking me into the seat and fastening my belt. What little I could see through my bad eye said he didn't look like the brute who'd thrown his fist at my face.

Didn't smell like the same either. This man had a different scent altogether, rich and earthy and soothingly masculine. He smelled *strong*, without giving off the nauseating musk I often picked up in the strip club after a full night passed with way too much testosterone swirling through the stuffy air.

"What's your name?" I whispered, wondering if he could even hear me as he slid into the driver's seat and started the truck.

"Name's Blaze. I'm VP of the Prairie Devils in this area. No need to bore you with more details than that. You just lay your head back and enjoy the ride, woman. You're safe with me."

Safe?

Nothing about my life felt safe right now. Somehow, the rugged confidence in his voice made me believe it, or maybe it was just the blow to the head.

I dozed on the short drive to their clubhouse on the outskirts of Python. He parked the truck, rounded to my passenger side, and plucked me into his arms again.

God, a lady could get used to big, strong, tattooed arms like his around her. Even if he was the last guy on earth who ought to be dating material.

I giggled softly through the pain as he carried me inside their place.

"What's so damned funny?" he asked, stepping toward the low lit bar.

"Nothing. The brain thinks stupid things when it's been rattled like this. You got any aspirin?"

He grunted in the affirmative and gently laid me down in a booth. I tried not to blush as his hands brushed near my breasts. No way did I want to admit to a silly crush I wasn't even sure I had.

My eye was still so damned swollen I couldn't get a good look at him. Blaze was just a sexy outline moving around his brothers in the darkness. He returned about a minute later packing aspirin, water, and an honest-to-God ice pack.

I wolfed down the pills, taking several handfuls before he snatched the bottle away from me. Bad eye or not, I could make out the sharp question in his eyes: *are you fucking crazy?*

"Sorry," I said sheepishly. "With the kinda jobs I've had, I'm used to this stuff. Haven't worked anywhere off my feet since I was sixteen."

Well, when there was work to be found, I thought with a shudder.

"Easy, baby. Can't let you do anything you'll regret while you aren't thinking straight. My fucking brother'll nail my ass to the wall if anything happens to you."

"Brother? Is he Maverick? The man with June?"

He nodded. "Half-brother by blood, full bro by patch. One notch higher than me as Prez of this charter too. Well, temporary President and temporary charter, really. Him and I are Nomads, same as most of the others in this club. My bro can't wait to hit the fucking road after we're finished here."

His words were soothing. I wasn't sure I fully comprehended what he was saying, but I listened anyway, loving the deep cadence in his voice. I pushed the ice pack deeper to my damaged eye, soothing the rough pain.

I heard a bottle cap hit the table, and realized he was cracking open a drink. His arm brushed mine as he took a long swig and set it down.

Sweet tingly fascination swept up my back, a strange interest in this man my body had no business feeling right now. Anytime blood shifted around in my veins, the throb went straight to my head, harsh as hell.

What are you doing? How much brain damage did that bastard's fist do?

I didn't want any awkward silences. Had to keep talking, and this time I'd try to focus on what he was telling me. Not just his natural cologne and intoxicating warmth only a few inches away.

"You don't sound real enthused. Are you enjoying this town?"

"Been on the road for a long fucking time. The long runs East and West get old, especially after the winter we just had. Cold enough out in Minnesota to make your Harley stick to your balls, when you can even ride at all. The valleys out here are warmer with more good riding weather. Gotta say, that's pretty fucking attractive right now."

I laughed. He was crude and coarse, just like I expected. I never thought about bikers wanting a change. Blaze spoke like a true weary soul, and that surprised me.

"They're pretty decent. Better than the Dakotas, anyway. I've been a Missoula girl all my life and the winters are okay in the valleys. It's the mountains you've got to watch out for."

He shifted, turning to me. "Yeah? What keeps you out here? You've gotta be pretty damned confident or pretty desperate to work at our strip joint."

I flushed, instantly regretting it when the blood touched my cheek around the damaged eye. Hurt like hell. Time to move the ice pack again.

"I'm just there for the money. It's family that keeps me here. Mom got torn up in a bad accident years ago and I'm the only one who can take care of her."

He gave me a respectful nod. I wished there were something else keeping me in town besides Mom and near poverty. Even my brother had flown the coop, and thinking about Jordan again made me sad.

"Hey...you know anything about the Grizzlies? I've seen them around town for years and everybody stays out of their way. Just curious."

"They're sick, greedy fucks." He slammed his fist lightly on the table. Any harder and I would've jumped, losing the ice pack. "Whole reason we're out here. Fuck, I could tell you some stories about what they did to your boss, that pretty little thing Maverick took under his wing..."

I swallowed hard. It seriously scared me to wonder where Jordan was now, or what he might be doing if he'd gotten involved with the wrong club.

"You'll keep your distance from those assholes if you know what's good for you, Saffron," he continued. "Consider yourself lucky for taking a fist to the face and nothing else. Their Missoula charter's done much worse. They've done the kind of shit that makes me want to start breaking skulls."

He flexed his hands on the table and cracked his knuckles for emphasis. It didn't take my full senses to feel the lethal energy coming off him.

Blaze looked me up and down. Then he turned back to his beer and shook his head, a low growl fading in his throat.

"Even what they did to you tonight is too fucking much. Shit's brewing, and it's coming to a head soon. I can feel it in my bones." He fixed his eyes on me, leaning in closer. "When it finally flies, you stay far away from work, this clubhouse, and everywhere else that isn't a Missoula suburb. You understand me, baby?"

Cold fear swept up my back. I nodded.

Nothing else was an option with the way he was looking at me, concern shining in his dark eyes. I only hoped it wouldn't happen the way he said it did and screw me out of more money.

Right now, Mom and I needed every dime. Disability stopped paying into the meds that actually worked for her pain. The stuff she needed cost a pretty penny, even on a stripper's pay, but I was happy to provide it.

I wasn't like Jordan. Loyalty ran in my blood. And looking at Blaze just now, I had a feeling the same spark was in him, badass outlaw biker or not.

"I understand. I really do."

The tense lightning in his eyes faded. His muscles relaxed, and he gulped the last of his beer.

God, he was intense. None of the rough looking posers who watched my act at Pink Unlimited exhausted me like he did.

For the life of me, I was relieved his energy was off me. Needed a break after that. I slumped in the booth. My head lolled to his shoulder, and I closed my eyes.

One hand reached up. He held the ice pack on my head while stroking my hair, a strangely tender gesture for a man with his size and power.

"Rest up. We'll get all this bullshit sorted out. Tonight, you got nothing to worry about. You never will when you're with me."

Sometime later, I jerked awake to explosive cheers. My cheek was chilled to the bone, like a solid icy ring around my head.

My vision was just slightly better. Maverick and June were back, and the big President had just finished shouting something about making June his 'old lady.'

Blaze gently nudged me aside, laying my head against the cushioned seat, and then made his way over. I watched the two men embrace in a big, manly bear hug as Blaze congratulated his brother.

Side by side, the resemblance was obvious. Blaze looked damned hot, and so did Maverick. No surprise that even a messed up girl like June fell for one of them.

Just glad she isn't after Blaze, I thought with a smile. Then I instantly pushed the crazy thought away, telling myself it was the pain and trauma tonight talking.

I didn't get schoolgirl crushes, especially on men who scared me as much as they excited me.

The whole thing was pretty startling too. I always thought an old lady was more like a powerless whore than a real girlfriend, but the way Maverick scooped June up into his arms and kissed her said otherwise. So did the looks the other bikers gave the couple. They were like the most badass faces you could imagine watching a wedding and wearing their approval.

I shook my head. Wasn't just my skull the stupid Grizzlies guy had knocked around. Between Blaze's kindness and the love lighting up the room, I had my whole perspective on bikers flipped upside down.

After the love birds disappeared, Blaze came back, carrying a blanket and a pillow in one hand and a glass of Jack in the other. He shifted past me so he could arrange the bedding on the booth, pushing the table away to make extra room.

"The other boys are about done drinking. They'll turn in for the night soon and leave you in peace. I'd offer you an extra room if we had one, but this'll have to do. I'll be right here in the morning to take you to your car."

For a second, I worried about sleeping out here alone, even if the guys were well behaved. Then he pointed to a sleeping bag at his feet.

Blaze was camping out next to me tonight, and that made me smile. Talk about going the extra mile.

"Don't think I do this for everybody," he said, as if reading my mind. "I'm a light sleeper. A few drinks don't faze me. I'll be right here to make sure you don't have a concussion or some shit. Sweet dreams, Saffron. Wake me up if you need anything to help with the pain. You'll feel better tomorrow."

He turned his back to me. Despite the awkward position, the pillow was surprisingly soft, and I quickly settled into a deep, dreamless sleep.

I woke to him running his fingers gently through my hair. "Hey. You good to go?"

Groaning, I sat up. My head still hurt, but it was bearable with his fingers on it. A girl could get used to this kind of medicine.

We didn't say much during the short drive to Pink Unlimited in the morning. I was grateful, but I didn't have a clue how to show it – at least not without making him think I was interested.

And I definitely wasn't. *No, no, hell no!* I thought to myself all over again.

Denying it was even harder in the dawn light when I could see him better. The pale sunlight shone down on his arms, bulging hills of muscle with dark ink and pale light spreading over them. They disappeared inside a leather jacket that was sleek and stretched across his torso, highlighting his powerful ridges.

Beneath the V. PRESIDENT patch and the 1% diamond, the leather and the way he made Jack and oil fumes smell like heaven, he was *built*. A gorgeous beast whose face crowned an otherwise perfect body.

I studied the stubble on his strong jaw, running up to his dark hair and bright eyes. God, suddenly I was glad I wasn't in such great shape last night. If I'd been in my right mind, spending half the night with him sleeping inches away would've been pure hell!

"All right, we're home, Saffron," he said at last, pulling into the strip club's parking lot. "Take care of yourself, baby. You leave taking care of the assholes who did you in last night to us. Call me anytime if they show up too close for comfort."

He reached into his pocket and pushed a number on a scrap of paper into my palm. I held it like a fortune teller holds her sacred leaves.

Woozy, I mouthed a thank you before hopping out and shutting the door.

Just in time. One more minute in his truck would've seriously tempted me to do some stupid like thank him in more than words.

"Shelly! Why haven't you picked it up? I'm fucking dying here!"

I tightened my lips before entering her room. Mom cursed like a damned sailor when the pain in her ruined knees hit her the hardest. Slowly, I twisted the door to her room and popped the door.

"Sorry. This is the last thing you want to hear, but the pharmacy's upped the price again. I'm…a little short this week."

I heard two gnarled hands slapping the bed. My mother spat pure venom for the next two minutes, crazy slurs like *cock-knuckles* and *satan's tits.*

Sometimes I wondered if Tourett's was one more syndrome worth adding to her long list of problems since the accident.

She sucked in a long breath after the explosion. "You telling me you ain't getting the hours? I don't understand, girl. What happened? Don't tell me your good boss went belly up!"

I bit my tongue to sharpen the blow. Today wasn't the day to tell her I'd been stripping, and much less about the whole damned club burning to the ground.

Mom sure didn't need more heart trouble. And telling her I was now an *unemployed* stripper without even a measly check from the state of Montana might push her into an early grave.

"No, it's just a little slowdown. Early summer, you know. The big tourist rush is coming, and I'll be ready. There's more generics at the drugstore if you need them…"

"Fuck the pills and fuck you!" I heard her reach for her cane next to the bed and thump the floor. "You know I love you, Shelly. But sometimes you really disappoint an old woman, almost as much as your god damned brother."

I left her alone and shut the door, blinking back tears. Was it any wonder I couldn't find steady work that paid more than minimum wage?

The whole world was cutting me down, and the pain in her brittle bones made Mom do it too. She couldn't help it. I understood more than ever with my busted eye, now more than halfway healed.

I told her I'd taken a fall, and she didn't press me further.

I couldn't spend a perfectly good summer day like this. She'd be breathing down my neck too, wanting me to bring her shit she didn't really need and then sending it back when it wasn't good enough. I grabbed my keys and left the shitstorm at home behind, opting to burn a dwindling tank of gas job hunting rather than take more abuse.

Driving beyond Missoula, I tried to forget. No luck, though. Anytime a girl tries to shove unwanted thoughts away, they come back ten times stronger, like a superstorm collecting wicked air as it rolls along.

One thing was for sure: I was really glad Mom didn't bother with the news.

If she'd watched it, she might have put two and two together. Shortly after Pink Unlimited was scorched to the ground, the Prairie Devils clubhouse in Python exploded. The cops found a bunch of charred Grizzlies inside the wreckage.

I followed the story closely, praying Blaze hadn't been hurt or killed in the carnage.

For awhile, it looked like the Feds were going to get involved since their little turf war had gone from MC clash to full blown terrorism. But I guess someone along the line must've paid their dues to the right cops, because the whole investigation blew over remarkably fast, and even the local reporters lost interest in the story.

No reports said anything about dead guys with different patches. Blaze was alive, and he'd kept his promise. The Grizzlies were gone, and I didn't need to fear running into them here anymore.

Near as I could tell, the Devils had taken their place. Last week at a gas station, I overheard two old riders on their bikes talking about how this was Prairie Devils territory now, and then they said his name.

Blaze. Not just alive, but President of the new charter they'd started up here.

I thought about him a lot. Had a feeling he was behind the new strip club opening next month, the old Dirty Diamond I was painfully tempted to interview with.

Tempted, desperate, and scared.

My money wouldn't last much longer, and then we'd be skimping along on Mom's disability. But it didn't make me want to dance for money again, especially not if it meant baring myself to violent assholes who'd punch me in the face or worse.

Or, hell, getting naked in front of *him.*

Just because the Grizzlies were gone didn't mean the new place was safe. And I vowed I wouldn't walk in there unless we were down to eating dirt for dinner.

It was a long day turning up empty handed yet again. On the drive home, I let myself think about him and his club, wondering if we'd ever cross paths.

Maybe better we didn't. I wasn't in any condition to date, and certainly not to lust after a man who probably wouldn't be interested in more than a quick fling. I hadn't been with anyone since my shitty stint at the community college, and it was just one boy who didn't do much to get the blood pumping.

The boy was a mistake I could handle. Blaze fired my interests in other ways, but I knew I'd pay dearly if I got too close.

No matter how much I wanted to lie to myself, I was a girl who liked red meat on a man. I didn't want rich or safe or normal, no matter how attractive it was supposed to be, or how much a guy like that would fix my life.

I wanted a badass with dark ink to flick my tongue against, and muscles forged in serious violence to hold onto while I rode the life out of him. I wanted a man who made me *feel,* fear and lust and savage excitement. And yeah, I really wanted a man who went beyond keeping me safe, a man so bad nobody would dream about fucking with him.

Blaze was all those things, and I was in lust.

One day, if I ever got my shit together, maybe I could have it with someone like him.

I wasn't a total idiot. Lust was never enough, no matter how amazing, and I wasn't in any shape to make stupid, sweaty mistakes on long summer nights.

I had to forget about bad boys – especially Blaze and the Prairie Devils – even if forcing myself to forget felt like one more stupid mistake.

23

It was a hot summer for Montana. The heat and humidity sapped my energy, and I laid out napping on our beat up leather sofa. Mom's tinny musicals played in her bedroom, distant and dismal as always.

She never got tired of watching those damned things over and over. The thick summer air sapped my energy so bad I didn't hear the pounding on the door at first.

Not until she began to scream. "Shellyyyy! Get your ass up and see who's bothering us!"

I rubbed my eyes. The wicked bruise around my poor eye was almost healed, but it hurt just a little to the touch.

A different kind of pain jerked through me when I looked through the little peephole in the door.

Two men in leather, one of them sporting a short wiry beard and a face I never thought I'd seen again behind it. I fumbled the locks and threw the door open.

"Jordan! Where the hell have you been?"

My brother grunted and pushed past me, another man right behind him. They both wore the thick boots I'd seen on serious bikers before. Their heavy footsteps clattered loudly on our old wooden floor, scuffing up the throw rug.

"No time to call, sis. There's shit going down and I needed to get here as soon as I could." He inhaled the stale air in the little apartment and snorted his disgust. "Fuck. This place never changes. You got room for Dubs and I?"

"Dubs?"

"Double Dice, but you can call me Dubs for short," the stranger said, looking me up and down.

I eyed him carefully, and then my brother. Dubs was a huge man, as big as Blaze and the guys I'd seen at the clubhouse. Unlike them, I wouldn't call him hot. Something about him was just…off. His skin was grayish, sickly even, making him look more like a walking Frankenstein than a hot bad boy.

Jordan was catching up to his friend in muscle and rugged looks. Also left no doubt about what my big brother had been up to the last couple seasons.

Idiot. He'd really gone and done it. He'd joined a motorcycle club. If it wasn't for my recent experience with the Devils, I would've been a lot more freaked out.

Then the big guy turned and I saw his patches for the first time. I recognized the big roaring bear right away, flanked with a bottom rocker that said GRIZZLIES MC, WASHINGTON.

I went pale and started to shake.

"Shelly? What the fuck's wrong with you?" Jordan caught me against the wall just as I began to slump to the floor.

"You're one of…one of *them.* Jesus, brother, I don't know where you've been or what's been going through your head. This is a big damned –"

Mistake. I almost said it, but Dubs was leering at me, a nasty smile pulling at his beard.

"What's that, babe? You got a problem with the Grizzlies Motorcycle Club?"

Jordan held my hand, helping me to my feet. My face remembered the way another member's punch felt against smooth bone, and the pain sealed my lips.

I desperately shook my head from side to side, forcing a weak smile.

"I'm just…surprised. That's all. Had no idea you were really going out there to join them, Jordan."

"Been a hang around for a long time with Missoula before those fucking Prairie Pussies kickcd the club out. I knew you and Mom would flip your shit if you found out. Well, now you know." He grinned, pointing to the second Grizzlies patch going up the side of his cut. "I'm the quickest prospect Spokane's ever patched in as a full member. And damned glad to be wearing it too."

Dubs nodded firmly. "You earned it, bro."

I didn't like the way his friend was looking at me. *Crap.*

Come to think of it, I didn't like a single thing about seeing my brother wearing the grizzly bear responsible for hurting me and so many others across the county. I would've rather seen him sporting a swastika.

I ripped myself out of his grip. The nausea racking my body settled to the point where I could stand without help. Good thing too because I sure as hell didn't want his.

"Fucking hell, sis. This place has gone to shit!" He sniffed again, then took a good look around. "Aren't you working?"

I shrugged, embarrassment boiling my blood.

"You know how it is…Mom doesn't get the right stuff, and all hell breaks loose. I lose my motivation. I've been looking, Jordan. Trust me."

"It's Brass now," he growled. "Call me by my road name."

"Whatever you say, *Brass,*" I emphasized it just the right way to let him know I disapproved, without getting Dubs' attention.

Whatever. He's still my big brother, and I haven't seen him in ages…

My hostess instinct switched on. Having company around here was pretty rare. Almost non-existent.

Without any prompting, I marched into the kitchen and started pulling out fixings for sandwiches. In the living room, the men flopped down on the couch, and I heard them speaking in hushed voices.

"You think Irons is really gonna approve a hit?"

"He'll do whatever it takes to make this Grizzlies territory again. This fucking town is ours, this whole fucking state, and we're gonna get it back. Those Dakota boys are bitches anyway. Got no business being here. Too bad old Ursa didn't see it coming…"

My head was spinning. Hits? Dakota boys? Territory?

I was going to eat one of my own pastrami sandwiches, but now just smelling it sickened me. Grabbing a couple beers and some chips, I carried the food out to them, and kept my distance near Mom's room while they inhaled it hungrily.

"Well? Who the hell was it?" Mom's voice croaked from behind the door.

Shit! I forgot Jordan's knock at the door woke her up. Just surprised she hadn't yelled about it sooner.

Jordan clacked his plate down on our old coffee table and stood up. He stomped past me and threw the door open, gazing inside through the bluish darkness. The only light came from the TV.

"It's me, Mom. I'm home."

Mom instantly teared up and then started to scowl. "You think you can just walk in here without asking to be let in, boy? Dammit, I can't walk without feeling hell in my bones, but this is still my house! I haven't forgotten what you said."

Oh, boy. Here we go. I swallowed hard.

"You called your own goddamned mother a worthless cripple. Said you were tired of living this way, like I haven't done my damnedest to give you two the world when I was able." She reached for her cane and pointed it toward him like an accusing finger. "You apologize, boy. Or I *will* have you ass thrown to the wolves."

I tried to get between them, but Jordan wasn't having it. His hand reached in his pocket and he stepped around me.

For one horrific second, I feared he was going to threaten her with something worse than words. No, the old Jordan wouldn't have done it. But while he was wearing that patch, I was terrified he'd do anything, no matter how awful.

"Here. How's this for an apology? You know I don't do words, Mom." He tossed a big wad of something dark on her lap. "Send Shelly out to get you something nice."

Mom's skinny hands reached for the lump, and held it up. My eyes bugged out right along with hers when she saw all the cash.

"Jesus, boy! What the hell's all this? There must be…" Her fingers flipped through it excitedly. "Two? Three thousand dollars here?"

She looked up, her eyes narrowed. I knew she couldn't see his cut too well in the darkness. Mom wasn't a stupid woman. She could still put two and two together. She had to realize he'd been doing something he shouldn't to get so much money to throw around.

You should talk, a voice said in the back of my mind. *Is his shit really more grubby and humiliating than flashing your naked body for a living?*

Jordan, never exposed himself to complete strangers. He never felt white hot pleasure flash through his system doing it either.

I was still ashamed there were nights when I actually enjoyed dancing.

Mom dropped the cash on her chest. One shaking hand reached out, and she winced at the effort. It hurt to move anything when it got this bad.

"You're still a little bastard. But you're my son. Welcome home, boy."

He gripped her fingers gently, and then turned back to me. His lips formed a thin smile.

Bastard was gloating. Jordan was throwing his new lifestyle in my face, showing me how wrong I was about him and his new friends. It couldn't be all bad if he shared the loot, right?

Hell no. That's a pile of fucking blood money right there.

I knew the Grizzlies were fucked up, and nothing was going to change it. Even if he didn't understand yet.

"Shelly! Take a few bills and go down to the pharmacy. Pick up some snacks. It's been a long trip, hasn't it, boy?"

Jordan nodded, never relaxing the same shitty smile.

"You got it, Mom." I took the money she was holding out, and my stomach did another flip, angry and unsettled.

It's blood money, all right. And now I'm touching it.

A loud roar from Jordan's pocket disturbed the near silence. He ripped out a cheap phone playing a crappy heavy metal ring tone and pressed it to his ear.

His eyes went wide when he heard whatever was on the other end. The phone snapped shut and he pushed past me.

"Wait, Jordan, where are you going? You just got here!"

"Gotta go, sis. Club business." He was almost out the door when he stopped and turned. "Go to the pharmacy like Mom asked. Dubs will go with you. There's shit going down, and I need somebody to keep you safe…I'll explain more later."

"But –"

The door flipped open, closed, and then he was gone. A minute later, I heard the roar of a motorcycle in the distance, a sound like the whole world fading away.

I tensed and slowly turned to face a man I really didn't want to see, much less be alone with.

"I'm all set, babe." He crushed a beer can in one hand and let it fall to the table. "Those sandwiches were fucking great. Love a woman who can cook."

Jesus, he must've been on his third or fourth beer by now. They hadn't even been here for an hour.

I nodded uneasily and threw on my shoes. It wasn't like I had much choice. Best to get this over with and hope for the best.

Dubs followed several steps behind me. I really wished he wouldn't because I could feel his dirty eyes on my ass.

In the parking lot, he caught up to me.

"Keys," he grunted.

"Huh?"

"Hand me your keys. I'll drive. It's not a bike, yeah, but I can handle a shitty old Toyota."

Oh, God. I listened to him swallow a hiccup. It was like I could hear the alcohol coursing through his system.

Crap. What if he started in somewhere else before he ever touched our beer? How much has this idiot had?

"Come on, babe, throw 'em over here!" He blocked my access to the driver's door. "You heard your bro. There's assholes out there who'll hurt you now that Brass is wearing the patch. Can't let them do that…especially not to a girl with such a sweet ass like you."

He moved his lips, almost pursing for a kiss. I flinched, disgusted, and threw him the keys.

Big mistake. All my instincts went off, shrieking in disbelief.

I should've listened to common sense. I shouldn't have climbed into the car with him, buckled my belt tight, and said a quick prayer we wouldn't wreck while swinging around the mountains or plow straight into a bear on the road.

We took off. Dubs drove surprisingly steady for having so much in his system, but he was still a little reckless, plowing straight through downtown Missoula and missing the shortcut to the pharmacy.

Maybe he was taking a different route. I hoped.

He blew a red light, narrowly missed a semi, and then we were outside the city altogether. I was so damned focused on getting to the drugstore and back home in one piece that I didn't notice where we were going.

"Hey...this isn't Missoula. We need to turn around. You know how to get back?"

"I got it, babe. Just because it says Washington on this fucking cut doesn't mean I don't know my way around these parts."

I swallowed the lump building in my throat. Ten minutes later, it was a hell of a lot darker, and now the city was just a distant glow at our backs.

He turned off the highway and rolled down a narrow road near the mountain, then toward an unpaved country path. Jesus, it looked like someone's driveway.

"Dubs…this can't be right," I said, tensing up and trying to keep breathing.

Panic was getting to me now. I wanted out of this car, out of this darkness, anywhere away from this weird asshole.

"No, it's right. I said I know my fucking way around, and don't you doubt it, bitch." His eyes beamed hellfire straight at me.

My heart began to race as we pulled up to a building. I saw it wasn't a house at all. More like an old cabin, falling apart and long abandoned by the looks of it.

He stomped the brakes and threw it into park. Then the engine cut and it was just silence, not a peep in the night except for the heavy breathing in my crappy little car.

I wasn't even sure if it was his breath or mine. I never got the chance to find out.

His hand fell on my thigh and pinched it so hard I screamed. I tried to bat his ugly arm away, but it just caused him to move quicker, cupping his dirty fingers between my legs.

Another awkward pinch *there* and I lost it.

"Get the fuck off me!" I squealed, jabbing both hands at his chest. "I don't want this…Jordan won't let this happen…"

Who are you kidding? Your stupid brother's the one who sent you out with this rapist in the first place!

"Come on, babe. Don't bullshit me. I saw the way you've been looking at me the second I walked through the fucking door. You like your men big and strong and rough, don't you? Probably the same way you like to fuck."

I twisted just in time to see his nasty wet tongue wagging out his parted lips, coming toward mine. I punched the lock as hard I could, and rolled, snapping off my seatbelt. I hit the dusty ground with an *oomph!*

Took off straight toward the woods, listening to him curse up a storm behind me.

I paused before going too deep, hoping I'd lost him. Shit. I wasn't used to running like this, and my legs and lungs were already crapping out.

Pushing myself into rugged forest was almost as bad as the beast behind me. There were bears out there in the darkness, not to mention the occasional mountain lion.

Still, I had to do something to get away from this crazy asshole, I had to –

"Fuck you for playing hard to get!" Dubs pawed at my breasts, wrapped the other hand around my stomach, and tackled me to the ground.

"You dumb cunt, don't you know anything about this fucking patch? Grizzlies share everything." His face was next to my ear; hot, menacing growls pouring into my ear. "Brass is family, and so am I the minute he became my bro. I haven't got laid since the run to Portland last month, and I'm pretty fucking pissed. Be a good little whore and give me what I need. Help me, bitch. Just the same as you'd help Brass…"

He pushed one hand to the back of my head and shoved me into the dirt face-first. His huge body covered mine, growling the entire time. I choked and sobbed, screaming through the earth when he started grinding against my ass.

Deep, guttural pleasure pulsed in his throat. He reached around, fondling my breasts, yanking on my nipple. I was sure there'd be a bruise tomorrow – if I was still alive.

"Oh, fuck. Nice little ass! Do I want your pussy or your asshole first? Bet they're both tight fucking suckholes, ready to be filled and fucked by a real man…"

My mind went blank. Numb. Exactly what I heard happened to other girls during this kind of nightmare. Just never thought I'd be in the terror zone to find out.

Dubs jerked me up savagely by my belt. My jeans ripped down my legs, and then I heard him working on his own belt buckle, ready to free something vile.

No! I can't let this happen. I won't have you in my body.

"Fucking tight ass jeans," he muttered, fumbling with his clothes.

Maybe it really was his pants, or else the alcohol he'd downed earlier making him clumsy. Whatever, it gave me a few extra seconds.

I groped around in the dirt, wriggling away from him, feeling all around me for something – anything! – to get him the hell off.

Shit, shit. All the little branches scattered on the ground were too fucking small. They wouldn't do a damned thing unless I jabbed it in his eye. My hand grazed a stone, and then a bigger one as I wrestled with him.

His hot, disgusting length pressed up against one ass cheek. I clawed my way forward, listening to him curse behind me as I got out of his grip.

"You little shit! Hold still! Now I'm definitely goin' for your fucking ass. Gonna make sure you don't shit right for a week for being such a bratty little slut…"

Easy. You've got one chance, I told myself, swallowing my fear to sharpen my focus.

I twisted, plucked the big rock out of the dirt with both hands, and threw myself forward. The asshole had his pants down, crawling toward me.

Luck finally gave me a wink and a smile.

Howling, I jerked up, smashing the big boulder on his head. I screamed so loud I drowned out the sick thud. Dubs cursed one more time and then fell flat.

He was down, and I didn't stop. It kept going, driving the stone into his head, beating the gory mess again and again. There was nothing here now but adrenaline and night. It thrummed in my veins, moving my fists to make sure he never, ever got up to hurt me again.

I only stopped when I felt the thick wet trickle against my knees. Dark blood, so much even the hungry soil couldn't contain it.

"Oh…oh, God…"

I dropped the stone. Clawing at the dirt, scuffling away from the body on the ground, I stared in disbelief at what I'd done.

I'd just killed a man.

Bloody fingers covered my mouth. The pain beating in my head was worse than when the punch to the face.

I covered my face with my hands and roared bloody murder, releasing my confusion, my horror, my guilt. I screamed and screamed and fucking screamed until my throat stopped working.

Then I went limp on the ground. This was it.

There was nothing left to do but pull up my pants, get in the car, and drive far, far away from this place. That's exactly what I would've done if I didn't feel the lump in my pocket.

My cell phone was there. I stood, flipped it open, and stepped gingerly over Dubs' body, still and messy as before.

No. Maybe there's another way…

My thumb tapped the menu to bring up contacts. I quickly scanned it, praying I hadn't wiped his number.

Found it. My finger hovered over the dial button, wondering if the number still worked, or if I'd just hear a robo-message telling me it had been disconnected on the other end.

I had to try. I was in over my head. I didn't know the first thing about murder, and much less how to cover up a dead body and get on with my life.

I needed to call someone who did.

Shaking, I held the speaker it up to my ear, and then sobbed when it began to ring.

If anybody could help me, it was him. So I hoped.

Blaze nursed a bad eye and protected me before...could he fix this too?

I wasn't sure. All I knew was that the first night had ended in blood, and my life would never, ever be sane again.

II: His Business (Blaze)

"Blaze? Wake up, hon."

Somebody was shaking my arm something fierce, purring in my ear. I opened my eyes and instantly felt the hum of way too much fucking Jack.

"Shit."

I jerked up. Marianne's skinny curves were attached to my elbow. When she saw I was up, she gave me a good squeeze, and moaned yet again.

"Hear that?"

Early mornings, I could do. But I'd never do the fucking things with a grin on my face and a song on my lips. My face tightened as I looked at her, shooting the whore a look that warned her this better be important.

Took a few seconds for my ears to tune in. Then I heard it, distinct and clear. Flesh slapping on leather, like somebody was hitting a bull.

"Better not be who I think it is. I already warned that asshole about his little workouts so early in the morning – right next to my damned room! Fuck me."

"Already did the fucking part, hon," she cooed. "Be a doll and stop the racket? My head's pounding after last night."

Yeah, whore. Me and you both.

I ripped off the blanket and threw my feet on the cold floor, scrambling for my boots and jeans. I threw them on, then went a little further for my shirt. It was right underneath my door.

I rolled it on and grabbed my cut off the hanger above. For a second, my eyes caught the mirror, and I saw my old leather stitched up with all the shiny new PRAIRIE DEVILS MC, MONTANA patches.

Turning my hips, I made sure all my shit was straight. Probably gave Marianne another view that made her drool – the woman loved a man in uniform – but I wasn't thinking about that just now.

As soon as club whores were out of sight, they were out of mind.

Just before I went for the doorknob, I caught the little rectangle sewn on my breast. The neat black letters read PRESIDENT.

I sucked in a breath, sparing a second to study it. Reminded me what I'd taken on, what I was doing out here in the goddamned mountains, what I'd devoted to my club when I was voted in head of the new Missoula branch.

"Blaze?" Marianne whispered again.

"Be right back. Go to sleep."

I didn't owe her shit. She was the club's plaything, a whore for me and every other brother to sink his dick into when we weren't busy drinking at the posh new bar in our fancy clubhouse.

But I didn't mind helping her get some beauty sleep — especially after the way she rode me last night, throwing her perky tits in my face.

The girl wouldn't win any beauty contests, but she knew how to fuck.

I grunted and walked on, closing the door behind me, just as Marianne purred and flopped in bed one more time. Better to think about sex than the way I was gonna lay into Tank when I got in the exercise room.

The neon lights and photographs hanging in the long hallway were like memory lane decked in devil red. I walked right past the most recent ones at the end, pictures of my last day as VP. My brother Maverick had his arm thrown around me, that pretty little thing he'd rescued at his other side, ready to ride off into the sunset to fuck knows where.

He was gone, and I was in charge now. Time to assert my fucking authority.

Nobody was stirring at the bar, even though it was getting close to breakfast time for some guys.

Slap-slap-slap.

The noise drew me closer. Sounded like a barely padded jackhammer the closer I got. I reached for the handle to the exercise room and tightened my hand around it. I threw it open so hard it hit the wall.

The machine in human flesh inside wasn't fazed. He looked right through me, throwing his huge fists into the old punching bag again and again. Sweat rolled down his shirtless flanks, right over the fading bullet wound that almost killed him last month.

"Hey, dumbass! What the hell did I tell you about doing this shit so early in the morning?"

He couldn't hear me over his fists. He was in manic mode, grunting and pummeling the big black slab in front of him. His huge head flushed bright red, and my jaw fucking dropped when both his fists disappeared inside the punching bag.

Next thing I knew, sand was spilling out all over the damned place. Tank looked down in surprise, panting and woozy from the psycho exertion. He staggered backward several steps and flattened his bulky body against the wall.

What were you thinking? I thought to myself as I approached him. *This is the fucking guy you backed for Sergeant of Arms?*

He finally looked up and focused his beady eyes on me. If he wasn't a giant who could pull my arms off, I would've slapped him clean across the head.

I settled for jerking forward, pressing my hands to both sides of his sweaty face, and staring him right in the eyes.

"Let's try this again. GOOD MORNING, ASSHOLE. Is anybody home in there?"

"Sorry, boss. I didn't know you were there…didn't see you coming. Didn't mean to make a mess either."

"Obviously, asking you not to start this shit up before the ass crack of dawn isn't working. If you won't do it for me, then do it for yourself. Are you trying to rip your fucking guts open again? You know what the nurse told you…"

His eyes glowed a little when I mentioned his crush. Jesus, the boy needed to get laid. If he'd blow off some steam with Marianne or the other whores we'd just recruited, rather than pining for the unreachable dove we kept on payroll, maybe he wouldn't be shitting up our exercise room before sunrise and waking my ass up.

"You're right. I wasn't thinking, boss. Bad habit." He smiled sheepishly.

I couldn't resist. I gave him one quick smack, right in the forehead, before I let go and turned away. My frustration was about to overflow like a badly shaken beer.

"Needs to change real soon, brother." I folded my arms and faced him. "You're an army vet, so I think you'll understand – this is my unit, my club now. I appreciate what you did during our fight with the Grizzlies as much as anybody. Doesn't mean I'm gonna put up with the same slapstick shit you put Maverick and Throttle through."

Tank lowered his eyes like a puppy. Make that a big, beefy, shirtless puppy covered in dark ink.

I shook my head. The boy still had a lot of learning to do.

He'd come a long way since screwing off at our mother charter in North Dakota, when Throttle got sick of his shit and dumped him on my brother while we were all Nomads. But he hadn't come far enough. Now, the giant was my problem, and I was convinced I could whip this fucker into line, the same as everything else I had in my grip.

My club now. Mine. That includes you, army boy.

"Grow a brain," I said coldly. Didn't take my gaze off him, even when he looked up. "We're not finished just because we settled with the Grizzlies. Those fucks are right across the border, and it's up to us to put some teeth into this truce while we make our money. Can't do that if you're fucking yourself over and everybody else because you can't follow simple orders."

He nodded. I moved to the door, satisfied I wouldn't need to have this talk a third time. I left him alone with his mess, glad the fucking punching bag was finished.

I headed for the bar. It was too damned early for Jack. Just black coffee and something to settle my stomach after last night.

I filled a mug from the thermos we always had stashed near the counter. Felt Lady Luck giving me the finger while I tried to pry my eyes open and shake off the hangover. Nothing else explained why I had to deal with such bullshit after my first night off since getting this place set up.

The new glossy marble countertop sparkled as I sat my cup down. I saw my PRESIDENT patch in the reflection.

Oh, yeah. Luck or not, that explains it pretty fucking well.

A hand clapped my shoulder. I swigged my coffee, pivoted on the stool, and looked at Stinger shooting me a grin that would've given a Cheshire cat a run for his money.

"Morning, sunshine. Thought you'd crash a lot later after last night."

"Whatever, man. Doesn't always work out like that. Hard to get any shut eye around here at all between Tank and our whore waking me up."

"I'm glad you're awake, Prez. We've got that vote on patching in Stone and Smokey."

I growled. I wasn't in any mood to talk about expediting our two prospects. Normally, we would've waited, but the Missoula charter needed every able bodied man it could get.

The operation out here was growing crazy fast. In just a few weeks, we had a few new legit businesses going up plus the blackhat stuff that brought in the real bucks moving through. Throttle wasted no time sending his boys on long runs up to Canada, and we were the crucial last stop before guns and drugs went north.

Hangover or not, my VP was right. He slid into the seat next to me, grabbing some coffee of his own. At least I was confident in one pick I'd made to lead this club.

"You think those boys are ready? Never heard of anybody being patched in with barely a month under their belt."

"They've been hang arounds for a full season when we were down in Python. Nothing's fucking ideal out there. We all found that out real fast last Spring. Gotta make do. You Dakota boys have had it too good for too long." I chugged my coffee and looked at my VP.

Stinger grunted and gave me a thin smile. Fuck, I didn't think it was possible to really insult this guy. Good thing too because my tongue was full of venom today.

"We've had our wars too," he said. "You know that. You were a Nomad long before you put on the Montana patch. Hell, these prospects will be the first native Montana blood we bring into this club. Might be good for ramping up our ties with the locals."

"Yeah, yeah. Save it for church, Stinger. What time is it, anyway?"

His hands slid over his pockets, and then twisted in frustration. "Shit. Must've left my phone somewhere else during the big bash last night."

I rubbed my cut, my jeans, and growled when I only felt my wallet and keys. I was just as fucked as him.

Downing my last swigs of coffee, I slammed the mug on the counter and jumped out of my seat. Despite being near dawn – or so I thought – it was dark as hell with all the lights turned low. The floor was a fucking mess.

I started crawling around in the overturned chairs, tossing empty bottles aside, hoping I wouldn't stick my hand right in somebody's mess from the night before. There'd been enough whores and groupies to bed every brother. More than that, actually, because we had a few guys with old ladies who stayed honest to their girls. I saw Roller running off with two girls last night.

"Fucking shit." I snarled, brushing aside a gnawed up chicken wing. "This is why I'm in no hurry to patch those boys in. We lose our prospects now, we'll have to hire a fucking maid to keep this place in order."

I heard a loud buzz. Right beneath the nearby sofa, a little ways away from the bar.

Stinger looked at me and shrugged. I dove for it, flipping over the couch. A cheap burner phone sat between popcorn kernels and grimy change.

I snatched it up and instantly recognized the scratch on the front. I put it there for just this reason, so nobody would confuse the damned thing when they were stinking drunk on whiskey or pussy.

"It's mine," I told him, flipping it open. "What the hell?"

Sixteen missed calls. All within the last two hours, starting at about one in the morning and going until three. It was almost four o'clock now, and there had just been another.

Hair prickled at the back of my neck. Either somebody was screwing around, or something was seriously fucked up.

My mind went through the possibilities. Didn't even have anybody out on patrol tonight since Grizzlies territory had been pretty quiet over in Idaho. Had something happened back east, maybe in Dickinson or

Cassandra? When mother charter squawked, everybody came to her aid.

I didn't recognize the number. Stinger came up behind me, nosy bastard, and pointed.

"Says you've got three voicemails. You know how to bring it up?"

I punched the keys. Hard.

"Sure do, asshole. I'm not a fucking idiot."

This was the third burner phone this year, and they were all pretty much the same. I glared at my VP as I tapped keys and listened to the robotic voice begin to drone.

His only problem was thinking he knew better than everybody else sometimes. Yeah, maybe I would've needed a lesson if I had an i-whatever in my hands, but everybody in this club could operate a simple fucking flip phone.

I ignored him, flexing my muscles and waiting for the pounding headache to stop. Almost as agonizing as waiting for this stupid drone to get to the messages.

Finally, a voice came on the line. Small, frantic, and female.

"Blaze...it's Shelly Reagan...um, Saffron. You've got to help me! Please, you're the only one who can. I'm in the woods all alone outside town. I'm ruined if you don't. Call me back when you get this!"

End of message.

The next message made my blood run cold. "Oh, God. I really, really need you out here. Call me. *Please.*"

There was no mistaking her whimper. It sounded even more strained than the way I'd heard her ooze pain when I tended her black eye. Something awful had happened out there, wherever the hell she was.

The last message hit me right between the eyes, and then went straight to my heart. Not an easy thing to do simultaneously.

"I killed him!" She sobbed, right before I heard a sound like something heavy being pulled on rough ground. "I'm fucked. Hopeless. You were my last chance…I was an idiot for calling you at all. Forget everything. You'll hear about it soon enough."

Her voice faded into more terror, more tears. I clenched my jaw, cleared the screen, and stuffed the shitty phone into my jeans.

"What's up, Prez? Everything kosher back home?" Stinger asked.

"It's not mother charter. Come on," I said, reaching for my keys and stepping toward the side door that led to the big garages. "See if anybody's awake in the back and get the truck. We need to get out there."

I whispered the name of the park. Seriousness crept across his face, and he moved fast.

So did I. A minute later, I had my helmet fastened and plugged the key into my brand new Harley's ignition.

The engine roared to life, dependable and calming. Saw my patches gleaming back at me, slightly distorted in cold steel.

This is it. This is what a President's business is all about in this MC.

Missoula and the surrounding counties were my territory. I was responsible for everything that happened here – all of it – and if this shy, sweet hottie was desperate enough to reach out, saying no didn't enter the equation.

I took off toward the light just beginning to turn blue on the horizon. It was a big park, reaching straight into the wilderness, but my whole life was an exercise in tracking down trouble. I'd find her, and I'd fix it.

Same as if some asshole's brought the trouble to her, I thought. After this morning, my hands were fucking ready to punch some fuck's lights out.

The whole drive beyond city limits, I thought about her.

Her short stint working at Pink Unlimited seemed like a small lifetime ago. Then the fucking place burned down and all hell broke loose with the Grizzlies. We lost a few battles, won the war, and set up shop in Missoula, a more stable place to control our new territories after the bears agreed to leave Montana for good.

Before, I rolled out of bed in a bad mood. Now, hot rage boiled in my veins, some seriously bad mojo every time I thought about poor Saffron suffering.

Wasn't the first time I'd thought about her since that night I took care of her at our old clubhouse in Python. My hands tightened on my handlebars, and my whole body stiffened at the memory.

Let it go, you dirty fucking dog... this is serious.

It was easy to hear good advice. Not so easy to act on it.

The girl obviously looked up to me. Saffron thought I was so kind, so sweet, so manly for tucking her in after that fuck with the Grizzlies patch put his fist in her face.

She was dead wrong.

Yeah, I was pissed, eager and ready to help her get some shut eye and patch up her beaten face. Too bad the thoughts rattling around in my head were less than charitable, and a million miles away from pure.

I wasn't a good humanitarian. I helped her because she was *hot*, keeping her warm and comfy while evil fantasies rattled in my brain.

If it were anybody else I had to look after, I would've done it. But I wouldn't have been so attentive, ready to kiss away her bruises if she asked, and then kiss, lick, and suck everything else on her tight body.

Thinking about her sent a whirlwind tearing through me, straight to my cock, tight like a fucking leash.

Saffron wasn't just another stripper, another whore, another throwaway.

She was absolutely beautiful, an innocent diamond in a dirty fucking rough. How she'd gotten caught up in this shit, I didn't have a clue.

I just knew one thing: this was the kinda girl I'd always had a thing for, the kind who made me twist and pulse in my darkest dreams, the one I saw when I was fucking the whore this morning.

Marianne said it was the hardest I ever came. If only she knew I was thinking Saffron, Saffron, always fucking Saffron while I swelled and unloaded in her pussy.

I had to do more than save this woman today. I had to have her, or else I was gonna end up in a goddamned straight jacket.

Blood pooled between my legs and circulated through my muscles, deadly as distant lightning.

Fuck, if anybody hurt her again...

I gave the bike more juice. The long ride past Missoula took half as it should've. I whipped around the mountains, navigating this beast with a growl that echoed what I was feeling in my veins.

I recognized her shitty Toyota from the road. It was up a ways on a hill, parked in a weird position next to an old cabin.

It bothered me that nobody was home. Even worse, the passenger door was open.

Aiming the bike up the path, I rolled on, then threw off my helmet and got off it in the early morning stillness. I drew my phone out of my pocket and dialed her number.

Damn it, there was no answer. The cautious thing would've been to wait for my backup, or at least dialed Stinger to tell him I was going in the woods.

Caution had never been my strong hand though, especially when people's lives depended on action.

I walked down a narrow path. Didn't take long to notice the flattened brush along the side. Followed it all the way until I saw the blood.

Fuck.

Wait.

If some asshole hurt Saffron and not the other way around, he probably would've done a better job covering his tracks.

This was an amateur job. And saying anything was covered at all here was being damned generous.

I reached into my other pocket, feeling for the switch blade stashed there. Wished I grabbed my nine millimeter before going out here, but I'd brought a knife to a gun fight plenty of times and came out on top.

Slowly, I moved forward, following the blood trail. Honestly couldn't tell what was worse: not having a clue what happened out here, or knowing whatever it was lay out in plain view for everybody to find.

The light on the horizon wasn't getting any darker. Just one old man out for an early morning walk with his dog would land us in a world of shit…

I got my ass into gear and hustled. Found her about a minute later, slumped against the body. Her face was puffy and red, but not any worse than the blood streaked on her hands, her knees.

"Blaze?" she looked up in disbelief, as if she'd just stepped off the plane from a long trip.

"Holy shit." I held out one hand, helping her up, and then instantly pushed past her.

A tall guy with some serious muscle was dead on the ground, wrapped in leather. When I saw the bloody Grizzlies patch, I fingered my blade, stiffening at the lightning surging through my nerves.

This is fucking bad, I thought with a growl.

"What happened out here?" I turned, grabbed her by the wrists, and pulled her close until we were face to face. "Tell me the truth."

"He got my keys…forced me to ride way out here with him. I couldn't say no –"

"Did he hurt you?" My hands tightened on hers. "Jesus, you weren't dating this piece of shit, were you?"

"N-no way!" she sputtered, furiously shaking her head. Her pretty chestnut hair flopped along her shoulders, flowing right down to those perfect tits.

No, dammit, this girl was too beautiful to lie. I trusted her.

"And you're okay? He didn't lay a hand on you?"

Dead or not, I was scared for what I'd do to the asshole at our feet if she told me what I didn't want to hear. I'd make Tank's little meltdown that morning look like a toddler pitching a fit.

"No…I killed him before he could. He was trying to." She cleared her throat. Her voice was weak and slightly hoarse. "Broke his face with a big rock. I tried to call you, but I couldn't get in touch…I pulled him here, out of sight."

"Baby, next time you take out the trash, don't leave a trail." I pointed to the blood.

She took one look behind her and wilted. Saffron threw herself at me, bawling and wrapping her arms tight around my chest. Any other time, I would've been on cloud fucking nine to have her sweet body pressed against mine.

Shit, I couldn't hold back the embrace, and pulled her in close. Too bad there was no fucking way it was gonna last. We had to move.

I ran one hand through her hair. Meant it to be soothing, but damn if it didn't make me think sexy. There was something about this girl, innocence overflowing, a sultry charm I didn't find with Marianne or any club whore I'd ever been with it.

Shit, bro. Get a fucking hold of yourself. The words sounded like Maverick in my brain. My older brother was always cool in these situations, even if he was a thousand times more susceptible to pussy than me.

I gave her one more squeeze, and then let go, taking a good look at her. Yeah, she was a gorgeous mountain girl, all right. Better not to stare too long, just like the sun, or else I'd go blind. I'd forget about the mangled fucker on the ground and think about her sleek long legs curled around my waist.

Just now, she was way in over her pretty head too. The sunrise wasn't stopping for us, and it threatened to burn away the rest of her life if anybody saw this grisly scene. Prison would take her away from me and everybody else. The very idea pissed me off, wiping away the last of my hangover as I sprang into action.

"We've got to get this fucker out of here. Now." I looked at the corpse again, and then at her. "Go to your car, Saffron. Stay there until I tell you otherwise."

"How're you going to take care of this? I don't understand. He's so big." Her lip quivered a little, but she'd cleared her head enough to listen.

"Not your fucking problem, baby. This asshole was a Grizzlies man, and that makes him our club's problem now. You worry about getting down to the car and keeping your act together. I'll worry about making sure this piece of shit doesn't reach up from the grave and fuck us all over. You see anybody who isn't wearing a Devils' patch, you start her up and drive. Just drive. Get away from this fucking place."

I stared at her intently until she obeyed. Her footsteps in the brush stopped on flatter ground just as I heard a roar a few feet away.

Stinger pulled up with Reb and Moose in the back. I was damned glad he brought support to make this job easier.

My boys passed Saffron, exchanged a few words, and then came running up to me. I was ready.

"Jesus Christ! The girl wasn't shittin' us." Stinger's eyes went wide when he saw the body. "What's this fucker doing here? Thought we had an agreement?"

"We did. Far as I know, our little truce with the Grizzlies isn't void yet. I'm gonna guess this is a one off fuckup unless we see otherwise."

"Sure hope so, Prez," Moose said, shaking his head so hard the full beard rolling down his chest flapped like a throw rug. "Can't believe they'd be dumb enough to sniff around for a re-match so soon."

"Grizzlies are assholes. They're not stupid. If they're up to something, we'll figure it out." I snapped my fingers. "Come on. Let's get him loaded up for disposal and clean up the rest of this mess. Stinger, you got that solution in the truck?"

He nodded. We always kept a little of that crap for mopping up organic matter in our saddlebags or in our trunks. Concealed the shit in antifreeze bottles so nosy cops would be none the wiser. A few splashes cleaned blood and bits of flesh like it never existed.

I didn't have to ask again. Reb and Moose had the body wrapped up in a shroud and Stinger was on the bloody trail with an efficiency that would've made a General jealous.

Only one thing left to deal with now...

Fuck. I almost forgot.

With things under control, I made my way to Saffron's car.

"Saffron?" I tapped on the window.

Took her several tries struggling with the ancient mechanism to roll it down. "What?"

"You said he was in this car?"

"Huh? Yeah. He's the one who drove us out here –"

"You need to get out now." I didn't wait.

I reached right in through the window, opened the door, and grabbed her. She squealed and jerked against me in protest.

"Blaze, what the hell's going on? This is my car!"

"And it's a goddamned liability right now. I need your keys. I'll have one of my guys drive it back to the clubhouse so we can scrub any traces of your friend."

"He didn't leave anything inside. I swear!" She struggled against me again, but I just held on tighter. "Please. I just want to go home."

"Home'll be there for you later. Baby, you don't understand." I drew in a big breath, frustrated and more than a little turned on after her little palms slapped my chest. "Your world, the civilian one, has room for mistakes. Mine doesn't. Guess which world you're in now? You want your life back, then we have to make sure nobody knows this ever happened."

Her face wrinkled up. I saw disgust, confusion. I pulled her hand, cutting right through it.

She knew I was right.

On the way to my bike, I heard Moose slam the trunk closed. The Grizzlies' body was inside. I threw him the keys.

"Get this hunk of junk to the clubhouse and look it over. I'm gonna get her out of here." I helped Saffron onto my Harley, trying not to let my fingers stray around her legs a second longer than necessary. "You ever ridden bitch before?"

"Excuse me?" Her jaw dropped, and I laughed.

"Means riding on the back of a bike. Nothing personal." That seemed to soothe her over. I covered her head with the spare helmet and then threw on my own. "Hang on tight, baby. Keep your hands locked on me and I'll have you back on solid ground in no time. We'll go slow so you get used to it."

Soon as my ride rumbled awake, everything felt better. Today was bound to be a bitch.

I needed to fill the club in about what happened out here and make some tough decisions, but this part?

I enjoyed it. Didn't matter that my head still throbbed with last night's hangover. Didn't fucking matter that Saffron just lived through murder, and it wouldn't be easy for her to live it down.

All that mattered was the wind passing through our hair and having her hands snug around my abs. Instincts raged in my system, the primal impulse made everything better.

I wondered if this was how my brother felt when that broken young thing he rescued rode with him. Then I listened to my own voice of reason piping up, telling me to forget about whatever crazy fantasies were wrapped around my cock.

You can't fuck her, and you sure as hell don't want to date her. Girl's been through enough shit.

Best to send her away in one piece. Get her out of this world, and make sure she goes running to safety, never looking back.

I nodded gently to myself as we rounded the mountains, riding into Missoula, down the streets that led to our brand new clubhouse.

That little weenie in my head was right – or was it in my heart? Regardless, the fucker overruled my cock. I had to do the right thing, no matter how much I'd regret it.

I couldn't have a fling. Not now, no matter how easy it would've been to sweet talk her into my arms. Especially when I could stick my dick in half a dozen whores without any complications. I had to get her safe and then send her packing.

With the Grizzlies on the prowl, the last thing I needed was to lose my shit over a woman. One Sturm brother had already done it, and I was damned if I'd follow in Maverick's footsteps without a fight.

Yeah, maybe she temporarily stumbled into our world, but she wasn't welcome here. She didn't belong. I was surprised the girl had ever shaken her knockout body for Pink Unlimited's short existence.

She wasn't cut out for any of this shit. It wasn't too late for her to do better.

It was a relief just to get home and flick the switch to close the gate. Soon as we parked, I brought my arms down, moving her hands off me. She held on, reluctant to let go, which only made this part harder.

I hopped off the bike and turned around. Saffron wore the same sad look on her face, a little bit of shell shock mixed with disbelief. I'd seen it before on guys who'd been through some close calls.

On girls, it was always an ugly fucking thing, and I instantly would've brought her the fucking moon to wipe it away.

"Let's go inside, baby. I'll have Miner fix you up real good with a few drinks. Anything you want to take the edge off."

She followed glumly. I was happy to see our club's oldest brother at his station. Miner didn't party as hard as the rest of us, but when he did, it was amazing to see him show up in the mornings like clockwork.

He was too old and beat up for serious club business. I never put him on any runs that went outside Missoula either. He'd been through all that shit in his younger years, and now he was there for moral support, a brother forever.

Also served up the best damned drinks I'd ever had. He was gonna be fucking irreplaceable when he stepped down later this summer like he planned.

"Hey, bro. We got ourselves a guest this morning. Get her something to take the edge off."

The old man stroked his gray stubble and cocked his head. "Must've been a hell of a night for this kind of breakfast."

"I'm not thirsty..." Saffron slumped on her stool, propping her pretty face up in her hands.

"Don't matter. You need to clear your head. My orders." I looked at him again. "Miner, figure something out. Have the prospects keep an eye on this place too. You got church in a half hour along with the rest of us."

I expected that was how long it would take to wrangle everybody up. Also plenty of time for Reb and Stinger to throw the body in one of the dumping grounds we'd set up in the Montana wild.

I'd return to Saffron later to get the truth. In the meantime, I went into the big waiting room and waited, staring at the giant Prairie Devils MC flag draped on the wall.

Needed some time to think.

Moose was right to be concerned about the colors on that dead bastard. We'd spilled plenty of blood and wrecked our old clubhouse to make the bears respect us. Took out our fucking bikes too, which was why all the brothers who'd been in Python had new ones.

Something didn't add up. Fang, their national President, was a backstabbing bastard, but he had his hands full with the cartels further south. We also paid the fuckers a pretty toll to haul our goods up through Seattle to Canada, where the Grizzles weren't welcome. They'd attracted too much attention up there and pissed off every MC north of the border, unlike us. We had good friends in the Canadian Snakes.

If the Grizzlies wanted to fuck us, they'd be fucking themselves and taking one hell of a risk on opening a two front war.

My men came shuffling in ten minutes later, one by one.

Stinger, Tank, Miner. Reb, Moose, and Roller. Our prospects weren't patched in yet, and sadly for them we had way more serious fucking business on our plates than deciding on their bottom rockers.

"Job's done," Moose said. "We buried that fucker deep in the caves. He'll be ash before anybody ever finds him."

I nodded. Several eyes went wide, especially Miner's.

"You wanna tell us what's going on here, Prez?" he asked.

"Here's the facts – one of our former girls from the Python skin shop got picked up this morning next to a dead guy wearing a Grizzlies patch. She killed him herself. Little girl did a fine job with a big rock to the head."

"Smells like trouble," Stinger said. "What the fuck was she doing with him in the first place? Grizzlies aren't supposed to be coming through here at all after we beat their asses."

"I'm about to find that out. Had to give the girl some room to breathe first. It's just one asshole. If there were others she was worried about, she would've told me."

Or she wouldn't have made it here in the first place, I thought grimly.

"You sure she's right for that?" Miner asked. "Soon as I served her some rum and Coke, she started sucking it like a fish. Girl's a goddamned nervous wreck."

"She just killed a man after he tried to fucking rape her, brother," I snapped, adding the last word as an afterthought. "Not the first time she's seen some shit. Saffron got punched in the face by one of the fucks from the old bear charter we ruined. But she's not used to this."

I tapped the small round patch beneath my PRESIDENT tag. SATAN'S SYTHE, it read, a special patch given to every brother after they'd killed for the club.

"Well, she better get used to it fast." Stinger rested his fists on the table, muscles tightening. "If there's really a war coming, she's gonna be right in the middle. You can't tell me she wasn't around any other Grizzlies. They'll know she was the last one hanging around their man."

"I already told you, we'll find out. You're right, she'll need protection if I smell even one more bastard with their patch lurking around her. I'll find out. No fucking around."

I meant it. Last thing I needed was any of my brothers doubting my officer patch. I'd pull it all out of Saffron, even if it upset her. Didn't have any damned choice.

The stakes were too high. Not just for her, but for the whole club.

"Should we bring Dakota in on this?" Reb asked. He plucked a small tin from his pocket and pinched some tobacco into his mouth.

Smug bastard. He liked to ask the hard questions. Just like I used to do when I was VP in the Nomads. Couldn't count the times I'd gotten under Maverick's skin. Now, I was on the receiving end, and it boiled my blood.

"Fuck no. Dickinson's still playing catch up after helping out our asses, plus mother charter the summer before. Cassandra doesn't need to know. Throttle's got his hands full just packing shipments for us to send on their merry way."

The mother charter in Cassandra, North Dakota, had become a full time shipping operation since the truce with the Grizzlies. We were the last stop before the long run up to Vancouver.

Guns, drugs, anything on the black market that turned a profit for the MC flowed through us, and it was our duty to keep it safe.

My brother got into it with the Grizzles when we first set up here, and earned himself Throttle looking over his shoulder. I wasn't gonna let the same damned thing happen to me.

Besides, I could make my own decisions for this club. Didn't need our national President to play babysitter, even if it would've been safer to have some support.

"Tank! You set up patrols and get the new guns unpacked and ready to go. We're not gonna be caught with our fucking pants around our ankles if the Grizzlies decide we're responsible for their missing friend."

"You got it, boss. I'll do my best. Rather play with guns than punch bags anyway." He smiled, trying to make good after our clash this morning.

I wasn't in the mood. Whatever, he could grin all he wanted. Just as long as goliath did his damned job as Sergeant at Arms.

"Before we go, is there any other business? I was hoping to have a vote on our prospects' patches today.

Obviously, that's out until we're sure those fucking bears aren't coming after our picnic basket."

Men laughed. Miner grunted, a blank look on his face. For him, this was just more bullshit, a bad rerun of wars between MCs he'd been balls deep in his whole life.

Nobody spoke up. I stopped twirling the gavel between my fingers and slammed it down.

"Church is over. Get out there and get back to work. I'll find out what's up from her and call another meeting if things get tense."

"She's a hot one, isn't she?" Stinger flashed his trademark grin. "I'd love to get on her protection detail. I could keep that safe all fucking night –"

"That's enough, asshole," I snapped. "Until you hear otherwise, the girl's a guest in this clubhouse. She's club business, and not the kind that gets your dick wet. Also means she's off limits."

The last word ended in a growl. Stinger's goofy fucking grin melted and he sulked away. He shot me one last look that said, *it was just a damned joke.*

Joke or not, I wasn't fucking having it. Saffron was my problem more than anyone else's. Last thing she needed was a bunch of brothers trying to take down her panties. Including me.

I was the last out and slammed the door behind me. The clubhouse was mostly empty. Even Miner stepped away from the bar, probably to take a long piss or do whatever the hell old guys do.

I pulled out the stool and sat down next to her. Had half a mind to steal some Jack, but it was too damned early and I needed to stay sober for this conversation.

Saffron looked at me and let out a loud hiccup. For the life of me, it was so surreal and out of place I fucking laughed. Then I reached for her back and let my hand rest, gingerly rubbing the warm skin beneath her t-shirt, patting her softly.

"Damn, woman. How many did he give you?"

"Three. You were right. I'm feeling a lot better now. The whole thing seems like a bad dream with this stuff in my system." She looked at me with those big bright eyes and managed a small smile.

My brain. My filthy, sweaty, evil fucking thoughts.

No, not just my head. The real culprit was a lot further down, and it pulsed something fierce when we locked eyes.

My head, my guts, screamed out for whiskey. But my cock only wanted one thing, and it wanted her a whole lot worse than the rest of me yearned for booze.

"Good. I'll cut straight to it. You mind telling me what the fuck led up to you bashing that fucker's head in with a giant rock?"

My fingers literally hurt when I forced them off her body. Without her warmth, I was ice cold. Frustrated. I wondered if a man could catch insanity, because she was driving me stark fucking mad. And it only got worse when she twisted on the stool, giving me a full view of her relaxed legs and the perky tits pushing against her shirt.

"It was a mistake...a big one. I didn't have much choice." She looked scared again, eyes darting quickly past me. "He's someone my brother knows. Jordan thought I'd be safe with him."

"Safe from what?" I demanded.

Fuck. If there were more threats to her, I wanted to lay them flat into the ground, and then lay into her...

"He's just a little jumpy. Jordan's been running around since Mom got really bad and left town. He just came back to us. Got himself into some bad business. Petty weed sales, mostly. You know...the usual."

Weed? That didn't sound like Grizzlies' business. They pushed harder shit, the kind of stuff that started wars with the Mexican cartels coming north of the border.

None of this added up. There was one question I had to ask point blank.

"Is Jordan a member of the Grizzlies MC?"

She looked at me intently. Her eyes didn't waver, and I watched hard, looking for any sign of hesitation or bullshit.

No, baby. Don't you fucking lie to me.

"More like a hang around. He supplies them with some stuff. The guy I was with was just passing through. Jordan had to take off, and I needed to pick up medicine for my mother. She's really sick. He pretty much forced me to take this guy, Dubs, with me. Said it was for my own good."

"Your brother sounds like a little bitch. No offense."

Could a guy say it at all without being offensive? Fuck it.

Saffron didn't take it too hard because she gave me that soft little smile again. This angel face wouldn't bullshit me, would it?

"That's all, then? It's just your brother involved? How the hell did he know Dubs?"

"That's all, Blaze. Just my brother being a fucking idiot. Jordan's his dealer, sometimes a middle man for other deals. Dubs was only passing through here, I'm sure. It's my rotten luck too. You saw how I was the lucky girl to get punched in the face when June was running the strip club…"

Girl had a point. Somehow, it made me want to help her even more. I wanted to throw myself between her and everything Lady Luck had in store while Luck was in bitch-mode.

"Jordan's dumb, but he meant well. He was trying to look out for me. Just like someone else I know…" She looked right at me. Fuck if I didn't stiffen. "Only he made a really, really bad mistake. Jesus, I'm not sure how I'll ever get back to normal."

I grabbed her hands with both of mine, fire rising in my throat. "You'll forget about this. Forget about last night. Forget about calling me. Forget about the dead man."

Her face twisted in agony. She looked away. I pulled her hands tighter, pissed at losing her when we'd been making progress.

"Can't we go to the police?" she pleaded, giving my fingers a squeeze. "They'll understand. They'll get it, if I just tell them the truth. It was self-defense! Anyone can see it."

"That's bullshit, Saffron." I grabbed her chin with one hand and forced her to look at me. "You killed a man. You called me up to help you dump the body and mop up blood. You did the right thing, but it doesn't change facts."

"It's Shelly," she said softly. "I don't use that stage name anymore. I'm not a stripper and I'm not a killer, Blaze."

I nodded. More than a little sarcasm burned through me. She couldn't be doing this to me. I had to get her fucking head straight.

"Blaze..." She wrinkled her nose, repeating my name. "What's up with that name anyway?"

"It's my road name, baby. Whole lot more exciting than Michael, don't you think? Some of us like a name with some spice. Wouldn't revert to my civilian name for the whole damned world."

"If it works for you," she said, turning her nose up slightly. "You really expect me to just walk away and keep this a secret?"

"That's exactly what you'll do. There's not a second option here, babe."

The girl picked up on my bullshit right away. She snatched her face away, and then her brow furrowed. Every part of me was screaming to go into asshole mode, but getting too deep into arguments and emotions was only one step away from embracing lust.

Careful. Gotta be real fucking careful.

Why doesn't she get it? It's not hard.

"I still don't understand," she sighed. "Civilian world or not, this is a job for the authorities. We're in too deep."

"Stop fantasizing, baby," I snapped. "I'll be honest: you tell the police the truth, you'll probably walk. Why do you think my club's still standing after our whole fucking clubhouse blew up in Python and our businesses burned to the ground?"

I watched the recognition light up her eyes, making her greens glow brighter. She opened her mouth to say something, and then quickly closed it. Satisfaction rolled through me. I knew a girl who didn't want to admit I was right when I saw her.

"Exactly. All the cops three counties over are on somebody's payroll. Mostly ours. But the Grizzlies could easily have some dirty money buying badges in this place too." I said it for her. "You squawk, you risk bringing some real trouble to your door. My boys will protect you as much as they can, but we're not all powerful. It's not the cops you need to worry about. If you end up in jail or hauled off to some shitty Grizzlies' clubhouse as a slave, who the hell's gonna take care of Mom?"

That sent her over the top. She threw my last hand on hers off, and then stood up, taking several furious steps away from the bar. I stood and eyed her.

Fuck. Shouldn't have said that last part, even if it worked to make her see the truth.

"Where's the damned door? Where's my car?" She was exasperated. "This is a mistake. I don't know what I was thinking calling you! I should've taken my chances out in the woods by myself."

"You know you don't mean that," I said, stepping closer. "I saved your pretty ass, and I'd do it all over again. Only thing is, I need you to *see* it, and listen to me. Stop fighting. Help me help you stay in one piece."

"I've had enough 'help.' Just let me go home."

I did a stupid thing. I reached out, grabbing her arm. She swatted back like a cougar and scratched my skin.

"What the fuck!" If she wasn't a woman, I wouldn't have hesitated to hit back. I swallowed my anger, hard and bitter and hot as hell. "You've lost your goddamned head, girl."

"I must've lost something to think about trusting a biker. Yeah, I see what you're thinking: I'm a stupid bitch, and I guess you're right. Just being here, being here with you, proves it." She spun away, her shoulders rolling, ready to strike if I laid another hand on her.

I wasn't that foolish. I stared at her, eyes going straight through her. Couldn't understand how someone so beautiful could be so stubborn.

Who the hell was she? Really?

"Where's the car? I've got better things to do today. We're done bickering."

The sass in her voice sent needles up my spine. I had a vision of hauling her back to my room and spanking her ass raw for being such an ungrateful bitch. Stupid fucking fantasies.

Took a lot to remember that was all they were, and all they'd ever be. When I pushed away the lust, only the anger remained, and I was getting madder by the second.

"All right. I'll talk to Moose and see if your damned car's good to go. Anything else comes up, you know my number."

She sniffed and turned away from me. I angrily walked to door leading into the garages and ripped it open, slamming it so hard behind me the entire clubhouse shook.

I found Moose outside puffing on his pipe. His goddamned tobacco smelled like shit. Didn't understand why he never bought the good stuff with the club stipend, which had only grown since the dust in Montana settled.

"Is this fucking thing clean or what?" I pointed to her rusted car.

"Good to go, Prez. Not a trace of the dead asshole on it. Even gave it an oil change for the road."

I took off without thanking him. Saffron had followed me outside, and she stood on the step next to the door, her arms folded.

"It's ready. Get your keys from Moose."

She wouldn't even look at me. Keeping my hands to myself was hell as she walked right past, grabbed the keys my big, bearded brother held out, and then thanked him.

Caught one more glimpse of her sweet, defiant ass before she disappeared inside and started it up.

Moose turned to face me. Bastard was trying not to smile. I barely noticed as I watched her whip around in the parking lot and drive toward the gate around our clubhouse, waiting to get on the road.

"Hope everything's smooth between you and her, Prez. Looks pretty pissed off to me…"

"Thank you, Mister Fucking Obvious." I leaned to the garage's wall and punched the opener for the gate. Saffron's car was gone in a heartbeat, as if it was never there at all.

"Have someone keep an eye on her," I said, hitting the button again, watching the gate slide shut. "She's safe, and it's my business to make sure she stays that way. Even if I have to protect her from herself."

"Your business or club business?"

I left him without answering, retreating to the bar instead. Smartass knew damned well it was both.

My head was buzzing with a clammy, uncomfortable beat inside my skull. Having the talk with Saffron left me stewing with more crap than I could handle at eleven o'clock in the morning.

Suddenly, that morning shot of Jack sounded awfully fucking nice.

III: Into Temptation (Saffron)

What an asshole!

I pummeled my poor Toyota's accelerator all the way to the floor, riding mountain roads on pure adrenaline. I couldn't believe what he said.

My rough and shameless savior morphed into Mister Badass Biker right before my eyes. And not in the way I wanted.

I felt like even more of an idiot for thinking what I did earlier on his bike. God, his abs were like hot stone beneath my fingers, rock hard hills and valleys that wound straight down into his jeans. Blaze was cut like an animal, all strength and perfect fury. I shouldn't have been surprised he'd acted like one too.

It didn't take raw shame long to catch up. I caught myself then, wondering what kind of sick slut I was for thinking about him at all. I'd just killed a man, after all, and there I was imagining myself under the rock hard man on the Harley!

"Idiot!" I muttered to myself, slapping the wheel.

I had half a mind to drive straight to the Missoula PD and tell them everything about what happened last night. Unfortunately, his blunt, arrogant, and totally asshole words were also completely true.

If I opened that box to outsiders, I was bound to end up in one, or else behind bars.

Blaze wasn't the only one who fucked up here. I lied to his face.

Didn't even expect to get away with it when I said Jordan was just a petty drug dealer. But amazingly, he believed me, and I saved my brother from a bullet in the head. I knew that would be his fate if they found out my brother wore the Grizzlies patch, and especially if Blaze learned the dumbass had blown back into town with a grudge to settle against his MC.

The cold truth hit me: I was fucked no matter what I did. I'd killed a man, lied to a man who helped me in his own messed up way, and stormed out, caught between two deceptions.

And the real killer? I hadn't picked up Mom's damned stuff at the drugstore yet!

That was my first stop. As soon as I had her pain pills and a few bags of chips, I hit the road, leaving the nightmare behind and crawling back into the safe, depressing shell of an apartment I called home.

I jiggled my key in the old lock and the door popped open. The TV was louder than usual. I almost dropped my bag when I saw Mom sitting in her wooden rocking chair in the living room for the first time in well over two years.

Jordan sat next to her. He turned his head and gave me a smile that made my blood run cold.

"Finally! Back after a long night on the town. You disappoint me, girl." Mom shook her head, sucking in a deep breath. "I give you money for a few simple things and you blow it on drinks and boys!"

"You're wrong, Mom. I brought your pills and picked up snacks too. Just ran into a little car trouble…"

The excuse was lame. It was all I could think of. My mother's sneer flattened into acceptance when I handed her the little prescription bag.

"Well, you're long overdue. Thank God I had your brother here to care for me. Not sure what I would've done if I had to suffer a minute more in the hell where you left me."

My heart sank. She was definitely high on something to be out here and to guilt trip me. I just didn't know if it was something Jordan had slipped or pure anger.

"You should've called me, sis. I would've come to get you. It's dangerous out there all alone, especially for a young woman at night." His face darkened and he lowered his voice. "What the hell were you thinking?"

I dropped the bag of chips, walked straight to the bathroom, and slammed the door. I wasn't in the mood for this.

Still had the stink of murder on my skin too, even if I was the only one who smelled it. I ripped off my clothes and showered quickly. I'd washed the blood off my hands at the clubhouse, but I could still feel it, so unclean it burned.

The water was cool and refreshing. I didn't care it came from an old spigot falling apart, just like everything else around here.

Water helped me meditate. If I focused on the steady beat of the droplets, I could forget about my rotten family, Blaze and his arrogance, the man whose skull I splintered in the darkness...

Shit, there was a lot to forget.

I'd just managed to clear my head and dry my hair when I heard a scratching at the door. I ignored it at first, but whoever was on the other side kept up. Annoyed, I cracked the door.

A hand reached through and yanked on mine. I almost lost my towel as strong male power jerked me out of the bathroom and twisted me up against the wall.

"Jordan? What're you doing?" I furrowed my brow, beaming pure rage at my brother. "I'm not your damned toy!"

"No, you're right, sis. You're more like a fucking puppy."

I looked over his shoulder. Wouldn't Mom hear us? We were only a few feet away.

He saw the fear rippling in my eyes and shook his head. "Forget it. She's asleep. Those pills give her the energy to get out of bed and then she collapses before the next dose. Nasty little side effect."

"Get on with it. You're obviously being an asshole because you want something," I said.

"Yeah. I wanna know where the hell you were last night, and why you never came back with Dubs. Irons said he hasn't checked in at all today. Something stinks real bad, and I don't like it one bit."

I swallowed hard and looked into his eyes. For a microsecond, I considered spilling the truth, telling him the man he called brother had tried to rape me in the woods.

But how would I ever explain killing him? The vicious bear patch on Jordan's leather jacket hadn't just changed the way he talked and the things he did. It warped his mind.

"Long story. I had car trouble, just like I said. Dubs said he was going to get a jump at the gas station or one of the bars up the street, or else find us a tow. Then he got a call and took off. Never came back."

"What kind of call?"

I shrugged. "Dunno. He left in a split second, wouldn't say what except it was 'club business.' It reminded me a lot of what happened to you last night. Just where the hell were you, anyway?"

Great. At least dealing with Blaze's shit gave me something useful…

"That's none of your damned business," he growled. "Jesus. I should've known. We're in an all out war and they've got to know we're here by now. Bastards!"

Jordan slapped his fist next to my head on the wall so hard it nearly punched a hole. I jumped.

"You didn't see anybody? No bikes? No cuts with patches that look different than this?"

"I know what the Devils' colors look like," I said. "I've been around here a lot longer than you in recent memory. Dubs left. Didn't see or hear anything. I waited on the side of the road until somebody pulled over to help me."

"Fuck. This is bad news, Shelly. Real fucking bad. I need to call Irons right now…"

That was the second time he said that name. I stared at him, questioning him with my eyes.

"He's my club's VP. He'll know what to do when we got a man down. I swear, we're gonna have to tear those fucking Prairie Pussies up soon, before we start dropping like flies."

He turned his back and let me up. Jordan walked right past Mom, stepped outside the apartment, and let the door fall shut behind him. I stared blankly ahead, dripping water on the carpet.

Crap. This can't go on forever.

I could only stack the lies so high for so long. Sooner or later, they were going to come crashing down on my head, and someone would definitely end up buried beneath them.

I drank and crashed and tried to forget for three days.

Jordan was rarely at home, and Mom retreated to her room when I was home. "Taking up a perfectly good couch," in her words.

Every time I heard a passing motorcycle's roar, my heart beat a little faster. Sometimes the loud engines woke me, and I'd jerk up, clutching my blanket tight and peering out the blinds.

A few times, bikers lingered near the parking lot, eyes on my car and on our window. It was hard to see their patches at night. Didn't think they were Grizzlies, though.

The Grizzlies all but had a key to our place with Jordan's insane trust in those maniacs. If Blaze had assigned protection to me – which he surely had – then these guys would keep their distance as long as I kept mine.

By the fourth day, I couldn't just wait.

I was up early, waiting on the balcony for the nightly drive by. As soon as I heard the growling purr, I threw on my shoes and ran outside. The biker was just about to peel away when he saw me approaching.

"Wait! I need to talk to Blaze," I said, running up to him.

It was the one they called Moose, a big man with an even bigger beard. He braked and steadied himself, raising one eyebrow beneath his helmet.

"That's fucking weird. Last I heard, I figured you two talking would be about the last thing you'd want. What's this about? Tell me and I'll send him a message."

I blinked, a little too long just to moisten my eyes. In truth, I was swallowing my pride one more time, vowing this would be my last lie.

"It's about a job. I know you've got more places opening their doors everyday here in Missoula. Surely, you need workers you can trust?"

Moose grinned. "Even the machine shop's got an online application. We're not Luddites. Don't you know how to fill those out instead of bothering the Prez, beautiful?"

Crap. Not the response I was expecting.

I smiled right back at the savage looking biker. "Look, I really, really need to make some money. I thought he'd be comfortable giving me a few minutes in person. I did take a blow to the head working for your MC, you know."

His smile melted. He stroked his beard thoughtfully.

"I'll see what I can do. No promises. Keep your lines clear and be ready to go when we call. If Blaze is gonna hear you, then it's gonna be on his schedule."

I mouthed a thank you, but Moose didn't wait around to hear it. He waved and took off, riding into the waning darkness, leaving me alone.

A sad look at my account confirmed I really needed a job. Damn it.

Was I cut out working for the Prairie Devils again? I refused to be a stripper. If there was something for me, it had to be in a bar, polishing tools, manning a register – anything that didn't involve taking my clothes off again.

If I had to be Saffron, I knew I'd wind up naked in front of Blaze. And that idea caused me to burn, equal parts horror and lust, an emotional knot with all the complexities the damned man wrapped around me.

"Grab me another cider from the fridge."

I cringed. Mom never took her eyes off the TV as she ordered me around. Whatever magic the pain pills had worked obviously wore off the last few days.

She was back to staying in bed all the time, watching her trashy shows and endless musicals, popping pain pills when she wasn't yelling at me to fetch drinks or junk food.

"You know what you're taking is pretty intense, right?" I picked up the bottle on her nightstand. "Says right here…no alcohol. May cause liver damage."

"Damn it, Shelly, you think I'm concerned about getting more fucked up than I already am? I said I want my bottle, and I want it now!"

I threw up my hands. There was no use arguing. I'd long stopped wondering if I was enabling her to a slow suicide.

I brought her the cider, all right. But I only poured half in a tall glass and filled the rest with water. If she was going to poison herself, I wasn't going to help her do it any faster than absolutely necessary.

"This goddamned country," she muttered after taking a sip. "Tastes like horse piss. Nobody can do anything right anymore."

She went right back to staring at the screen. There was an old show playing, one of those sit coms from the early nineties. The episode was ending, and a family shared a group hug after suffering some petty and hilarious misunderstanding.

I remembered why I never watched TV or movies anymore. Their problems were easily solved with a laugh, an explosion, or a flick of the writer's pen.

Real life didn't work that way.

I got up from the rickety chair next to her bed. Then a hand shot out to my wrist, so fast and sudden I gasped.

"I was wrong the other day, Shelly. You're a good girl. At least you try. Your fucking brother thought he could buy me off..."

I didn't know what to say. Receiving a watery eyed compliment from my mother was almost as alarming and unexpected as hearing her criticize Jordan.

"You put up with a lot of shit for me. I appreciate it. You deserve better than this." She sighed, real tears lighting up her eyes. "A woman does a lot of thinking when she's stuck in one place like this. At least when my damned legs aren't setting my brain on fire and I can actually think straight."

"Yeah?" I said quietly.

Her candidness was freaking me the fuck out. Had something finally broken inside her? Or was it some strange cocktail of drugs going straight to her head and making her feel guilty?

"Go. Make the most of your life, baby. Stop working these shitty jobs and don't you *dare* get into the same bullshit as your big brother!" She bared her small sharp teeth. "I see right through him. Those thugs he's with have got him by the nose, and he's too damned stupid to see it.

I don't care how much money they throw at him, and he throws at us. They're using him."

I nodded. She definitely wasn't wrong.

"Make something of yourself. Do what you love with people you love. Find a good man. I'm not getting any better…you still can." She looked at me very intently.

I studied her eyes, wondering who the hell was lecturing me. The senile fog that often clouded them wasn't there. They were as vivid and sharp as my own reflection, and it made me want to cry.

I squeezed her hand tight. Mom slumped down on the bed and started to cry. For the first time in well over a year, I gave her a hug, and she squeezed me back with one withered hand.

"We'll figure something out to make this better. It's not too late, Mom. Maybe we can get you some better help, or I'll have Jordan take shifts with me. I'll *make* him do whatever you need and stay away from that stupid club!"

If only it were that easy, I thought with a cold shudder. *But I'll try.*

"Stop bullshittin' me, girl," Mom said, throwing water on my mad hopes. "I'm not letting any strangers insert their nosy asses in our lives. I'm beyond help, and so is your big brother. He left a screwed up child and came back to us a fucked up man. You keep away from him." Her breathing grew tense and shallow.

"He's lost. Probably my fault. But you…God, you, girl, still have time, despite my screw ups. Please don't waste it."

She stopped talking. Rough sobs ripped through her body and I held her tight, shedding tears myself. Whatever was behind this emotional cascade, there was no doubting it was real.

I held my mother until she settled into a soft sleep. Then I picked up the cider, poured the rest down the drain, and got ready for the night.

I prayed it would be the night to deliver me from this.

My phone rang just as I started to doze off. It must've been around five a.m. I'd waited all damned night for something to happen, and now I was pissed I'd have this conversation with the sandman's dust in my eyes.

"It's Blaze," the voice said on the other end of the line. I instantly tensed up. "Come by our clubhouse in the next hour. Make sure nobody sees you. Trust me, my guys have seen Grizzlies in the area lately, and they've been hanging way too close to your place for my liking."

"Okay. I'll be there." I spoke to a dead line.

Asshole. He couldn't even wait for me to reply.

I changed into fresh clothes and then got into my car. My heart almost stopped when I got to downtown Missoula. A man on a motorcycle stopped next to me at a red light.

My hands shook on the steering wheel as I forced myself to look over at him.

Jesus. It was just an old man out for an early morning joy ride. Probably some guy who'd picked up a Harley and a new woman to feed his mid-life crisis.

Much as I didn't want to admit it, dickhead Blaze had me rattled. All this crap did. I needed to get a grip.

I got to the Prairie Devils' gate and blew my horn. A second later, the gate opened, and I rolled inside, parking next to the row of bikes.

The garages were open but none of the lamps overhead came on. The only light came from the cracked door leading into the clubhouse. I watched a shadowy figure approach, thinking it was somebody Blaze had sent for me.

I started to get out, only to come face to face with Mister Bad Tempered Bastard himself. I slid backward, pushing my door shut, and then straightening up fast so I didn't look like a total pushover.

"I never expected I'd see you back here. What's so important you want me involved, Shelly?"

My eyes went wide. It was strange to hear my real name on his lips. Part of me regretted giving him something so intimate. The other part – the one I desperately wanted to silence – purred its approval.

"Can't we go inside?"

He gave me a cautious look and then nodded. I followed him into the clubhouse. If he went berserk when I spilled the truth, I hoped there were others around.

I could pretend all I want, but this man scared the hell out of me. Almost as much as Dubs, except that disgusting creep didn't press other buttons like he did. And right now, just looking at Blaze played me like a piano, sending me through the full spectrum of flushed, sweaty heat and taboo shocks throttling my system.

"No drinks this time. If we're gonna talk, we're both gonna do it sober. Come on." He grabbed my hand and led me over to an empty table.

I didn't resist. The place wasn't a mess like the last time I saw it. Someone had cleaned recently, or else the men had laid off their wild parties for a few nights.

Blaze held out a chair and didn't sit until I was seated. His gravity was like a tiger's pacing around the table, finally settling in front of me. He even smashed his palms together and flexed them like a big beast testing its claws, its power.

I shuddered.

"I'm sorry about before," I choked out. "It was a long night. I shouldn't have been so hasty to flip you off and run."

He shrugged, as if I'd done nothing worse than step on his toe at a crowded dance. *Damn!*

How could a man be so infuriatingly smug and sexy at the same time?

"Stupid things were said on both ends. What's done is done. I'm more interested why you've put insults aside and returned to my clubhouse. Moose said you were pretty damned insistent about having this talk."

I closed my hands, lacing my fingers together in a tight nest, mirroring him. I tried not to sigh too loud, collecting ill thoughts into words. Better to get it out sooner, rather than later.

"I lied to you. My brother, Jordan, isn't just a stupid weed dealer. He went out West and joined the Grizzlies before coming home. He's been a full patch member for at least six months."

I forced myself to look directly at Blaze. The raw, dangerous heat growing in his eyes was like having a gun aimed at my head.

"I'm so, so sorry," I offered, knowing it wouldn't do much good.

I'd betrayed him, and everything about this rock hard man said he wasn't one to take treason lightly. Slowly, he leaned in, focusing his gaze so hard I couldn't take it anymore and had to look away.

He went for my hand. When his big calloused palm went around my wrist, I screamed.

"Tell me something new, baby. Saw right through your lie the day after you told me."

"Huh?" My heartbeat picked up even faster. "You knew?"

It was hard to process.

"Yeah. My guys saw him coming in and out of your apartment. Sporting his MC's colors the whole time, proud as a fucking peacock."

A dozen terrible thoughts surged up at once. Oh, God, Jordan hadn't been around for days, and Blaze knew about his patch. Was my brother even alive?

"He's still breathing," Blaze whispered, as if reading my mind. "Already got one dead bear on our hands. No point in making another unless those fuckers give us a damned good reason."

"Then...you're not mad? You understand I just wanted to protect him? I thought you'd hurt him or..."

Blaze took his hand off mine. He moved like lightning, slamming both fists on the table, and jolting out of his chair.

"Of course I'm fucking pissed! You lied to me, Shelly. You spat right in my face, right in the face of our whole club with your bullshit."

He turned around and pointed at the grinning devil on the back of his cut for emphasis. Then he faced me again, calmer.

I was shaking. Cowering, actually.

Blaze wasn't just some foul tempered guy to piss off and walk away from. He showed me his true nature, reminded me what he was, a walking storm in leather and fury.

All bets were off right now. I blubbered like an idiot and started mouthing apologies.

"Sorry, sorry, sorry..." Just like a broken record.

"Stop it!" He growled. "I've heard enough apologies. You're a lucky girl, babe," he said, moving to me like a panther and snatching my hands in his.

I whimpered. Jesus, no matter how many times I thought I was ready to face him, to feel him, I was wrong.

Seeing him up close, enraged, and sexy as a loaded weapon completely wrecked my sanity, my self-control.

Melting into him, he pulled me closer, shifting his hands off my wrists and around me. My breasts pressed against his chest, adrenaline hardening the wicked need in my nipples.

"Lucky? Why? I sure don't feel like it, Blaze." The words came out like mush.

"You are. You're maybe the third person I've ever given a second chance. Only because your brother's stint in the Grizzlies directly affects my club, and because I know you're not a born liar. People do very stupid, very shitty things when they're afraid."

"Are you going to kill Jordan?" Point blank. I couldn't hold it back anymore, even if I was afraid to hear the answer.

He shook his head. "No. Not yet. Kid's barely finished prospecting. He lives on two conditions."

I sucked in a breath and held it. Blaze held up his fist and extended a finger.

"One: he keeps being useful and feeds me information I can use to find out what the hell the Grizzlies are doing. Your brother's a sloppy fucker. Doesn't take much to keep eyes on him with our brothers and hang arounds."

"What else?" I whispered.

"Number two: he doesn't hurt anybody in my club, and he sure as hell doesn't hurt you. I swear, Shelly, the instant he lays a hand on you, he's dead. Don't try to hide it from me. I'll find out and I'll rip him apart with my own bare hands if I have to." Eyes glowing, he closed his fists and pressed them together.

Fear and unwanted arousal pulsed through me. His muscles bulged like a champion fighter. No, better than that.

Blaze's sculpted his body in fire and violence. Not at a gym like most guys who would've fled at the first sign of danger.

Lighting zipped up my spine. I shivered in place. Muscles deep inside me clenched, spilling heat through my belly, tingling around my womb.

Fuck him. Fuck him for making me feel like this after he threatened Jordan's life.

More heat shot through me when he closed his arms around me again, yanking me tight to his chest. I shook again in his rugged embrace, a slave to his words.

"Let's try this again," he continued. "You're scared right now, and you should be. I'm giving you and your family one more chance to stay in one piece. But, baby, if you bullshit me again, I'm handling things *my way*. I won't hesitate and I won't hear you out. If that means putting a bullet in big brother's head, so be it. If you're coming to me up close and personal like this, then we're starting over with a clean slate, and you're gonna tell me the truth about everything. *Everything*, understand?"

He repeated it in a whisper so sharp it tickled my nerves. There was no denying he knew his power, his insane ability to turn a girl to putty against his big strong slab of a body.

I melted. I moaned. I got hotter than hell. He rocked his hips forward, and I hissed when I felt his hardness between my legs.

Now who's bullshitting who? The pure smoke rolling off his hard body told me there was more going on here than club business.

Reaching deep, I found the last little smidgeon of courage I had.

"Is that all this is, Blaze? Club business? Is that what I am?"

"More," he said firmly.

One rough, full, lightning hot word. It was a prelude to the total inferno that came when his hands bound me tight, dragging me tighter against him to connect with his lips.

I couldn't even remember the last time I'd been kissed. In all my life, it was nothing like this. No man held a single fucking match to the explosion he ignited deep inside me.

He clutched at my skin, rolling his tight fingers up my back, inch by agonizing inch. I moaned into his mouth, and he sucked harder, devouring my little breaths.

His tongue pushed its way past my lips, exploring my mouth, seeking to tame everything he found.

The fire boiling within shot to my extremities in long tendrils, shocking my toes, my fingers, my nipples, and especially my poor tortured clit.

He wanted truth?

Well, he found it in my body, tasting my mutinous desire for a full minute before he jerked back. Breaking the kiss was like being cut adrift. If his hands weren't still on me, I would've fallen right to the hard floor and knocked myself silly.

"Fuck, baby. What do you think you're doing?" It sounded like a real question he needed an answer to. He pulled me close again, but stopped just short of another kiss.

Truthfully, I didn't have one. *I don't know,* I wanted to say, but really I just wanted to taste him, feel him, fuck him a whole lot more. I wanted us to stop using words to speak, and start using skin instead.

"You can't do this. Won't let any woman toy with me. Moose told me you want a job. Is that true, or was it just a bullshit excuse to talk about your bro?"

"Yeah." It was hard to even think straight after having his lips on mine.

If he went any further, I was sure I'd be sucked speechless. Possibly for weeks.

My panties were shot, scorched to tatters. Or maybe just soaked so thoroughly they'd stick to me forever.

Job? What the hell is that?

"Got ourselves a new skin shop at the old Dirty Diamond. Don't tell me that's what you're thinking?"

I shook my head. No. Hell no!

"Something else. I'm not Saffron anymore, Blaze. I told you that. Isn't there something I can learn? I don't care if the money's less or it's menial and boring. I'll do it.

I need to get on with my life, and unfortunately I need to make money to do it."

His hands tensed on me again. Damn it, the man was sexy all around, even when he was deep in thought.

My eyes flashed to his neck. I saw the very tips of dark fiery tattoos, and wondered what he looked like with his shirt off. His chest must be just like his arms: hard, rough, and fully inked. The perfect bad boy recipe for making a woman lose her mind.

"Here."

"What? I thought you only allowed brothers at the clubhouse?"

"We're gonna have a job opening. Miner's about to go into retirement. Emeritus, if you wanna call it that."

I raised an eyebrow. Never knew bikers were so educated to have fancy Latin words in their lexicon.

"He'll still come to church and fuck around at parties," Blaze continued. "We're gonna need a new bartender, though. Also somebody to make sure the prospects stock up the booze and keep this place spotless."

I shook my head. "How much work would I actually get? I don't know the first thing about bar tending. And, uh, I know you guys drink a lot…surely you don't need somebody serving drinks all the time?"

Blaze laughed. The rich baritone sound echoed through the empty clubhouse.

"What do you think this place is, baby? This is more than just a glorified bachelor pad with Harleys parked outside." He winked, his lips curled in a damned tease of a smirk. "This is our home and a place where we do business. With the deals going down, we always need somebody on hand who can serve up the goods for our associates. And, yes, for whenever we need a few quick hits too."

What he said made sense. It also made me feel like a complete moron, a stark reminder of how little I still knew about the MC life.

"You do it right, you'll make almost as much as you did stripping some nights. We all share the wealth around here." He leaned in, flattening his hand along the small of my back and pushing me into him. "What do you say? I'll have Miner train you in."

Damn! It was a little painful to give in so easily. But my body couldn't lie, and neither could my ears.

His proposal – if it was as clear cut as he said – was actually pretty generous. I answered him with a kiss, standing on my tip toes to reach up to him, sucking at his bottom lip until he groaned.

"Hey, Prez!"

Blaze dropped me. He spun around, a pissed off whirlwind. I looked over his shoulder in horror.

Stinger stood there with a wide grin on his face. God, for all I knew, he'd seen the whole thing go down!

"Why don't you ever knock, asshole?" Blaze muttered. "Gonna hang a goddamned bell around your neck one of these days. That and change your name to Smiley."

Stinger laughed, but quickly swallowed it the longer Blaze's icy glare held him in its grasp.

"Got a special delivery for you. The Dakota boys want you out there personally so our guys can unload it."

"All right, fine." Blaze took off, marching toward the garage. I was worried he'd completely forgotten about me until he turned around and stopped near the door. "Miner will be in for his shift shortly. Tell him I sent you."

I nodded dumbly. Stinger lingered long behind his boss, and put out a hand to stop me when I tried to walk past to the bar.

"Don't mind him. You're doing everything right." He looked me up and down and I quietly fumed.

Damn it, is every one of these men a pervert who thinks he's entitled to a woman?

Stinger was tall and a little scruffier than Blaze. Not too bad on the eyes by any means. Still, that didn't mean I wanted him ogling me – especially with that big grin of his.

"I'm not sure what you mean," I said, hoping he'd let me pass.

Nope. The VP stood in my way, crossing his arms.

"I think having a girl will be good for old Blaze. Just one thing, babe: if he turns you down again, you're fair game. I'm giving you a fair warning: every brother without an old lady's gonna be all over you if you're not claimed. Especially if you're gonna be working this bar all day."

My heart pounded. Well, shit.

I hadn't even considered that. I knew biker culture meant the men went after ladies with an intensity that would've been considered total harassment anywhere outside the clubs.

"Soon as work's done outside, I'll be by this afternoon to sample your goods. Hope the brain behind that pretty face is just as hot as the rest of you." Stinger smiled wider, reached out, and pinched my ass.

I almost hit the ceiling. My hands flew at his back, punching the leather and patches.

Didn't seem to faze him. He just laughed and thudded away, leaving me fuming all alone between the tables.

Asshole.

It would've been one thing coming from Blaze – much as I didn't want to admit it. But I definitely didn't want all these big badasses trying to drag me onto their bikes or into their beds like fucking cavemen.

Saffron's old stage show fortitude burned in my heart. My eyes pierced Stinger like daggers as he stepped outside and slammed the door behind him.

Okay, fine, I thought. *If I need to make more than just money, I will. I'll earn some respect and be the best damned bartender this club has ever seen.*

Miner stood behind me, guiding my hands. He'd shown me how to make the Manhattan three times and I still fucked it up.

I didn't mind having his hands on mine. The old man was the only guy I'd met here who didn't give off a *need to fuck you now* vibe.

"Everybody wants to give you shit over this over this drink," he said softly. "You give it right back. If they don't tell me what they want, I trade some bitters for a cherry. Put it on the rocks and make it a little sweet."

"You mean the guys and, uh," I paused. "Business contacts really go for a drink like this?"

I turned. This seemed way more sophisticated than gut burning whiskey shots. He looked at me seriously.

"You better believe it. We've got international folks coming down from Canada every so often. Sometimes all the way from New England and Europe too. You'll get a request a couple times a year, maybe more than that if there's a big deal going down. You'd be surprised how many bastards who look all rough around the edges like to look all complicated at the bar."

I nodded. *Okay, let's try this again.*

Miner stepped back so I could repeat what he'd shown me. I threw together the ingredients, gave it a good mix, and tossed the cherry in with a plastic pirate sword going through it. The little toy hilt had a skull with horns growing out of it.

Pretty appropriate for drinks served up by the Prairie Devils MC.

Miner reached for the glass and took a long pull. Listening to him smack his lips gave me a small smile.

"Better," he said, putting the drink down. "We'll pick this up tomorrow morning. Feel free to hang around as long as you like and serve some drinks. Most of our boys never ask for anything except cold beer and Jack anyway.

It's the outsiders you gotta watch out for. You good? I've got some accounting crap with Roller."

I told him I'd take care of it, and then I was all alone.

Moose and the two prospects came by for drinks. The simple stuff – just like Miner said – was on the house for full patch brothers. The prospects paid a small fee. Everybody left great tips, and I ended up making more than I would at a crap job with way more stress.

All in all, I was feeling pretty happy. It was going on six hours at my station when Blaze came in.

He saw me, turned, and headed straight for the bar. My knees went a little weak and the heat roared through me.

Jesus. Right or wrong, fierce or smiling, kind or merciless, he always looked good. And leaving it at "good" was one hell of an understatement, the kind my brain heaved up to try to keep my senses straight.

"What'll it be?" I asked, stealing Miner's trademark phrase. Also flashed him a smile that hopefully didn't betray too much.

Blaze saw right through me, peering straight to my hot, wet desire. But I wasn't going to make it any more obvious, dammit. I wasn't going to show him how badly I wanted to feel his lips and stubble steaming across my flesh, how bad I wanted to reach between his legs and squeeze the thick hard-on I'd felt earlier…

"Straight Jack," he said, not even smiling. "And a tall glass of water."

I turned, reaching for a bottle of mineral water and then the whiskey. I felt his eyes anchored to my ass while I reached for the shot glass. I had to grip it tight not to fumble, and end the day with an embarrassing mistake after doing so well.

"Getting hot out there, isn't it? I'll bet you're thirsty."

He grunted an affirmative. God, I sounded like an idiot, babbling meaningless small talk – the only weak defense I had against him just now.

"No." He reached past his water and grabbed my wrist. "I'm only feeling the fucking heat in here. Your shift over after this?"

The raw need in his eyes was solid, unwavering. I couldn't have missed it if I tried.

Fierce warmth hissed through my veins and a jolt coalesced between my legs. I leaned into the bar, meeting his gaze, collecting everything I had to steel myself against it.

Against *him*.

"Yeah, and I've got things to do for Mom. Need to get home and squirrel away this money. You weren't kidding about the tips."

"Wasn't kidding about what I said before either, baby. I got another position that's a lot more fun for you than hooking us up with drinks all day. My new apartment. Ride there with me."

My hands shook as I gently pushed his shot glass toward him. Blaze never took his eyes off me as he took it, drew it to his lips, pausing to caress the rim. Then he knocked it back in one gulp and slammed the empty glass on the counter.

"Blaze...look..."

If only it were that easy. Truth was, I didn't know where to begin. I let the fear in my brain take over running my mouth.

"Yeah? You gonna finish what we started this morning, or what? Can't wait any longer, baby. You're killing me." His eyes locked on mine.

"Blaze! I can't – I can't work here if it's going to be like this!" I tripped all over my words, but they were out. "You're hot and you know it, and you're using it against me. I'm really, really sorry. I'm just not ready for this. I want to be a professional here and do the best job I can without any complications. Even if another part of me wants to do the exact opposite..."

Every inch of me burned. Shame and lust and regret crashed together like heavy waves, electrifying me all over.

"Another shot." He pushed his glass forward.

I blinked, wondering if I'd just imagined the whole conversation. I shakily poured him his whiskey, watching him down it a second time. When I heard the glass clink to rest, I furrowed my brow.

No response? What the hell was he doing? Was this some weird pickup tactic to melt my panties?

"Are we okay?" I asked softly.

"We're square. You don't want it, I get that. I got other girls. No skin off my back." He stood up, moving his eyes swiftly over my body. "Take care tonight, woman."

They stopped at my chest before they shot to my face one last time, and then he turned and started to walk, back toward the offices down the long hallway.

"Blaze!" I called after him. "I don't want it to…"

Be like this.

No use. Never got to the last three words. He was gone.

I grabbed the towel I used to wipe up the counter and twisted it so hard my knuckles hurt.

"Bastard!" I spat, glad the bar was empty.

He really knew how to turn a rejection on his head. Just one of his many talents, I guess.

Now I felt like the idiot for turning him down, as if he were the one who dropped me like a used condom. And what the hell had he said about "other girls?"

I gritted my teeth, quickly mopped up, and tucked away all my cash.

I should've waited for Miner to pick up, but he was due to be along shortly, and I couldn't take the clubhouse's dark atmosphere anymore. I fished out my keys and stepped out into the warm summer evening, wishing it were as easy to banish Blaze's bullshit as it was to dash away the shadows.

At least I had some good news. Mom would be thrilled to learn I had an honest-to-god job. I could tell her I was serving drinks without hiding it. Just couldn't tell her *where*.

The last thing she needed to hear was that both her kids were mixed up with violent outlaw MCs. I stopped at the drugstore for her pain pills and picked up some kitchen sink ice cream for myself.

Not the healthiest choice, but dammit, I was going to forget about Blaze by partying with the most caramel, nuts, and dark chocolate a company could pack into my mouth at one time.

I must've been in a daze. I never heard the motorcycle revving up behind me, following me all the way to the apartment until it dropped off and parked about a block away behind an old abandoned sport's shop.

No sooner than I got inside with a smile on my face, Brass pushed me against the wall. I dropped the ice cream and yelped as he held me down.

"You lied, sis. You were with them – *them!*" His breath stank like whiskey, so strong it rolled around my ear to the other side of my face. "I saw you leave their fucking clubhouse myself."

"It's just a job, Jordan! I'm serving drinks. You're the one who's mislead. It's not too late to get out. Just leave this stupid club and forget about all this…"

I was braver than I expected. Maybe I'd had my fill of crap for the day, and now I didn't care what happened.

My big brother begged to differ. He picked me up and slammed me against the wall again, harder, then flipped me around to face him.

"Jesus. Jordan, you look like shit."

He was way past drunk. He was on something else, something that sucked the color out of his skin and left him clammy.

His long brown hair was all greasy and messed up like he hadn't showered for days. He'd always been a big guy, muscular and tall, but now it looked like he'd lost some serious weight. I'd never seen him so skinny, so dark, so tired.

So damned soulless.

"Stop being a know-it-all-bitch, Shelly. This isn't fucking grade school anymore. The guys you're hanging around will rape you and kill you when they get the chance. I need you to work with me and stay the fuck away. If you want a job, I can find something. I can –"

"You won't! And I don't want your help." I snatched my hand away with a huff. "I don't need you, big brother. Our family's managed for years without you."

His face darkened. He looked genuinely hurt, and I almost felt bad. Then he went and grabbed me again, twisting my wrist at a nasty angle. I shrieked and dug my nails into his palm.

"I tried to ask nicely, you know. I thought you'd understand. You don't know what the hell you're dealing with, sis. You don't know these men are fucking killers –"

"Just like you?" I snarled.

His eyes went wide. "It's different. We do what we need to protect our club. The fucks you're working for killed a whole charter of good men last Spring to take this area for themselves. We should've wiped them out then, and we would've, if our national President hadn't lost his balls…"

He clenched his jaw. His eyes were bloodshot, enraged with anger and exhaustion. Then his face loosened, relaxed with the realization he'd nearly said too much.

"Forget it. Everything's gonna be all right just as long as you listen to me. Here's what's gonna happen. You're gonna stay the fuck away from their clubhouse and let me do the runs for Mom's shit. You'll stay in this apartment until I say otherwise. I'll send some guys around to protect you."

"No!" I screamed and scratched so furiously it caught him by surprise.

I couldn't handle getting raped or hurt or having to kill a second time. Let alone a whole group of vicious thugs I didn't have a prayer against.

"What the fuck?" Jordan muttered. "Why, sis? Why you got to be so fucking difficult? This isn't hard…I know you want to work. I'm trying to save your life and you're too stupid to see it."

He laid a hand on my shoulder, trying to be comforting. I threw it off, facing him with new vigor.

"Leave, Jordan. I'll say it again: we don't need your help and we don't want anything to do with your MC. It's too late for you. Best thing you can do is tell those guys to pack it in and leave. Get on your bikes and ride, go far away, and just forget about all this."

"Not an option." It came out so low and rough it sounded like a growl. He stepped forward, his body flattening me to the wall.

"We're doing this one way or another, sis. The Grizzlies are my family, and that makes them yours too." He reached for my purse.

I started thrashing around when he got a hold of it, but he was too strong. I elbowed him hard when I heard him break the strap, and then he was digging through my things.

No! I clawed at his huge arm, using my nails the same way I'd used them on Blaze. Even with less meat on his bones, he was still nearly as ripped as any of the Devils.

"What the fuck! Get out of there!" I wanted to bite him.

He let the purse drop and all my stuff spilled across the floor. He held up my phone, opened it, and began pressing keys.

"Where's their fucking number? You call them right now and tell them you'll never be back. Change of plans." I looked at his hard face and shook my head. "I told you I'm not fucking around anymore, Shelly! Stop being a dumb cunt and do what I say!"

I was about to take a serious beating. I'd have to scratch out his eyes or kick him in the nuts.

Family or not, he'd crossed a line. The Grizzlies poisoned his brain and twisted the man, the brother I once knew, turned him into a demon that couldn't think for himself.

Crack!

Something flashed straight across Jordan's ribs and he roared. I looked up and saw Mom half-crumpled on the floor. The cane flew out of her hands when she hit him in the stomach. It must've taken all her strength.

Winded and stricken with pain, he stood up and turned around. When Jordan saw her, his eyes were just as wide as mine, filled with teary surprise.

"Get out," Mom said hoarsely.

"Mom? I need to protect you both...I need to do what's right...you understand?"

No way. Jordan's words were like whispers, the rage and confidence he'd used against me suddenly leveled.

"I said get the hell out of my house," she said again, clawing at the wall to stand. "No son of mine threatens family. I didn't raise neither of you right, I get it. But at least Shelly inherited some damned common sense and a good heart. You, boy, are your father's son."

Time froze. I stared at them, forgetting to even breathe.

Jordan spun with his fists outstretched, moving like a wild gorilla. I thought he was about to punch me in the face, but he made a sharp right for the little table next to the door. He snatched it up and hurled it against the wall.

We shook when it broke apart, sending wooden pieces flying everywhere.

"You'll both regret this!" he roared, pushing me aside to get to the door. "My own fucking family. Irons was right...it's just goddamned unbelievable!"

Just like that, he was gone.

.

The door slamming shut sent an earthquake through the apartment. I stood like an idiot for a full minute while Mom sunk to her knees and wept on the ground.

Slowly, I picked her cane up from the floor and went over, holding her tight.

"It's okay. We're okay," I whispered. Over and over.

Say it enough times, and you'll believe it, I hoped.

Hot tears stung at my eyes, but I refused to let them out. I stared at the broken wood, the oily footprints in the rug left by Jordan's boots, the little carton that rolled out the plastic bag and landed next to an old bookshelf.

Shit. I knew my fucking ice cream was completely melted.

IV: Jealousy's a Bitch (Blaze)

Other girls?

What a bunch of bullshit. Having that cute little thing at the bar turn me down pissed me off like nothing else.

I treated it like a shot to the gut. The last thing a man does when he gets stung is show weakness.

The truth? I had exactly one woman I fucked regularly, and that was the club's best whore, Marianne. Woman had a mouth like a fucking vacuum cleaner lined with velvet. Great rack, great ass, a pussy that stayed tight no matter how many times all the brothers used her…

And I would've traded her away forever just for one night with Saffron.

Fuck, I couldn't even think straight anymore. I wanted to lay my hands on her from the first night we met at the old strip club. The urge hadn't simmered down one iota since we dumped that piece of shit she killed and I was fool enough to hire her to fill Miner's place.

After she went home that night, I found Marianne freshening up in Tank's room. I was all ready to use her sweet cunt to forget all about Saffron. Least until the next morning when I had to see her again.

But the whore was with Tank.

Fucking Tank.

Bastard probably split her in two and loosened her up if whatever he had between his legs was just as big as the rest of him. Sloppy seconds never appealed to me.

"It's not what you think," she said, seeing the sour look on my face. "Tanky just wanted a massage, so I gave him one."

She lifted her hands and flashed me a sexy smile. I didn't feel a thing, upstairs or down, even when I smelled the seductive oil and perfume on her skin.

Marianne tried to rub my neck, but I turned away with a growl. Tank came plodding out of her small bathroom, dripping wet with a towel around his waist. He took one look at me and smiled.

"You need her, boss? I'm all done."

"I'm always ready for you, Blaze. Always." Her hot breath purred in my head reassuringly.

"Massage?" I pushed her hands off me and turned to Tank. "What the fuck? Since when are you more interested in getting lubed up and pampered than getting your dick wet?"

He laughed and shook his head. "Ought to try it sometime, boss. It's great for the muscles. Keeps a man limber after a workout."

Marianne leaned in and whispered. She cupped my ear in one hand and rubbed the other across my thigh. What a fucking Siren.

"He never touched me. Ever since he started crushing on that pretty little nurse, Tank's the only boy here who won't fuck me, but that's okay. More for you, Blaze. So much more."

She shuddered with delight and pushed her tits into my back, tempting me. My cock jerked, begging to get down and dirty with her, but my brain wouldn't let go of Saffron.

No way was I fucking the whore with somebody else burning up my brain, the gal I really wanted. Wasn't fair to me, wasn't fair to Marianne, and it sure as shit wasn't fair to Saffron.

I growled again, stumbling a little as I pushed her away. Took real strength to overrule by traitorous cock.

Tank stared on in amusement.

"Blaze?" The whore looked surprised. I ignored her.

"Don't you have shit to set up in the armory? The new gear Throttle sent us isn't gonna test itself."

"You know it, boss. I'll head out there right now," he said with a mock salute. "Stinger says he hopes you'll leave something for him when you're done with her tonight."

I heard Tank grab his clothes and cross the hall to the nearest bathroom to change. He took his work seriously, at least, and the bastard knew when to scram.

Too fucking bad I couldn't get my VP to do his job without mouthing off through proxies. Marianne's long nails were on my neck again, sexy and unstoppable, vying for attention.

What the hell's going on here? Really?

I should've been uncontrollable, hard and raging with lust. My dick was steel, all right, but I couldn't stop seeing her, couldn't blot her out long enough to turn and take the willing blonde pussy begging to purr.

Something had changed since Saffron started hanging around, something I didn't like one bit.

"Not tonight," I muttered, putting some real distance between us as I neared the door. "Can't give my asshole VP the satisfaction. Go hang with somebody who needs you, girl."

She looked genuinely disappointed. Probably wasn't just an act either. Wearing the PRESIDENT patch did amazing things with the ladies. I could've rotated girls every damned night if I'd wanted to.

Of course, it wasn't as fucking exciting as it sounded. Marianne was the best of the bunch, and if she couldn't get Saffron out of my head tonight, nobody else would.

I stalked over to the empty bar and took a snort of Jack. My third shot in just a couple hours, just the right amount to make my brain buzz numb.

Maybe I could fuck Marianne if I shut that fucker up and let my dick do the talking. Still, something gnawed deep inside me, a heavy, irksome disappointment that told me again and again I wouldn't be satisfied with anything less than Saffron.

I heard my asshole brother laughing in my head. I'd scoffed pretty hard when Maverick started to get pussy whipped. If he could see me now, the shit Stinger gave me would've been like a fucking joke.

Shit, at least my bro was nailing June not long after he started crushing on her.

I couldn't say that. Something was always in the damned way and I hadn't taken her. I just thought about Saffron and jerked off to her sweet memory like a goddamned kid.

Frustrated, I slid my hand over the bar, and reached for more Jack. Hoped to hell there wouldn't be any urgent business tonight. If there was, I'd be too blasted to move like I needed to.

Hang on, baby, I thought to myself. *You don't get off that easy.*

Maverick never took no for an answer, and neither will I. Sturm blood doesn't cool when it knows what it wants. Not until you're wedged between me and the wall and I'm pumping between your long legs.

You're teasing a volcano, and you don't even know it.

You're gonna end up under me, Saffron, one way or another. Won't fucking stop until I'm coming deep inside you, bleaching every other woman I've ever lusted for out of my skull.

Tonight, woman, you're mine.

"It's deserted." Stinger came back to us as we waited by the parked bikes, shoving his handgun back into his pants. "But they've been there. Come see for yourself."

The run-down building looked like an old drive-in diner. It wasn't suitable for a petty dope dealing racket, let alone an MC's clubhouse. Not even an MC that shat where it slept and ate like the Grizzlies.

I followed my VP through the break in the fence, toward the rickety old building. Tank was right behind me, with Reb and Roller at the rear.

Scoping out the site where we'd tracked them should've been a welcome distraction. It got me away from the clubhouse when she started her shift, plus I didn't have to sit around in the office with Moose and Miner, listening to them drone on about boring accounting stuff.

I could handle money laundering and legit business receipts, sure. Did I want to fuck with them a second longer than necessary when our legit businesses were only a small part of our earnings out here? Hell no.

"Watch out. Stinks like a sewer once you get inside," Stinger said.

My VP wasn't kidding. I had to throw my head outside the battered door for fresh air as soon as we were in.

"Holy shit. Forget the stench. Look at this place, boss!" Tank gawked and pointed.

For a club that styled themselves after grizzly bears, these assholes lived like rats. Old food containers were strewn everywhere, mixed with empty overturned ammo boxes. Half the floor was ripped up and dirty.

In the corner, used needles sprinkled beat up mattresses. If these guys were shooting up themselves, then it was a miracle they could ride without wrecking their bikes.

Reb leaned over an old mattress and carefully reached for one of the old syringes. The smell hit him in the face and he coughed, spitting tobacco everywhere.

"Fucking shit. These guys are blasted out of their gourds. Look at this, Prez." He dangled the syringe between two fingers.

Damned thing was more dirty and stained than most I'd seen. I grunted. We found enough stubbed out roaches, melted spoons, and dirty needles to choke an elephant heard.

The only telltale sign the Grizzlies had been there at all, besides the lingering stink of motor oil outside, were the big black letters graffitied on the wall.

D.D.I.G.C.

"Fuckers knew we'd show up sooner or later," I said.

Everybody's faces turned when they took a good look. Anger flashed through Reb's face. Roller was so pissed he had to go out for a cigarette, his face turning bright red beneath his spiky hair. The rest of us were older, more sober, but we knew damned well it meant trouble.

"Devils Die In Grizzlies Country," I said quietly, spelling out the full phrase.

Tank stepped past me and crouched toward the ground. The lazy fucks had left their spray paint right beneath their war motto. Either these guys were really disorganized, or they'd hauled ass away from here pretty damned fast and did a hack job leaving us a calling card.

Tank stood, shaking the can. He pushed his big finger down on the nozzle and black paint oozed onto the wall.

"Still some left, boss. You want it?"

Without a word, I snatched it away, and then aimed it over their bullshit letters. I wasn't in the mood for anything fancy. Tank watched with approval glowing in his eyes as I covered their shit in a thick dark layer, warping each letter until it was unintelligible.

"Let's go," I said, waving him to follow.

"What do you make of that? Haven't seen such a shithole since me and Throttle's boys wiped out the Raging Skulls."

"It means something's really fucked up here, brother," I said, grateful to be outside with the fresh mountain air. "These assholes were hunkered down hardcore. Calling that cesspool Grizzlies' territory is a fucking joke, and I think they know it."

Stinger stroked his chin thoughtfully. "You're telling me this is a recon job then? Just some bullshit to test our defenses?"

"No." I looked at Tank and the other men gathered in a small circle, one at a time. "I think somebody's on their own personal crusade, doing this shit under Fang's nose. This isn't a run up to another invasion so those bastards can reclaim Montana. This is the invasion, and there won't be any reinforcements for these guys. We're dealing with renegade bears on the loose."

Stinger's eyes widened. For once, I'd actually gotten my VP by the balls. All the guys looked at me like I was Sherlock Fucking Holmes.

Right about then, I guess I was.

Another church meeting led us to beef up our defenses. If the fuckers creeping in on us really were renegades, it made them even more dangerous and unpredictable than a war with the whole Grizzlies MC.

Sure, they didn't have the huge numbers a proper Grizzlies threat would've brought. But these fuckers were bound to strike sooner or later, and fight harder because they were desperate. They didn't care what it took or who got in the way, as long as they gave the Prairie Devils a black eye, or else cranked up the heat so high in Missoula we couldn't do business.

We'd taken a gamble during our last battle. Blowing up our old clubhouse in Python and killing off their old Missoula charter nearly brought the Feds down on us. Took some really sharp lawyers and a lot of fucking money from national to put the brakes on.

We wouldn't get any do-overs. No more fireworks.

One shootout or bombing in a town as big as this was bound to bring in all the alphabet soup organizations, and then the whole club would be under the gun. When the Feds decided to squeeze a club's balls, they held on tight and didn't let go until they were crushed forever.

I couldn't let that happen. Not on my watch.

I played dumb when I called up Throttle to talk about the latest shipments. Fortunately, the renegade Grizzlies hadn't done shit except flip us the finger and threaten Saffron. That was bad enough, but it could've been a whole lot worse if they'd tried to bomb the clubhouse or hit our boys on the road during a run.

Filling him in when I didn't need to would only invite more trouble. The man who headed mother charter had his fill of fun out West. If he caught wind of what was happening, I knew he'd have Fang on the line, and the Grizzlies President would want to come after anybody using his club's name and colors without his authorization.

No MC took kindly to posers, rogues, or false flags. Ever.

Then there was the little problem of Saffron's fucking brother. I'd promised not to kill him, and I meant to keep my word. The kid was as good as dead if he had a hit put on him by either the Prairie Devils or the Grizzlies. No different than the crazy bastards above him who'd obviously roped her big bro into something he was too young and too stupid to understand.

"What is it, Prez?" Moose came into the office for some files. Running a black market business was no different than a legit one. The limbo we danced for Uncle Sam was never ending.

"Trying to put my finger on who's stupid and motivated enough to go behind Fang's back and fuck with us. We wiped out Vulture's whole Missoula crew except for the old President above him. Can't believe that fucker would chance it. My brother said he was Fang's bitch through and through, more like a figurehead than an active President."

"Those boys must've been some nasty motherfuckers," Moose said.

I nodded. Thinking about how we'd nearly got our asses pillaged and killed by Vulture and his guys while they raped Maverick's old lady still kept me up at night. I didn't need to relive that fucking story again.

"You in the mood to take your mind off this shit? We've got the big bash tomorrow night. Shelly's gonna be working late to serve up drinks. Can't wait for the fucking hog." He patted his gut, and then his eyebrows went up in surprise. "I'm talking about the pig…not her."

Good times and pig roasts were indistinguishable.

"Be nice to blow off some steam," I agreed. "You bringing your old lady?"

"You know Connie! That lady won't miss it, and neither would I. She gets hot as the day I married her after these things. Must be something about all the partyin' and smiling guys in their cuts that makes a girl feel young."

I grunted a reply, and he took the signal to leave me alone.

I hadn't so much as seen Saffron up close for about a week. Going home to my new apartment most nights made it easier to avoid her, especially when there was plenty of club business to tend to.

Far too long since the night at the bar when I vowed to claim her ass.

On the few afternoons when I watched her from a distance, it looked like something was eating her up inside. Didn't worry about it, though. I'd ordered Miner to tell me if anything was going on with her bro, and he hadn't breathed a word.

I kicked back in my chair, cradling the back of my head in my hands. Dammit, this was one of those times when being President meant a dozen brush fires popping up at once, and I was short on limbs to stomp 'em all out.

Maybe I couldn't put them all out on my terms. The one Saffron left blazing between my legs was the biggest by far.

This fire, I could control. I had to.

Tomorrow, at the pig roast, I planned to have words with her, serious fucking words that would stomp the love-hate cinders between us for good. And if those words didn't lead to me throwing her on my bike and flinging her pretty ass into my bed, then I deserved to have those renegade fuckers eat me alive.

I managed a whole fucking charter in dangerous territory. Why the hell couldn't I manage this stubborn, sharp tongued, irresistible woman?

Everybody was deep in their drinks except Tank. Him and the prospects stayed sober to bang the alarm if any of our fucked up friends decided to hit us in the nuts while we were all tipsy.

I seriously double they'd try to raid our clubhouse during a party. And what a fucking party!

Every brother without an old lady seemed to have two or three whores hanging on his arm, in his lap, or around his neck. The first hog got eaten up so fast we had to roast a second, and its rich sizzling scent filled the air, mingling with booze and sex and leather.

These were the times when a man remembers what this lifestyle was really all about: freedom, good times, and living to the goddamned limit.

Some Jack and chit-chat with my brothers plus a couple Dakota boys who'd been passing through and joined our bash had me feeling pretty fucking revved up. I circled the bar every so often, catching Saffron's dark eyes through the throngs of supporters and loose women.

I caught her eyes a few times. She always glanced away when she saw me looking, or else somebody walked by, blocking my view.

Wasn't until a couple hours in that there was enough of a break in the crowd to get a good look at her. When I saw what she was wearing, my fucking eyes nearly popped out of my head. Meanwhile, my cock pulsed hard in my jeans.

Oh, baby! You naughty, nasty, sweet little thing. You want attention that bad, or are you just trying to make me lose a load in my pants?

She was the sexiest bartender I'd ever seen. No exaggeration, and I'd been to plenty of bars in my time where the babes served cold beers topless.

The V running down her cleavage was cut wide and lacy, a push up bra easily exposed behind the low cut top covering her perfect tits – and it stopped well short of covering much at all. When she rounded the bar's counter to help the prospects bring out some drinks, I saw the short black skirt she had on. Beneath it, her long legs were decked in fishnets gliding all the way up to her butt.

My blood started to roar. Now it wasn't even a question of what I'd do when I got her alone. My cock knew.

I was gonna rip that shit off, pin her to the nearest surface, and ram my way straight between her thighs. I was gonna fuck her until she knew there were no ifs, ands, or buts about who her sweet ass belonged to.

My beauty, my toy, my vessel…my woman. My Saffron.

And if there was some fucked up miscommunication along the line, then we'd sort it out with sweat and come and passion, the only fucking language I could understand when I saw her like that.

"More Jack?" A voice said behind me.

Fuck, no! I nearly said. *More like the tallest, coolest glass of water you can find. Gonna need it to keep me from self-combusting when I start sucking and fucking this girl.*

My hard-on deflated when I saw it was Miner. My eldest brother held out the bottle and gave me a wink.

I took a quick swig and then looked past him. "Where's the damned water cooler?"

Some fuckers must've carried it off. Our tap wasn't in its usual place.

"That really what you're looking for, Blaze, or were you gawking at something else?"

Bastard knew. Hell, I wasn't sure if there was a single brother around who didn't know how bad I needed to tame our newest, sweetest addition to the bar.

"I just need some fucking water. This place needs its air conditioning cranked up. It's like a goddamned sauna in here with this many people on a hot summer night."

"Feels pretty damned comfortable to me. You sure you're not coming down with a different kinda fever, Prez? Maybe there's plenty here who can help you out. I hear Marianne's starved for attention tonight. Too many new girls showing up who just want a Devils' ride they'll remember, if you know what I mean."

Miner rolled his hips and grinned, laughing the whole time. Fuck, I did not need to see that. I had to get up close and personal with Saffron *soon* before my lust died an untimely death.

"Jesus, bro. You're like seventy." I put up a hand and began to walk, but there were lots of drunken floozies and big leather backs in my way.

"Sixty-five!" Miner called after me. "And I'm partying way fucking harder than you, Prez. Step it up! Don't want to see a guy like you get your ass beat by a retiree."

His laughter disappeared in my ears as I finally pushed through the crowd. I stepped around more guys feeling up their gals and sucking face when the urge hit fierce. I headed straight for the shitty drinking fountain by the bathroom. It was better than nothing.

A long, cool drink gave me back my senses.

Okay. No more fucking around. Time to head for the bar, grab her by the hand, and take her someplace where "no" isn't even a damned option.

When I rounded the corner, I looked all over for her. She wasn't at the bar anymore. I saw her near the open door leading outside where the fires were going, her silhouette framed in a flirtatious pose that screamed sex.

Saffron wasn't alone. Rage shot through me when I saw the big hand on her shoulder, and then doubled when I noticed the big goofy face with his eyes locked on her pretty face.

"Stinger!" His name rolled on my lips like a curse.

Mother. Fucker.

I didn't do him the courtesy of a tap on the shoulder. I threw my hand down on his shoulder, hurled him around to face me, and pinned him to the wall.

Several floozies behind us screamed, and Saffron's shocked gasp was mixed into the noise.

"Blaze? What the fuck are you doing, brother?" Stinger had his fists ready to go, but forced them to relax when he saw it was me.

"Keeping you from sticking your damned dick where it doesn't belong. You leave her alone," I growled. Relaxed my grip just enough so the observers we'd collected wouldn't think a brawl was about to break out.

Not that I wasn't ready. Took every fiber in my being to keep my fists from pummeling any man who looked at her like that, even if he was my own VP.

"What're you talking about? You snorted too much Jack tonight or what?"

I flashed him an evil grin. "Totally sober. You're not welcome around Saffron. She's not another club whore to sink your cock into."

"Shit, tell me something I don't know!"

I didn't like his tone. Bastard was dripping sarcasm, and he knew it. I grabbed his leather clad shoulders and shook them hard, not stopping until he squeezed my wrists with his.

"Shut the fuck up and listen!" I hissed. "Saffron's off limits. I don't give a single shit if you don't like my reasoning. I'm the main in charge here, and my word's the fucking law. You and the other brothers are gonna tuck it in when you're around her, be real polite, and never, ever give her that goofy fucking smile while you're wearing a hard-on again."

His eyes narrowed angrily. "Funny. I didn't see anybody's patch on her. She's not an old lady. Nobody's laid claim to her pretty ass, and you know it. Since when do we have to lay off pussy that's not another brother's?"

"Since I hired her to take Miner's place at the bar," I growled. "How the hell do you think that'll go down if you start fucking her? She's part of this fucking club and nobody's gonna treat her like a whore. She's nobody's toy to drag around and fuck off with."

Nobody's except mine, I thought. Stinger could practically see the cold truth in expression, a terrible mask reflected back at me in his wide eyes.

"Why's that? If this is a change in charter policy, I think we get a vote."

"Because I say so. You get a vote for club business that's life and death. We're not voting on your fucking cock and where it belongs. I'm telling you where it doesn't, and that's good enough, understand?" He nodded reluctantly. I eased my grip, backing away. "Go find some other shit to dig into. Anywhere but here."

Stinger didn't look happy. Knew he'd be pissed for a long time, but that was the price to pay for bringing down the gavel. He didn't breathe another word about challenging my executive decision either.

I watched him slink away through the crowd, deflated hard-on tucked between his legs. Satisfied, I turned to Saffron. Couldn't tell if the tight mask on her face meant she was horrified or impressed. Maybe a little of both.

"Did you hear all that?" I asked.

"How could I have missed it?" she whimpered. "Blaze…Jesus! You may be my boss, but I didn't know it entitled you to tell me who I could hang around with at a party."

She was pissed. The stiffness in her body said everything, and so did her voice. But damn, the tension looked goddamned sexy anyway.

I grabbed her by the wrist and she tried to bat me away. Not good enough.

"Come on. We need to talk. This is about a whole lot more than you and some fucking idiot in a patch looking for pussy."

"I don't think –"

"Don't make me ask again."

She flushed. Her resistance crumbled as I threw one arm around her shoulders and led her along, inch by inch to the door. I led us to the edge of the clubhouse's gate for some privacy.

I shook my head, thinking about what a full animal house the place was tonight.

"You can't keep doing this," she said softly. Her eyes were closed, but at least she opened them and looked at me.

"I'll keep doing whatever it takes to protect you, baby. Bad enough to have your fucking bro fall in with the Grizzlies and bring them pawing at your door. I'm not gonna let a brother take you for a ride you'll regret just because you haven't figured everything out with this club."

"What's there to figure out? It's a job!" She shook her head, frustrated.

"Stinger and everybody else wants a piece of you. If I didn't put my foot down, they'd keep pressing until they got it too. You're an unclaimed woman on our turf. Yeah, I gave you a job, but it's not like any job you'd ever have in the civilian world. When you agreed to this, you stepped into *my* territory, Saffron, and that means working with our rules, our ways, and our needs."

She let out a long sigh, shaking her head. "And you really think I'm cut out for this? Here I thought Stinger was just being nice to me…I didn't think he'd…"

"Fuck you?" I said it for her, letting a little smirk pull at my lips. "That's what he was after. Trust me. I did you a favor. Nobody takes kind to being turned down by a woman at our clubhouse who isn't another man's old lady."

"Maybe this is all wrong, then. Maybe I'm wrong for you." She forced herself to look at me. "For this job, I mean."

"That's where you're the one who's wrong, baby. There's only one way you're gonna get along here and do your thing without me constantly whipping my boys back into line." I paused. "You've got to get under a man's protection. The *right* man's protection."

Now it was her turn to smirk. Shit, her sweet lips called to me like nothing else. I threw one hand over her head, leaning on the gate, flattening her little body against mine.

"Don't tell me. You've got the perfect guy in mind?"

"Matter of fact, I do. Make no mistake: what I said back there was all about club business and chasing off any fucks who wanna get in the way of you doing your job. This here is about you and I. And I'm damned close to saying all I can say with words. You really want to understand me, then it's time you learned my language…"

I moved in. My cock pulsed so hard it felt like a bolt snapping through my body when I pressed my lips to hers.

Yeah, my little tease was ready. No fooling.

She put up a good show, but the second we melded, I tasted her sweet moan. She oozed eager, wet, and ready.

My heart beat hard and fierce, sending hot blood roaring in my ears.

My chest pressed closer, sandwiching her against the gate, feeling the pebbles beneath her shirt. Her nipples were flaming peaks, and my balls churned when I thought about what they'd feel like against my tongue.

Fucking-A! I'd had it with those thoughts, these fantasies. It was time to find out.

"My bike. Right now." I tugged at her arm, ready to drag her to the little side area where we'd corralled our Harleys for the party so there'd be more room in the garage.

"But my shift! I'm supposed to be serving drinks..." The reluctance, the hunger, in her voice was clear.

"Forget about that shit. Bet you've made tips hand over fist tonight already. Miner will figure it out when too many cups run dry." I paused as a thunderous masculine jeer exploded behind us. "Besides, a lot of these bastards are already close to having their fill. You did your job, and did it damned well."

She nodded, a little more seriously than if she was just agreeing. I saw the recognition of what was about to happen flicker in her eyes.

Fuck yeah. She was ready, and it was a beautiful sight to see.

Then I smiled and pulled on her hand, leading her out the gate to my ride.

Honestly, sweet Saffron didn't have a fucking clue what was coming. Yeah, she knew I was gonna throw her down on my bed and fuck her for hours, but that wasn't half of it.

She didn't know I'd been starved, thinking about her for weeks. She didn't know I'd pent up all this fire for her, and when it came out it was gonna be just short of fucking apocalyptic. And the girl definitely didn't know once I started, I didn't stop.

I'd throw my body between her legs and keep it there for hours, power fucking her until she forgot her name, until she forgot what it was like to do anything except come on my cock. Once I had one taste, there was no going back. If it meant I had to tie her down spread eagled and tattoo my name in her flesh with my mouth, I was fucking ready.

"Hold on tight," I warned, fixing her helmet tight and pushing her arms around my waist. "It's a hell of a ride from here."

Her eyebrows shot up in surprise and I saw a shy smile light up her face in my mirrors. The girl was onto what I really meant – I made it pretty fucking obvious.

But still, she didn't have a damned clue. Not really.

Luckily for both of us, she was about to find out, and I'd savor the long, hard, screaming night we were about to have for the rest of my life.

V: Like a Rollercoaster (Saffron)

I was blushing like a virgin all over again.

My hands shook as I locked them around his abs, which seemed bigger, harder, and hotter than before. It wasn't just the amazing way he smelled or the rock solid beauty of his body beneath my fingers.

It was the way he'd fought for me, taken me. Would I ever be able to look at him again without seeing the fire? I saw what it said, clear as day: *You're coming with me, woman, and no isn't an option.*

Ending up with Stinger wouldn't have been the worst thing in the world for a throwaway night. Of course, I instantly would've regretted it the next morning, no matter how much booze and sweet talk it took to coax me into bed.

Blaze and I had done this dance for too long, and I was tired of fighting. Seeing him nearly come to blows with his VP for me battered down my last defenses. I hadn't realized it at the time, but I'd dressed like a slut for him, hoping to draw him to me before any other whores laid into him.

Well, mission accomplished. I just wasn't sure what I'd won beyond fire, stubble, and muscles.

I squeezed Blaze tighter as he steered the Harley along the little mountain roads to Missoula's other side. He drove more confident than ever, and why shouldn't he?

He'd proven he took what he wanted, what I needed, even if I was too stupid at the time to listen.

Well, I was all ears now. No, make that two tingling nipples and a pussy that felt like it would drown if it didn't get filled with raw iron.

My lips parted. I released another moan into the open air, grazing the very edge of the stubble on his cheek with my lips.

Blaze stiffened, and turned his head just enough to speak over the roaring engine. "Careful, baby. You do too much of that and we'll never make it home in one piece. Goddamned tragedy if I got cut down before hearing you scream my name while you're coming like lightning."

Lightning? Oh, yeah.

It tore up my spine harder as soon as he said it. All I could do was lay my head on his shoulder, fully drunk on his rich musk and little snorts of the bike's oil, running my fingernails across his abs as the road blurred past.

I prayed it wouldn't be too long to get to his place. There was no way I could take too much thunder between my legs with the wicked need building there, the fire that reached up and rattled my brain until it was totally consumed in sex.

Sex, sex, sex.

Filthy, dirty, sweaty fucking.

God, if he really did the things he said he would, I knew I might not leave his place alive. It had been eons since I'd been with a man, and never a man like this.

Lust and nervousness roiled my stomach. I wondered if I even had the stuff to satisfy a ruthless badass like him. At least something drew him to me, a strange throbbing magnetism that forced our flesh together, no matter how much we wanted to ignore it.

We roared up next to a small, neat looking building and he threw his bike in park. I shuddered as his fingers swept across my face, winding through my hair, tugging my helmet away.

What a damned mess he'd made me. My panties were a hot, soaked heap, and I felt them twist uncomfortably when he tugged me up with one arm, the only thing that could get me moving. I was grateful they wouldn't be staying on long.

Blaze's place was barer than I expected, a real cave with hard floors and sparse furniture. Not that I expected a man who was just getting settled to have much – especially a man who lived like an outlaw. He needed to be ready to move again at a moment's notice if things got crazy.

I couldn't stare too long. Blaze tugged on my hand again, his thin smile warm, but insistent.

He didn't have to ask twice. I followed him eagerly to the room, just a few steps behind him. When we were inside, I saw the bed in the darkness.

He got behind me and ground his hips into mine, urging me deeper still, all the way to the bed.

"Blaze! I –"

He wouldn't let me go another way. He moved against me, forward, forward, and then I went over the edge.

I crashed down on the mattress, laying on the bed all wrong, but he didn't care. He fell on top of me, pushing his way between my legs, hands circling up my thighs to make sure I stayed open for him.

The feel of his hands *there* caused me to gasp. My hips thrashed, bucking up into his, and my brain melted into a hot, steaming mess when he rocked against my ass. He was huge, hard, *everything* a man should be, and it was all burning for me.

I moaned and bucked gently. He wasn't having it. One hand went behind my head, twisted my hair in one fist, and aimed my chin up to him until our glowing eyes met perfectly.

"One more thing I forgot to mention back at the bar: you don't dress like this in the clubhouse anymore. The only time you wear this shit is when we're alone and I've got you good and hot. This sweet skin's mine, Shelly – every inch of it – and that means what's on it too."

Bastard! I almost spat the word right at him.

Then I thought about whether he was trying to rile me up more. The little flash of anger and irritation mingled like hellfire with the lust prickling my nerves, one little strike away from lighting me up in a way I'd never walk away from.

"I get it," he said, his smile getting wider. "You don't wanna listen. Not to bullshit words. Neither do I. You listen to this instead."

He kissed me so deep and fast I nearly swallowed his tongue. Pleasure jerked through me, delight and a need to taste more, exhilarating when he sucked in my bottom lip and needled it with his teeth.

"Then listen to this," he said, breaking the kiss.

His free hand yanked my low top to its breaking point. He grabbed one breast, raked his stubble across my cleavage, and forced aside my bra.

God, what the hell was I thinking? At some base subconscious level, I definitely wanted this to happen tonight with the trashy outfit I'd picked out. The bra was an old hangover from my time at Pink Unlimited, and Blaze had noticed.

Noticed, and enjoyed it. His teeth dug deeper into my flesh, stopping just short of my nipple, where the terrible pulse seethed for his sweet mouth again and again.

Damn! I pushed hard against his chin, but he was intent on teasing me, bringing only a little relief when his face moved up to mine and he pinched both breasts hard.

My tongue slipped into his mouth. He tasted me losing my mind, tasted the little quakes shaking through my system.

"Blaze. *Please.*" I sounded pathetic. The only thing worse was the brutal burn between my legs, the mad fire pushing against his hard cock as he held his bulge against me.

"Not until you listen, baby. Have to know you're gonna be a good girl from now on. *My* fucking girl."

His hands swept up my breasts and took my shirt with them. The top popped off and I was glad to see it go. I pinched my legs tight around him.

"No fair! You get to see them, feel them…what about me? I'd like to find out what those tattoos I've seen crawling up your neck look like." I was literally begging now. Blaze stared at me with flames mounting in his eyes.

We both knew what he wanted, and he wouldn't give in until he had it. It still took two more nipple twists and his lips teasingly pushing on mine to make me submit.

"Okay! Okay. I'm yours. I'll listen. I'll be your good girl. Just as long as I'm yours. I –"

He rose up and stopped my words. I watched as he crouched, dropped his cut off his shoulders to the floor, and then dragged the shirt beneath it up over his head.

Holy, holy shit. He's…

Magnificent.

No other word was suitable. What else could describe the total perfection locked in his muscles, rolling hills gliding from his neck to his belt, hills and deep canyons lining his torso and stretched across his arms?

I wasn't sure there were any words at all for his ink. Jesus, seeing his tattoos – really seeing them – caught me off guard. They were a hypnotic canvass, dark lines across his muscle like a second skin.

A raging devil face was emblazoned on his chest, same as the big patch on the back of the club jacket. The flames spiraled up and rolled around the his neck while others burst straight down, running into yet more tattoos.

Without anymore whining from me, Blaze stood up and turned.

I saw his back. No surprise, it was just as ripped as the front. Pitchforks flanked his sides. There was a huge one right between his shoulder blades with elegant words scrawled around it.

The phrase *Straight to Hades* was scrawled in a half-circle, arranged around the giant pitch fork like a top rocker on a biker's cut. Beneath it, I counted eight little skulls, each one a slightly different shade of red ink.

Looked like they'd been added over time, as I knew from the flower pattern I had going up my hip. It was a work in progress, something I added to whenever I reached another milestone.

After tonight, I'd be adding more buds to the rosebush. Maybe even a full bouquet. I wondered what his project was all about.

"What's that?" I said, pointing stupidly as he opened his belt and dropped his pants.

"The skulls..." I whispered, losing my mind. Seeing the hard mountains of his ass beneath his tight boxers made it hard to focus on anything except feeling his hard flesh on mine.

"Missions I've done for the club," he said, returning to his place between my legs. "I like to keep track and I'm proud of my career. Some bros do patches. Me, I like to wear it on my skin so I'll never forget. Everything I do for the Prairie Devils is part of me. All part of what you're about to suck and fuck, baby."

Crap! Did he really have to remind me?

He did. And then he sent me another reminder with a new deep kiss, running his hands down my legs when I pushed up against him. He was done messing around with my skirt.

His hands reached for the waistband and it raced down my legs so fast I shuddered. I helped kick it off, breaking out in goosebumps when I caught his eyes fixed on my tattoo.

"What?" I smiled. "You didn't think you were the only one with a little ink?"

"It's beautiful. Fuck, do they taste as good as they look?" One stray finger caressed the blooming flowers, rounding my hip, stopping at the top of my panties.

I couldn't stop him as he sank low to the pattern. Nor did I want to.

No man's breath ever made me gasp, but then nobody had ever shown interest in it before like Blaze. He stopped next to my skin, breath coming slowly, inhaling my scent. Then his tongue darted out, circling the first rose, tracing its way along the thorny stem to the next.

My hips jerked. I had to grab his head to steady myself. Big mistake. It only encouraged him to kiss harder.

When he started pulling at my panties with his teeth, I whimpered. The gentle strokes he'd used on my tattoos became a savage need to get me bare, to discover the ends of my tattoos.

Blaze passed my panties into one hand with his mouth, and then he returned to my flesh, vibrating a growl up my sleek thigh. I pinched my teeth tight and hissed, all I could do to keep from exploding.

Now I understood why guys got so embarrassed if they lost it too fast with a girl.

He hadn't even touched me there yet, and I was ready to cream myself. Blaze was dynamite packed into a beautiful man's flesh. Nothing would've prepared me for him, certainly not the way he dove between my legs as soon as I was naked, trailing the last of my ink with his tongue and letting it guide him lower.

Lower...lower...oh! Too low!

No such thing. My body jerked hard at his lips on my pussy, before rolling forward again. His tongue opened me up, kissing past my lips, plunging deep into my slickness.

He fucked me with wet warmth the same way he kissed. Rough, eager, and unstoppable. My fingernails raked their way down through his hair and rested on his shoulders.

I must've clawed him half to death when his rhythm increased. Raw electric pleasure pulsed through my core, through the wetness, feeding the need spilling into my blood, brain, and bones.

I was on fire, a human pyre ready to combust for him, to burn into so many pieces only he could put them together again. My body accepted it, and I thought I was ready.

Then his tongue swirled up, pulling my clit in his mouth.

Thick long strokes circled my little nub again and again. The fire I thought I'd accepted was nothing compared to the molten tsunami ripping through my spine.

I had just enough time to look down between my legs, digging my claws into his tattooed back. Blaze had his head turned, staring up at me, and his eyes said what is mouth couldn't.

Come for me, baby. Come your pretty fucking brains out.

Helpless, I obeyed. I jerked, thrashed, convulsed, imagining how incredible his cock would be inside me if his mouth was this good.

Blaze pulled me in as I came, clenching my ass and thrusting me to his face. I rode his sucking, tonguing, rough lips hard, diving into the rough pleasure swallowing me whole.

He relished my screams. My clit locked between his teeth and he held it there, thrumming it in slippery heat again and again, holding my spasming cunt on his face.

I gushed like nothing else, a geyser of wet, hot pleasure drowning him between my legs.

When it was all over, he set me gently on the bed, and wiped his mouth as he got up. His tongue swept through his lips, wiping away my cream, his hot breath flaring out his nostrils.

"Shit. Nice to feel a girl come on demand. I'll never go back to whores with you, baby."

Big words for a badass biker. I was still too dazed to answer, but I looked at him, wondering if I should be scared or flattered.

Just how many whores had he fucked? I'd seen the blonde one around, the girl he pushed off to other guys as soon as he started getting into me.

Blaze covered my small body with his. He made me taste my sex on his lips, kissing me deep, stroking his tongue against mine with the same hot passion he'd poured between my legs.

"You ready for this, woman? Wrap your legs around me and hold on really fucking tight. Told you the ride gets rough from here."

New heat pulsed deep inside me and I grinned. I looked up into his face, trembling with desire when I felt his bulge crease up and down my slit. His *very naked* bulge.

He'd lost his boxers sometime in between changing positions. I flattened my palms against his tattooed chest and pushed against him.

"What's up?" he growled.

"Are you safe? I'm on the pill…but you've been with a lot of women."

His face darkened. "You think I'm so far gone thinking with my dick I'd put you in danger? No, baby. Never been with anybody dirty and the whores stay fucking clean. Just because I ride a Harley doesn't mean I'm immune to physicals either. If I caught a bug the last few months, my doctor would've told me."

I sighed. That made me feel a little better, but I still wasn't sure. Then his hips rocked against mine, rubbing his huge, full, eager length against my opening. His tip coated itself in wetness and slathered my clit.

"Oh! Holy shit," I moaned, poising the tips of my nails on his chest. "I…I think I want this."

"Yeah, you do," he said, not a shred of doubt in his voice. "You'll take it good and get damned used to it. I'll never do you wrong. Fuck your worries into the ground. They're over. From now on, there's only one pussy this cock's going into."

His face didn't show a single line of deception. He was actually serious.

It could've been the lust, forcing us together with magnetic intensity, but I believed him. Plus being the *only* girl this crazy, overprotective, rock hard man wanted swelled my heart like nothing else.

I nodded. All the signal he needed to sink low, hard, and deep.

"So. Fucking. Tight!" Blaze said each word like a curse when he pushed into me.

Pleasure exploded inside me, overwhelming the last few impulses my mind still controlled. My arms and legs wrapped tight around his perfect body. I hooked myself to him and drew him closer, urging his cock deeper, even when he'd gone to the hilt and rested his balls on my ass.

Blaze opened his eyes and looked at me. I gave him a shallow nod, hoping he saw how badly I needed him just now, how badly I needed him to ravage me.

Let go and fuck me. Please.

His large cock slid back and he plunged in again, adding more force to his hips. No doubt about it: he was big, and I was tight. It took my inexperienced cunt several strokes to loosen up and accommodate him, but when it finally did, we fit together like we'd been made for this, designed for each other.

Rising vigor shuddered in his muscles as he picked up speed. Each time he thrust all the way in, his arms bulged out, hard and steady. I watched the devil tat on his chest glistening with sweat.

Blaze fucked like a conqueror, a *man*. Not that I expected anything less.

When this man got what he wanted, he savored it, and now it was my body's turn to be worshiped. I pinched his hard ass with my ankles and began to buck back, swallowing him whole, not stopping until I heard him groan pleasure.

"Fuck me!" I urged, my thoughts spilling out loud. Ecstasy soared like hot smoke inside me. "Fuck me deep, Blaze. Give it like you want."

I had a dirty mouth and I knew how to use it. Thankfully, I'd finally found a man worth it.

Blaze took me harder, spiking down and pinning my hips to the mattress. Springs snapped and squealed beneath our weight.

"Where's my good girl gone?" Blaze asked, amusement shining in his eyes.

I dug my nails into his neck and lifted my head. He swore as I lifted my head to his chest and bit tenderly around one nipple.

"Oh, fuck. You wanna play rough with me, baby? Be careful what you wish for…"

He lifted one hand, fisted my hair, and shoved my teeth away. He pinned me down and bit my bottom lip in a long kiss, increasing the speed and pressure from his hips. He rocked into me harder, grunting feral pleasure through my lips.

Our sweaty flesh meshed perfectly now. His cock glided up to my womb with fluid perfection. Hot, insistent lightning zapped my brain each time his friction caught my clit.

Feels so fucking good, Blaze. Don't ever take this body away from me. Don't ever leave me alone again.

I was too beaten by sex to say it. But I thought it as his thrusts grew fiercer. He clawed at my hair more desperately, swallowing my rising moans with his lips.

When I came, it was like shrapnel ripping through me, each little pellet charged with pure carnal energy. The buckshot burned through every muscle, every nerve, and sent my eyes rolling deep in my head.

"Blaze! Michael. Take. Me." I stuttered, my last words gurgling into incoherent bliss.

He fucked me even harder, excited by hearing his real name.

Orgasm stole my breath. I tightened around his cock and exploded, shaking beneath him, losing myself in an endless cascade when he rammed his cock through my spasms.

I thought he was about to break the bed and come with me. But Blaze had something else in store, and he didn't release anything as he happily rocked my body.

I collapsed back, still feeling him shaking my flesh and bones. He woke me from my stupor, grabbing one breast and bringing it to his mouth to get needled with a love bite.

"Up. Flip over for me, baby."

I did as he asked, resting on my hands and knees. He entered me from behind and immediately pawed at my breasts, using them for support as he mounted from behind.

If I thought he fucked me hard before, I didn't have a clue.

The angle, the energy, the position was perfect to ratchet up the fire. His balls slapped my tender flesh furiously and I began to scream, the last orgasm's numbness melting into new desire.

His muscles hit the backs of my thighs with a steady tempo. Mostly, I felt him inside me, bigger and harder with every stroke, his maniac lust carrying me away.

"You want it inside you, don't you? You want me to shoot my fucking come where it belongs?" He jerked my hair, breathing hot smoke on my neck.

"Tell me, baby. Only gonna give it to you if you beg and come for me again."

His hips rocked for savagely.

God, what a devil. Bastard. I forced my hips back, trying to make him lose control before he was ready, but it just caused my sex to suck and pulse closer to climax.

Blaze laughed. "No more play, Saffron. No more fucking around. You want to take it in you, or what? I need to brand you deep, baby, and this cock won't take no for an answer."

Neither would my body. My mutinous, evilly honest flesh worked my lips. I turned my head, jerking my hair a little tighter in his hand. Damn, it felt strangely good with his thrusts down below, like the tension in my scalp increased the pleasure humming in my pussy.

"I want it, Blaze! Want it bad. Want to feel you come inside me. *Please.*"

He wanted me to beg? Fine.

If shallow jerks of my hips against his cock didn't make him lose it, maybe words would, and I was more than okay with that. His hands went to my ass and clamped on hard, fingers like vices.

"You say it again and I just might shoot." One hand went around my thigh and found my clit, and he began aggressively rubbing it. "Tighten up that sweet cunt and ask again. Make me believe it."

What the fuck? Does he want me on my hands and knees?

Well…I was already there. But I wasn't going to spill it and blubber like a schoolgirl. That is, until he started to thrust deep, hitting just the right spot inside me with his cock as his fingers gyrated around my wet clit.

Pleasure foamed up in my brain. I was one breath away from coming, and the only thing on my mind now was how good it would feel to have his warm come flooding me.

"Do it," I grunted through my teeth. "Fill me, Blaze. Take what's yours. Pump it deep 'til I can't hold another drop!"

I sounded desperate. And apparently, desperation was good, especially with orgasmic tension possessing us.

He grunted, shifting his hips faster, power fucking me in longer, more savage strokes than before. I screamed and felt everything below the waist turn to warm, mushy cream. I was one neuron firing away from coming when he slammed himself forward, holding my ass until it hurt with one hand, and pinching my clit so hard with the other I thought he'd blow my brains out of my head.

My pussy contracted right as he shot his first jet. Blaze's cock swelled and jerked inside me, and then it happened again, filling my slick emptiness with his seed.

I let out an animal scream and came. We shook together, sweating and rocking and melting, two bodies flowing into one.

His fire darted into me again and again, each time a little higher and deeper. My screams were loud, but they were punctured by his masculine roars, his guttural passion rushing out as my sex milked his cock for all it was worth.

It was the hardest orgasm of my life. Pleasurable, but hard, so hot and intense it blinded me and sucked my lungs empty.

I toppled head first to the mattress and Blaze was right behind me near the end, his shallow growls moving with his breaths. He caught himself just in time and propped himself up before he fell and crushed me.

"Fucking hell, baby. You ride better than a hundred whores."

For some reason, I laughed. "I'll take that as a compliment."

I twisted my head and caught him in a kiss. Not long after, he pulled out and we rolled over. I mingled around him, rubbing my fingers over his muscles, loving the way our sweat lubricated his skin.

Blaze's shoulder was turned and he had one arm around me. My nails stopped over the top row of skulls near his shoulder and I studied them.

"Just eight? Thought it would take a lot more jobs than that to become club President."

"They're not jobs," he said coldly. "They're people I've killed."

Slowly, I drew my hand away. The sexy warmth inside me shriveled up a little. I looked at him hard, wondering if this was a joke, but the way he looked at me said *no way.*

Shit. Laying here naked in bed with this gorgeous man, it was easy to forget just how dangerous he really was, and how differently he lived from every other man I'd known.

"You must've had good reason…" I whispered, more to reassure myself than because I believed it.

He nodded seriously. "Always. I'd do it all over again too, kill every last one of those fucks. I don't think I need to tell you about the group of men we got into it with when you were working at the old strip club."

I remembered the fist slamming into my face and swallowed away the painful memory. At least it wasn't all bad. If it hadn't been for that, I might not be laying with him here right now.

"The skulls are for them? The old Missoula Grizzlies?"

Blaze shook his head. "Nope. Can't take credit for any of those kills. The whole club was in on it and my brother was the mastermind. Blew those fuckers to hell and gone along with our clubhouse. Just in time too. They were about to rape and kill my bro's old lady."

Jesus. My chest tightened up.

"Poor June." I sighed.

He spoke about it with only a hint of anger and disgust. Not the head spinning horror any other person would've used. This was his world, and killing was a natural part of it.

Something about the deadly tone in his voice made me nuzzle in closer to his chest. I inhaled his scent, his rich, masculine, calming musk, basking in it as I pressed my cheek to his tattooed flesh.

"Don't worry, baby. This club doesn't draw blood unless there's a damned good reason. I kill because I have to every time to protect my brothers. And right now, I'd kill for you too."

He squeezed my chin in his fingers and forced me to look at him. I wanted to be afraid and sick, but the stark shadows in his eyes were as reassuring as his spicy smell.

"What about the name? What does Blaze mean anyway?" I had to ask.

His lips quirked in a smile. "Got it for the first two skulls on my back. Twin brothers. I was in the Nomads then, and were out in Iowa patching over a support club. These jackoffs didn't take kindly to having the Devils' patch on their cuts and on their little businesses. You can guess they didn't do the sensible thing and walk away from it all."

"What did they do?" I asked softly.

"Raped the top girl at the strip joint we took over. They used their bodies and a broken bottle. Tore her up so bad she never danced again. Thank God my sister, Aimee, was around to help her get some other work after she healed." He cleared his throat, focusing on the darker, bloodier part again. "Maverick and I fucking destroyed them. He ran their shitty bikes off the road and we found 'em in the ditch. They were pretty beat up. I poured the gasoline on their coward asses and threw the match."

I winced and twisted away. Blaze suppressed a dark laugh, only barely.

"Poof!" I jumped at the loud noise he made and watched him spread his hands apart, slowly settling them on my skin again. "They went up in a blaze. I got my name and my full patch, along with the first two skulls on my skin. Haven't looked back since. My name's a reminder, babe, and I'm proud to have it. It tells me every damned day what I need to do if anybody fucks with my brothers or anybody else I care about."

I studied him hard, eyes questioning.

"I'll raze their fucking bones to ash. No hesitation. Won't feel bad about it neither. This is the life I choose, baby, and I'm not afraid to kill the motherfuckers who deserve it. Hope you'll respect that."

There was no denying it. This man was a monster and killer. A noble one, maybe, but beyond all that he was a cold hearted savage. And right now, at this point in my life, I needed one.

He made me feel safe and loved. That alone was a whole lot more than anyone else had ever given me.

Was I crazy for loving him? Maybe.

If this was insanity, then I wanted to be committed, locked up in his arms and rough heat so tight I'd never escape.

I leaned in for a kiss. Blaze's lips took mine eagerly, working them with wet, possessive pleasure.

His arm covered me and pulled me in. A new erection pressed against my thigh. Wouldn't be long until we were at it again

This time my body, mind, and soul were ready.

I often think about this first blissful night with him and want to call it the second night when I realized who I was and who I was meant to be with. The way we shuddered, screamed, and fucked late into the darkness gave me memories I'll never forget.

But there's still two more nights that were even more powerful. Two unforgettable long dark nights that split my soul in two, and then stitched it together anew.

"Let's go, baby. You need to wake up."

I laughed sleepily. Something prickly and soft nudged my neck. I opened my eyes and saw a tangle of dark hair that could only be his.

He kissed me awake. I sat up, wondering why it was barely light in the dark apartment.

"No need to start your shift early, but I need you to come with me to the clubhouse anyway. Got some shit to take care of, and I'm your ride to work today."

I let out a giant yawn and stretched. Felt like we'd only slept for a few hours, and the slight soreness between my legs reminded me why.

It had been worth it. Blaze stood, his pants already on. I watched the dark ink inscribed on his granite muscles disappear behind his shirt, and then the cut that went over it.

I got dressed quickly. With some horror, I realized I'd be rolling into the clubhouse stinking like sex.

Will anyone even notice? I had to wonder, expecting a mess after the huge bash that went down last night. More than a few couples had stopped at the bar while I was serving drinks, just one more scrap of clothing away from getting busy in front of me.

Shit. I sure hope Stone and Smokey aren't drunk off their asses. Need somebody to help me clean the place up.

"You can fix yourself up in the infirmary," he said, as if reading my mind. "Come on. Doubt anybody else will be rolling in too fast, so you can take it easy."

A couple minutes later, I rode behind him, his Harley roaring beneath us. The sun was barely up. It reminded me of the morning when he'd come out into the boonies to help me with Dubs.

Good thing this one was a lot more pleasant. Today, the tiny light twinkling over the mountain peaks filled me with hope. Leaning into him and inhaling his sexy fragrance filled me with even more.

We were about three blocks from the clubhouse when the other bikes appeared. They roared in from both sides of the street, loud dragons snorting ferocious threats.

I jerked up from his shoulder, thinking they were his guys. Didn't take me long to see the strange colors on their jackets and feel the way Blaze tensed up beneath my hands.

I had to grip his shoulders for dear life as he spun the motorcycle. It skidded to a stop, less than a foot from plowing into a nasty looking man with hard eyes and a shaved head.

The thug with the Grizzlies patch smiled, and then pulled out a long knife. He took a slash at us and I screamed, ducking as it just barely missed my neck.

Next thing I knew, Blaze's hand was pawing desperately by my thigh. A compartment popped open and something heavy brushed past.

He held the pistol up in the air and fired off three shots. Then he took us on another stomach churning zigzag through the bikers. There must've been at least five, and they were all circling us like sharks.

I looked around desperately, trying not to throw up, wondering if Jordan was among them. I didn't see him anywhere.

"Hold on!" Blaze yelled.

More bikes roared nearby, and there was a sound like metal scraping on raw concrete. I screamed when three more bikes blazed past us, charging straight for the Grizzlies. It was a small relief recognizing the Prairie Devils patch on the back of their jackets.

Several Grizzlies whooped like cavalrymen charging into battle. Gunshots went off. I screamed again, practically spearing my nails into his stomach as I held on and prayed.

Blaze aimed his pistol more carefully this time and fired. A man howled in agony, his bloodcurdling scream cutting straight to the pit of my stomach.

Holy shit. There was nothing left to do except tighten up and hope. Our perfect morning ended with lead and daggers flying back and forth, a hellish crossfire.

Engines roared, drowning out everything else. Blaze spun the bike and I crashed against his back as we jerked to a stop a moment later. I realized he'd driven through the open gate and parked next to my shitty Toyota.

The other bikes came roaring in a few seconds later. A man barked orders, straining like a wounded bear in between his words.

"Close the fucking gate! Get everybody else on the line…don't give a shit how hungover they are…fuck me…"

"Jesus Christ!" Blaze threw my hands off and jumped up, running toward one of the other bikes. "Not you again!"

I lifted my head. The world was still spinning, and it took a solid minute for my eyes to focus like normal through the dizzy blur.

The loud voice grunted, this time clearly in pain. When I could finally see, I saw the two prospects and Blaze hauling him off his bike. Blaze's face was red with rage, and he pressed both hands tight to the man's hip.

It was Tank, and his bright red blood gushed out between my lover's fingers. I got up and approached, not thinking as I tore off my shirt.

I ripped it apart in one go, fashioning a makeshift tourniquet to stop the bleeding. It felt good to rip and claw at something after I'd been helpless while bullets and knives flew around me.

"Sonofabitch! Somebody reach in my pocket and get my phone. Dial Emma. Tell her we need her ass here to fix this, right now!"

The prospects were still holding Tank up by the shoulders. He was so huge it took one man on each arm.

I pushed my way through the mess and nudged Blaze. He saw what I was doing and let me in, and I worked quick to wrap the torn shirt tight, getting crimson blood all over my hands in the process.

"Fuck! We can't risk moving him. Put him down here!" Blaze looked at me and saw I had his phone, searching for the name Emma. "You better not bleed out, brother. You got the shittiest luck in the world."

"Don't I know it, boss," Tank said weakly. The pale hue creeping across his skin made him look like a wax giant.

"I can't...where the hell is it? Emma?" I shook my head, frustrated.

"No, no! Look under nurse. Nurse, baby!"

Found it. I auto-dialed the phone and shoved it to Blaze's face. Almost dropped it several times in the fury. All this blood was pretty damned slippery.

"Emma? Get your ass down here for the club. Stab wound. Yeah, it's him. Again."

Blaze's face was hard and furious. Even so, he looked at me with gratitude. He kept me next to him while we waited for the other brothers and the nurse to arrive. Tank groaned and bled, but he seemed stable with the pressure on his bad leg.

I curled my fingers into fists, ignoring the drying blood.

If I'm going to live this life with him, then I'll do my part. I'm not afraid, I told myself.

It was easy to say just then. Easy-peasy.

I had no clue just how fucking real things were about to get.

Talk about dead. The clubhouse was on red alert, and nobody even came to the bar to calm their nerves after the attack, leaving me all alone to wipe the counters.

By mid-afternoon, I gave up any thought of making any tips. Really, I didn't care. I was just glad Blaze and I were in one piece. A lunchtime snort of whiskey helped calm my nerves.

Blaze and his guys all filed into the meeting room and stayed there for hours after making sure Tank was getting the attention he needed. They were still there when the door to the makeshift infirmary burst open.

The grim faced nurse closed it gently and headed straight for me. I scrambled off the stool and stared. It was surprising to see the club's only medic, of all people, wanting something.

"Tall beer and two big glasses of water," she said, flinging her hair back behind her shoulders. "It's been one of those mornings. Help me take the edge off."

I guessed one little beer wouldn't mess with her judgment too much. I got her what she wanted and slid the beverages onto the counter in front of her.

"Emma, right?"

"That's the name. Thanks." She sipped her beer and gave me nothing more than a brief glance.

"Is he going to be okay?" I asked, eyeing several dark red splotches on her scrubs.

"Definitely. It's not as bad as last time, when he was shot. Poor Tank has the worst luck…it's amazing how nobody else takes a beating here."

I swallowed. A few wrong turns on Blaze's bike, and I might've easily ended up back there, or worse. I didn't want to dwell on it, but I couldn't ignore what had happened.

Those Grizzlies looked like they were coming for me. They didn't seem that interested in Blaze and the Devils.

My chest tightened. Did my own stupid brother put my life in danger?

I shook my head. My brother was fucked up, possibly beyond repair, but I didn't want to believe it.

Emma drained her beer fast and clinked the empty glass on the counter. She grabbed her water to start in, but paused before taking a sip.

"No offense…you're not looking so hot yourself. Everything all right?"

"Just personal stuff," I said gently. "I'm still new to this. It's easy to forget there's danger breathing down your neck until it hits you in the face."

"These guys have a rough life. Seems to touch everybody who gets in their circle." She took a long pull on the water. "They've got their reasons. This is the second time I've patched up goliath in there, and he's always adamant about one thing: no regrets. He'd die for this club. You have to admire a man who's committed to something."

I understood. I really did. Despite the wild melee this morning, I wasn't having second thoughts about anything.

It wasn't just the men who were dedicated. Now that I'd gone to bed with Blaze, I wanted more, no matter how wild or dangerous things were about to get.

"It's our world too," I said. "We'll never ride around and fight like the boys, but they couldn't do it without us. I'm glad you're here. It's nice to have another woman around to remind me I haven't lost my mind getting into this."

Emma and I shared a long look. We were on the same wave length, two girls who realized our place was here in this strange, violent world.

"You're Blaze's girl?" she asked.

I blinked in surprise. *Crap. What am I supposed to say to that?*

I was closer than ever to being just what she said after last night. Still, nothing was official. He'd rebuffed Stinger, but he hadn't called me his old lady in front of his other brothers or anything. I didn't even know how the claiming process worked.

"I'm...the bartender. New hire. Yeah, Blaze and I are pretty tight."

Emma flashed a knowing smile. Damn, why did I bother hiding it? It wasn't hard for a girl with her education to fill in the gaps.

"How about you? Got an eye for anybody here?" I leaned in, beaming a smile her way. I decided to give her a taste of her own medicine. "What about Tank? He's pretty hot."

She looked away, but not before I saw rosy red lighting up her cheeks. "No way! I mean, I like the club and the fat paychecks every time they call me in. Tank's a nice guy too. I don't think I'd ever get deeper into this than I already am. It's crazy."

"Uh-huh. That's what I told myself at first too."

Emma made a sour face. She gulped down the rest of her water and then tapped her nails on the counter like she was preparing a rebuttal. Then the door to the meeting room swung open before she said a word, and both our eyes were on the brothers.

"What's the latest?" Blaze stopped at the counter and looked at her.

"He's stable. This isn't like the gun shot, but he's lucky they missed some crucial nerves. Your guy lost a lot of blood too. Keep him off his feet for a week or two and he'll be solid. Make sure he gets his antibiotics and pain pills."

"Fuck," Blaze growled. "Not a good time to lose my Sergeant at Arms. Can't spare anybody to place babysitter either. Will the hospital let you flip your hours to spend more time here?"

Emma opened her mouth to speak and froze. I wasn't sure if it was her job or the idea of spending more time with Tank that left her paralyzed.

"I'll watch him for a few." I raised my hand. "Doubt you boys will want as much from the bar right now anyway."

Blaze looked at me for a second and snorted. "Not much choice. Gonna have to keep you by my side anyway, baby. You're under lock and key, so you might as well make yourself useful."

Now it was my turn to freeze up. "Hey, I still have to go home to check up on Mom, you know."

Blaze stepped closer, his eyes dark. Emma knew when to scram, leaving me alone with him as the last few brothers disappeared into the garage.

"You're not going anywhere without somebody watching your back. Preferably me. The shit that went down this morning changes everything." He folded his arms, giving me that stern *I'm not fucking around here* look.

"Fine." I mirrored him, crossing my arms. "Then you'll get a guard for my mother too."

Blaze turned around and cursed again, running one hand over his face before he turned back to me. He was still shaking his head. If things weren't so damned serious, I would've laughed at his crazy frustration.

"You know what you're asking, Shelly? I'm sure we've got more men than the fucking Grizzlies, but they've got plenty to raise hell. You want me to spare men to guard your damned apartment when you're not even living there? There's no one else to check on mama?"

"No one. I've got my family. You've got yours."

Amazing. I had him by the balls. Blaze's lips twitched angrily, but the furious calm said he understood.

"She can't stay there. Your ma's coming here, or else we're putting her up with somebody like Miner. Easier to keep tabs on this side of town."

Holy shit. Does he have any clue what he's asking?

"We…we can try," I said softly. "She won't go easily. Hasn't been outside the apartment for years, except for a couple check-ups."

"Try me. I can handle some stubborn old woman. I've had plenty of practice with the ornery gene in your family tree."

I didn't have a clue what he thought he could say or do. Still, the effort made me smile for the first time since before the attack, and I reached out to embrace his massive shoulders.

"Thank you," I whispered, brushing my cheek on his stubble. It was always a joy to feel his muscles twitch at my touch.

"Just wait here. We'll go have our talk soon."

We didn't get going until near sundown. Blaze and I rode ahead of four guys, a formation I had a feeling he had to take as club President.

Moose, Reb, and the two prospects parked behind us outside and waited. They were there for extra security so we couldn't be ambushed again.

He hadn't said a word about Jordan yet. If my brother was still with the rogue Grizzlies, then he'd sealed his fate.

I couldn't argue anymore after this morning. All I could do was pray that Jordan came to his senses and beat it. Thinking he helped set up the deadly assault was too much to handle. If he had anything – *anything* – to do with attacking us, then he wasn't my brother anymore. He was dead to me, and he deserved whatever the Prairie Devils had in store for him.

"Mom!" I called. "Sorry I'm late. Work held me over. There's someone here I need you to meet…"

I walked through the apartment, up to her room. Last thing I needed was Blaze seeing me shaking like a leaf. This was beyond tense, and I knew it wouldn't go down easy.

No answer. Strange.

The place smelled more stagnant than usual. What the hell? I hadn't fallen behind on upkeep that much since I started working for the club. Every night I came home, I did everything I could for her and then cleaned up.

I shook my head as I pushed against her door. She still hadn't answered me. I figured she must've really been out of it.

"Mom?" I nudged the door open.

It took a few seconds for my eyes to adjust to the darkness. I looked at the floor and saw her cane laying there. It had fallen and twisted awkwardly, several feet from the bed.

My heart began pounding like a heavy drum before I even looked up. My brain refused to make sense of the torn, bloody pile laying in her bed. I dropped to my knees, screaming and crying at once.

Blaze was there with his gun drawn in an instant. He flipped the light on and I screamed again, shielding my eyes.

"Jesus Christ!" He lowered his gun. I heard him shuffle forward slowly, amazed he was able to move closer to the abomination there at all.

"Don't look, baby. Don't. Fucking. Look."

His large body blocked out the worst of it, but I still saw the messages scrawled in blood on the walls.

YOU DID THIS, CUNT.

IT SHOULD'VE BEEN YOU.

NO MERCY.

DDIGC!

God. No. No. No!

Blaze spun and ripped me up, burying my face in his chest. He clapped one hand across my eyes, repeating the same mantra over and over.

"Don't look. Keep your eyes closed. Don't look, baby."

I cracked my eyes and saw him rooting around on the floor. He stood up a moment later with a sheet and laid it gently across Mom's broken body.

"Turn around," he said softly. "If you can walk, stand up, close your eyes, and go straight outside. I'll take care of this."

His words rang deep inside me like hypnotic commands. It would've been so easy to do what he asked, anything to get away from the brutal scene that ripped out my heart. I didn't get up.

Blaze reached to my level a few seconds later, picked me up by the armpits, and pulled me close. I lost it. Buried my face deep into his leather, his chest, the very beginning of all the mourning I'd do for the woman who raised me.

"I'll take care of this, baby, I promise you that. I'm not gonna tell you what'll happen to the men who did this because it's not the time and place for that shit. Right now, we need to get the fuck out of here and I need to call up my man in the Missoula PD."

"No!" I pushed away from him, stumbling back into the narrow hallway between her room and the bathroom. "Let me handle this. It's my mother...Jesus! She didn't deserve this, Blaze. I can't abandon her and pretend it didn't happen."

He approached me, unwavering, only stopping when he was outside her room to reach for the door and pull it gently closed. Then he moved fast, grabbing me by the shoulders, holding me in a bear hug so tight it almost hurt. I freaked out and tried to claw him, scratching at the leather stained with my tears.

"Let me go! This wasn't supposed to happen…never would've happened if her kids hadn't gotten fucked up in all these stupid gangs!"

I was practically daring him to hit me. I knew how much bikers hated having their MCs called gangs, comparing them to loathsome street thugs. Shit, maybe I wanted him to slap me out, to knock me unconscious so I wouldn't have to feel my heart crumbling to ash.

"You're right. She's an innocent victim. I'm not gonna argue against the cold hard truth."

My eyes opened. I stopped pawing and struggling, watching him cautiously instead. I wasn't sure why his response disgusted me.

"That's it? You're going to pussy out just because you're feeling sorry for me?" I shook my head, letting out another sob that shook me to breaking point. "I hate the Grizzlies. I hate Jordan. And I really fucking hate the Prairie Devils too."

"Enough," he growled, his fingers tightening on my skin. "You'll have your say in this. If you wanna pick up the damned phone and call the cops, I won't stop you. Thing is, if you don't go through the proper channels, you're gonna get a whole heap of unexpected bullshit. You don't have a clue what a fucking mess you'll make if the FBI and everybody else descends on this."

I shook my head. Selfish prick!

Shouldn't be so stupid. This is all about him and his stupid club, just like it always is. God, why did I ever think about changing my life for this asshole?

"I don't care!" I shrieked. "I'll give up the job. I'll move where I have to. I'll take witness protection. I don't give a shit anymore. I want justice."

"Justice? That's what you think badges will give you?" He stared at me with hard, dark eyes.

I shook my head. What the fuck was he getting at?

"You want the same thing I do, Shelly. You want the fuckers who killed her dead. Me and my club can deliver. The Feds can't. First whiff the Grizzlies have of badges getting involved will have them blowing this fucking town. My club won't be able to hold down our own business, let alone pursue them. You get the cops involved, and you'll keep those sick motherfuckers breathing. There's no goddamned justice in that."

I stared back, too numb to cry anymore. I wanted him to be wrong. Jesus, I wanted to hate him, to see every idiot with a patch hauled away in handcuffs.

But he was right.

Blaze was always, always right, and I couldn't unsee the ruthless truth that curdled my blood. I watched him reach into his pocket. He held out the same crappy cell phone I'd used to call in Tank's stabbing.

"Here you go. You want to do it your way, then you take it. Show me what you really want so I can get my fucking ducks in a row either way."

I looked down at the cell phone waiting in his open palm. He loosened his grip on me, and I stepped away, taking several steps backward into the dark bathroom.

"No. We'll do it your way. But you *promise me*, Blaze!" I steadied myself and walked toward him again. Swallowing took all my energy because my throat felt like it was full of cotton. "You'll kill them all. Everyone who did this. Even Jordan. Give me justice."

I never wanted anything so badly in my life. I started trembling, not from fear or sadness anymore, but from blinding hot rage.

"Baby, it's not even a fucking question. You'll have your blood. I'll deliver their fucking hearts to you on a silver platter." He reached for me and pulled me tight, firmly running his fingers through my hair.

"No. I need them on Mom's grave instead. This is for her."

Blaze nodded coldly and gripped me tight as I began dry sobbing all over again.

"You'll have them, woman, if it's the last thing I do."

VI: The Demon Instinct (Blaze)

We were buried in shit. The best night of my whole fucking life turned into a toxic sewer. I had a bad feeling the ambush that got Tank stabbed was just the first ton of manure hitting the windmill.

As soon as I saw poor Saffron's mother ripped to hell, I knew I was right.

Didn't blame her for reacting like a wild animal. It would've been worse if I hadn't edged her out of there and covered up the body. She hadn't seen it like I had.

The Grizzlies were the fucking animals here, and that went double for this rogue charter. It hadn't been enough to stab a helpless old woman several dozen times. The bloody mess they left between her legs where they took turns raping her turned my fucking stomach long after we left the putrid apartment, and I'd seen some nasty shit in my time.

The memory shined in my skull like a star straight from hell, a star that wouldn't stop blinding me with its evil fucking light until I darkened it with blood. Same as the bullshit threats they'd splattered on the walls, messages I was used to seeing when shit got real between clubs.

Too bad those barbaric words were never, ever supposed to poison the civilian world.

It was hell sending Saffron away with my boys. I wanted to stay with her, but the world wasn't so merciful. I called up Stinger and had him bring the truck around for a full escort to the clubhouse. No fucking way was I leaving her exposed on a Harley anymore, even if she was pressed up behind me.

No more chances. No more mercy. Just cleanup, mourning, and then a laser sharp focus on murdering every last bitch who'd hurt my club through an innocent woman.

My badges showed up promptly, and the cops knew what to do. They'd split their payoff with their friends in the media to keep it quiet too. That was the easy part.

Filling in the rest of the club wasn't gonna be as simple. Things had turned too fucking serious to keep this a Missoula only problem. Now that the fucks had rattled us, they'd probably hit the supply lines running northwest, anything to rub our noses in bear shit.

Like it or not, I had to call in mother charter on this. Talking to Throttle was the last thing I wanted, but I'd dial him up a hundred times over if it meant savaging every last fucker in Montana wearing their greasy patch.

"Got to be Ursa behind this. I had a rotten feeling something was up when the little bitch didn't show up in Cali like I ordered." Fang's gravelly voice rumbled on the other end of the line.

"The old fart looked like he was gonna shit himself when we made our deal back in the springtime. Guess he really couldn't handle his old charter getting blown sky high." Throttle was a snarky sonofabitch sometimes, but he knew when to give it and when to pull back.

"We don't talk about that shit!" Fang snarled. "They were bastards, but they were *my* bastards. Right now, all that matters is what we're doing with these fucks who aren't mine."

Silence. My cue to weigh in on the three way call.

"We're all in agreement? A full wipe? I've got the manpower to take care of it. Can't be more than a dozen we're dealing with. I told you guys about the ratty shithole we found. It wasn't big enough for a full Grizzlies charter. This is a skeleton crew."

"You sure you won't fuck it up?" Fang insisted. "If I get wind these cocksuckers are still riding around next week, I'm sending in my own guys. Grizzlies ought to be doing this job anyway. They're wearing our fucking patch when they got no right."

No. Fuck no! I wanted to say, but it was up to Throttle as national President.

"Blaze will take care of business. I don't need to remind you what he and his brother did before the

172

truce…if you got any doubts, Fang, you come to *me*. I'll sort it out."

"One week. That's all you Missoula boys get before I'm handling things my way. You're lucky I got enough going on here in Sacramento, or I wouldn't be giving you two any chances at all. Consider yourselves lucky. I want their asses buried."

"We'll do it," I said harshly.

There was a clicking sound. Throttle coughed. The Grizzlies President had obviously dropped off.

"Take care of it, Blaze. Don't make me come out there again to keep you from shooting up Fang's crew and the renegades. I've already spent too much fucking time out West this year."

"It'll get done, brother. This shit's personal now. I'm not just talking about Tank or the old woman…"

"Damned right. Keep soldier boy out of the fire this time if you can. Poor bastard's spilled plenty of blood this year between you and Maverick getting him in harm's way." Throttle paused. "What do you mean 'personal?' Is it the girl? The dead woman's daughter?"

Fuck me blue. I'd slipped up and said too much. I flexed my fists on my desk, pissed at myself for being so sloppy when we needed all the fires hot and clean.

"You know what, I'm happy about this," he said. "Nothing like a woman you got a hard-on for to give you some real skin in the game. Now, I know you won't let me down."

Fucker. I could practically feel him grinning through the phone.

"Whatever, brother. You know I'll do the job one way or another. I'll send you their patches when we've ripped 'em off their backs."

"You'd better. Fang's gonna want to take a look at those. It's a small miracle the asshole's letting us play sheriff over this without sticking his nose in."

I snorted. "Miracle? It's called the cartels. We both know he can't handle a distraction right now on his northern front. Same reason he let us have Montana in the first place."

"Hard won. Let's make sure it stays that –"

A crying baby was bawling in the distance. I heard a woman's voice shouting his real name – Jack. Probably the little virgin girl he'd hitched as an old lady and a wife last year. The woman had given him a son in no time, making our badass king of all the Prairie Devils clubs a soft family man in his off hours.

"Shit. I got other business here," he said quickly. "You know what to do. Dial in when there's good news."

My turn to smile through the phone. Not for long, though, because the line went dead. I hung up and sat in my office for a minute, thinking about all the shit I had to shovel.

Then I thought about Saffron. She was sleeping off the utter hell that descended on her life in my old club room.

Maybe Throttle was right.

Having her at my side gave me an extra kick in the ass to do this right. No, I wouldn't let a single one of those fucks escape Satan's Scythe sweeping toward their necks.

I couldn't. I had to give her blood for blood, and make it clear to her MC life could protect as well as destroy. Had to make her believe it if she was gonna be my old lady.

And after all this fucking agony, I secretly hoped she'd still accept when I claimed her.

The rain was thick, a living cliché at the funeral. Nobody else came to honor her Mom except me.

Big surprise. From what Saffron told me, mama had been bad off for years and cut the few social contacts she'd had as a working lady. Her last few relatives were far flung and obscure, the kind who didn't give a rat's ass about a dead cousin, or a young woman who'd lost everything.

She'd suffered plenty, yeah, but I wasn't going anywhere. She hadn't lost me.

I stood by her, feeling awkward as fuck in an old suit that was one size too small. I hadn't worn the damned thing since I was in my twenties at my own father's wake.

I kept one hand on Saffron's shoulder and squeezed when the priest finished his speech. Rain pattered on the tent above us so loud it drowned out half his words, and I knew my girl wasn't hearing the rest. His sweet talk wouldn't bring the old lady back or avenge her.

That was my job.

The look she wore right now I'd seen a hundred times. Saw it on good men who lost their brothers, families who lost their men, even my own brother when we had to put dad into the ground.

She slipped from my grasp. I stood behind her, ready to comfort, as she stepped over to the casket and lovingly caressed it one last time.

I was surprised there weren't more tears. It was like the whole fucking world decided to cry for her. As far as I was concerned, even one drop was one too many.

I watched it slide down her cheek as she returned to me and nodded to the priest. Then the waterworks switched on. I held her tight, rocked her against my chest.

A mountain wind blew rain sideways, sending stray droplets into our tent. They splashed against me, but I didn't give a shit. Only wished it were as easy to block the heartache from stinging my woman.

God help me. If the fucking renegades tried to surrender, I was afraid for what I'd do.

Nothing was gonna stop me from ripping into them. What I had waiting for them was a hundred times worse than what they'd done to the poor woman in the casket.

These men were going to suffer. They'd signed their death warrants. I'd drown their scrawny asses in cold blood before they burned in hell.

When the casket was lowered into the ground, I gently traced a line up her cheek, tilting her head to look at me. Bright determination and anger shone through the tears, an anger that matched mine.

Good. I can't have her speaking any second thoughts. I need to kill all these motherfuckers.

"Don't you worry about this, baby. I got it. Your mama won't be forgotten. I'm not gonna let you down, Shelly."

"Call me Saffron," she said coldly. "It's the only name that means anything now. Only one that's right for this world."

This world. I thought about what she meant, and decided it wasn't right.

The only world she belonged to now was mine, and I ruled it with an iron fist. If she thought her world was pain and darkness, then I was gonna show her how fucking wrong she was.

I took her straight to the clubhouse. No work for her today. My boys could pour their own damned drinks or have Miner do it if they wanted.

On the way home, her shitty Toyota snorted. I was in the driver's seat, one more thing to help her ease the burden.

"Fuck, baby. We've got to find you something better when things calm down." I looked at the car's control panel and saw the gas gauge was completely broken. "Uh, not just because you deserve it. Driving this thing around with the renegades out there's bound to invite trouble. Your bro knows this car and the asshole we mopped up did too."

"Whatever. You don't want to be seen behind his rust bucket's wheel?"

I flexed my fingers defensively and glanced over. The meager smile on her face surprised me. Didn't expect her to crack a joke, however lame. I smiled back, but mine was real.

Despite all the bullshit the world had thrown at her, she wasn't broken.

The rain and the funeral created a lazy atmosphere at the clubhouse. I laid next to her for a good hour, cradling her in my old bed as she fell asleep. The raindrops pattered against our windows, cruel and relentless, incessant reminders I had some serious fucking work to do.

The landline was ringing as I unlocked my office. Hoped it was just one of my guys reporting in from patrol, and not Throttle.

I snatched the receiver and pressed it to my hear. "It's Blaze."

"Hey, asshole. What's this I hear about you tripping all over yourself for a girl? Never thought I'd see the day, Michael."

I clenched my jaw. My dickhead brother chose the worst time to call.

"Aaron. Maverick. Where the hell are you?"

"Sunny Iowa. June and I are hanging out with little sis before we head up to Minnesota. I saw the shit out your way rolling in. Glad I'm where things are a hell of a lot prettier right now."

He was talking about the weather, but it could've easily been our lives. Fuck, why couldn't I have a little of his luck?

"Whatever, bro. I know you're not man enough to admit you miss the Wild West, Grizzlies and all."

Maverick laughed. "That's right. The bears are your fucking problem now, brother. Hope you put 'em in their place before Throttle sends our asses up there as reinforcements."

"It'll never be a full war like we were looking at before," I said coldly. "Nomads won't do us any good. I got guys here who'll defend this territory like their own because it really is."

I practically saw him shrug over the line. Awkward silence. Normally I would've razzed back a lot more viciously, but the funeral killed every shred of wit and humor.

"Now, what about the girl? Heard it's the brunette with the flower tattoos my old lady used to manage. Saffron, right?"

Jealousy shot through me. Didn't want to think about any man who knew about those tattoos, though my brother was far from the only man who'd seen them. Her time up on the stage meant there were hundreds of guys who'd seen her the only way I should.

"I'm not in the mood for this shit. Whatever brotherly wisdom you're thinking about coughing up, just say it and let me go. I got a lot of work to do."

"What's going on up there? Really?" His tone lowered and thickened with concern. "Heard there was some kind of killing."

"Saffron's mother. Gonna pay the fuck's back big time. Not that it's really any of your fucking business seeing how you're hundreds of miles away. Neither is my love life."

"Yeah? You sure stepped into mine when June came around, scared she was influencing me too much." He paused. "I'm not interested in payback. I'm just trying to help your clueless ass, Michael."

Bastard. He always had to get in a few insults. Same as me.

"Clueless how?"

"If you want her, now's the time to show her how fucking much. Throttle wouldn't have mentioned her if she was just another lay. If you're serious, then you need to claim her, brother. Get your brand on her today."

"I already told the brothers where they can stick it," I growled. "They know she's off limits. Plenty of whores around here lately to keep their cocks wet anyway."

"Then where's the brand? She got your patch? How about your name on her skin?" Maverick paused long enough for my adrenaline to surge. "Didn't think so. Don't bullshit me, Blaze. I moved in and took control when June needed me the most."

"Her fucking mother just died. Romance has gotta be the furthest thing from a sane woman's mind after something like that."

Maverick laughed. God damn I wanted to reach through the phone and grab his thick neck. It'd probably end in a draw, just like all the fights we had when we were kids.

"No, this is when she needs you even more. That goes double if the girl's got nobody else. I know you're new to relationships about more than getting your dick wet, but you need to trust me on this."

"I don't need to do shit, bro. We're equals with the same patch. I make my own fucking decisions."

Hot anger flared out my nostrils. He was getting me more worked up than I should've let him, but I'd been under him too long as his VP. Last thing I needed was his fucking input on the most important decision in my life.

"No disagreements about that. Just trying to get you to man up as a brother. Come on, Michael. You've always been the asshole when it came to girls and club business. Right now, I'm taking over so you don't have to be. You know what to do."

I relaxed a little. He was a forceful sonofabitch, but he was my brother by blood and patch. Much as I hated to admit it, he was right too.

"I'll do what I need to. Next time you hear from me, all this shit will be in order. All of it. Take care out there. And say hello to Aimee and June for me."

"No need to!" June's voice came on the line and I heard a small scuffle. "You were wrong about me and you're wrong about this. Listen to Maverick and *man up,* Blaze. Rock her world so hard she forgets all about the pain and suffering. It's the best thing a man can do for his old lady."

More curses and playful slaps as my bro and his old lady fought over the phone. Gave me a few seconds to think.

"Blaze? You there?" I told my brother I was. "Just be glad you're hearing it from us. Aimee knows about the girl too and she wanted to deliver the same message we're giving you. She's anxious to have you follow in my footsteps."

"Whatever. Thanks. You've given me something to chew on, brother."

I ended the call. He was right, my blood would've boiled twice as hot having our junkie-turned-clean-and-loveable sister on my ass.

I went to work and checked in with my guys. Everybody bitched about the rain, which kept coming in strong bursts throughout the day. No sign of the renegades, and it wasn't much surprise.

Nobody wanted to be out driving around on a day like this, much less on Harleys.

When I saw everything was clear, I phoned Emma. She figured I was calling about Tank, but I really needed to talk to her mother, the owner of a seamstress and tailoring business in town.

If I was gonna get Saffron with me and breathe some light into her, then I had to do it right. I wanted her to sport her colors as my old lady and let the whole club know.

Almost as bad as I wanted to find her shithead bro and the rest of the assholes who'd caused us so much grief. Almost as much as I wanted to feel their spines snap beneath my fingers, piece by brittle piece. *Almost.*

But almost wasn't fucking good enough. No matter how hungry I was for blood, I wanted her more. Nothing else came close to having Saffron happy, safe, and mine.

Mine forever.

"Wake up, baby. We've got shit to do tonight. You've rested long enough."

She fought me at first. I gripped her skinny wrist, gently shaking her when she tried to shrug me off.

Saffron looked pissed as hell. Who could blame her?

She sat up, lips pursed sourly, especially when she saw the glass of water and aspirin I shoved toward her.

"What's this?"

"Something to make you feel human. I'm not gonna let you sleep your life away. Club's having a little bonfire to take the edge off recent bullshit. You're coming."

She crashed back on the bed and stuck her head in the pillows. Shit, this was gonna be harder than I thought.

I set the water and pills down on the nightstand and dove on top of her. Knocked the pillow clean off her head and then pushed my face to her ear. She struggled, but I wasn't going anywhere until I had her in tow.

"I know you're in pain, babe. I let you sleep this shit off for a solid week. Not tonight. Give me a few hours.

Need to see you realize your life didn't end at the fucking funeral too."

She sat up to speak. Wondered if she was about to sink her little teeth into my finger.

"Jesus, Blaze. You think I want to suck down booze and listen to a bunch of drunken idiots mess around with their whores?"

"It's not like that. Just the brothers and a few guests. Not a fucking party in the proper sense. No women whoring around. Come on." My hands tightened on her wrist and I pulled her up.

This time, I wasn't letting go.

Saffron tumbled into my lap and I had a good look at her. The long dark hair flowing down her shoulders was a mess. Her eyes were still puffy and slightly red, despite the near coma she'd been in since the funeral.

Yep, no two ways about it: the girl needed tough love.

I wouldn't let her follow her ma into an early grave. She was mine, dammit, and it was my job to reignite her whole world.

"Let's get up and move around. This shit's not healthy. It's giving into the assholes who murdered her and tore your heart to smithereens."

"What do you know?" She hissed. "It's called grief, Blaze. You wouldn't understand."

"Bullshit. You don't think I've lost people? I lost my own damned father and plenty of good brothers along the way. We have funerals and we mourn just like anybody else. But you know what? Give it a day, a weekend, or maybe a solid week, and life goes on. Your Mom couldn't get out of bed, could she?"

"What's that got to do with anything?" Saffron looked like an angry mess.

Didn't fucking matter one bit. She was *my* mess, and she looked as beautiful as she did on the only mind blowing night we'd shared. Must've been a strange kinda magic to be so pretty and so fucked up all at once.

"She *couldn't* get up and live. You want to think how pissed she'd be if she knew her only daughter was living the same way when she doesn't have to? I'm not saying get over it, because you never really do. But you don't have to let this shit poison your life. You can have any life you want, baby. Anything."

She stared at me. Resistance flickered in her eyes, but she couldn't deny what I'd said. There was no enthusiasm as I pulled her onto her feet. I practically fed the pills and small sips of water down her throat.

Whatever. I got her moving, and that's all that mattered.

The clubhouse was dead quiet except for Emma. She came by to check on Tank, who was rebounding nicely, and to drop off what I'd ordered from the family business.

"Outside." I pointed, stopping at the door to the little courtyard we'd made behind the clubhouse. "There's lots of good spots out there. Don't be afraid to sit down next to my boys and just chill. I'll be there shortly."

Saffron shook her head and opened her mouth. "But, Blaze…"

185

Her eyes were pleading. *I'm not ready for this,* they seemed to say.

I wasn't having it.

No more talk. I beamed a warning back at her, and it worked. She closed her pretty lips and turned, sighing as she pushed her way out.

Hurt like hell to see her go. I'd learned a long time ago that tough love is never fucking easy, and this was the toughest yet.

The door to the infirmary opened and slammed shut just as I was approaching. Tank staggered past me, a pissed off look on his face. He didn't even look at me as he went on his way, pounding the cane he'd gotten into the ground while his leg healed.

Didn't take a psychic to feel the bad juju bristling around him. I coughed, annoyed and wondering what the hell was going on. Just when I reached for the door, it flung open again, and Emma stepped out.

Red eyes and lots of wrinkles in her young face. Christ, she looked a whole lot like Saffron. Was everybody in this fucking place bawling their eyes out today?

"What's wrong?" I demanded.

She didn't notice me until I spoke, and when she did, her eyes went wide. I looked down and saw the big package wrapped in plastic.

"Here. I brought it along, just like you asked. Hope it's right. Mom worked with what you gave her. If you need any alterations, just send it back. I...won't be here for awhile unless you really need me. Tank's good to get along without my supervision."

"Yeah? Didn't look real good when he came stomping out ahead of you. What's up?"

Her eyes narrowed and she gave me an ugly pout. "I'm here to do my work for you, Blaze, and that's it. I'll make sure my personal crap doesn't become club business. God, I'm such an idiot…"

Emma shoved the carefully wrapped jacket into my arms and took off. I took one step toward her, getting ready to yell, but fell back at the last second.

Fuck it. Not my problem; not my business.

The evening was off to a shitty start, and there was no guarantee this was gonna go like I hoped. Last thing I needed was to become a goddamned counselor. Especially for giants with bum legs and nurses who really didn't have any business here beyond patching up my boys.

I walked around the corner and stopped, tearing away the plastic. Finally some fucking good news. The short women's cut was just like I wanted. Looked a lot like the one Moose's old lady Connie wore when she was younger.

On the front, it was sleek and smooth, all leather, just like a standard riding jacket with long sleeves. I held it up and inhaled. Shit, it even smelled good, fresh leather meant to mingle with my woman's scent.

I turned it over. The club's cocky devil was on the back, the same face I'd dedicated my life to. The patches surrounding his grin were the real important part.

PROPERTY OF BLAZE, PRAIRIE DEVILS MC, MONTANA.

It was perfect. No joke. I couldn't wait to see it on her, if she'd do me the highest honor a man can receive when he takes an old lady.

All I knew was I wasn't taking no for an answer.

I tucked the jacket under my arm and stepped outside. The guys and a tiny gaggle of girls were drinking near the fire.

I found her sitting glumly by herself underneath a tree in a fold out chair, well away from everybody else by the fire. She didn't see me coming.

"Pretty cool this evening when you're not by the flames. I want this to keep you warm." I draped the coat over her shoulders and steadied it there when her shoulders flinched.

That got a response. She looked at me in surprise, bringing one hand to her opposite arm to caress the leather. I watched her fingers pinch at the material and roll down it, giving it a good feel.

"What's this? Looks like something you'd wear."

"Stand up. Open it so you can see. Read the back."

I held in a smile as she obeyed. A man only gets a few serious moments of truth in his life, and this was one of them.

She gripped it by the arms and spread it, carefully mouthing the phrase PROPERTY OF BLAZE to herself. Fuck, just seeing her lips forming those words sent a jolt straight to my cock.

Maybe I was an animal for feeling the urge when she was in so much pain. Couldn't be helped, though, and I didn't regret it for a second either.

"It's yours, baby, if you'll have it. It's more than just a leather jacket." I stepped closer, and she looked at me, eyes questioning. "I know what you're thinking. The property part's a compliment in this world. Means nobody else will even try to lay a hand on you, much less anything else, or I'll make them fucking sorry they even got the thought in their stupid heads."

"Okay…" Her cheeks reddened. She looked so small, unsure.

I reached out and clasped her in my embrace, smashing the new jacket between us. One hand pushed flat against her back, drawing her into me, until we were face to face and only inches apart.

"I'm asking you to be my old lady, Saffron. A new chapter for your life, for us, right after another one slammed shut. You gonna help me write it?"

I couldn't remember the last time I held my breath. Maybe during the vote to make me President of this charter, and the outcome here was much less certain.

She looked up slowly, blinking a couple times.

Damn it, woman, hurry up. I'll fucking suffocate here if you don't give me an answer.

"Blaze! Blaze…Blaze…Blaze…"

She pushed against me firmly. Her sweet tits flattened on my chest and she leaned up, pushing her cheek against my stubble. I grunted, inhaling her scent, wondering why she was on the verge of tears and calling my name over and over.

"Is that a 'yes?'" I asked. Shameless and impatient.

"*Yes!*" As soon as the word steamed into my ear, I squeezed her tight, running my hands down to her ass.

"It's been so hard. The danger, the funeral…"

"I know, baby. You got nothing to fear. I told you that a hundred times. This is what's right."

"I don't doubt it anymore. Just a couple weeks ago, I wasn't sure, but I'm not having second thoughts anymore. You're right, Blaze. This is where I belong," she said softly, before giving me a look with more life than I'd seen since we fucked. "I'll wear this and do you proud."

Just what I wanted to hear. I reached up, cupped her chin between my fingers, and brushed my lips over hers. One little prelude to the deep, hungry kiss that came next, obliterating more than a week of pure loneliness without her lips on mine.

Lust wasn't far behind. The familiar demon roared in my blood, hungry to get her alone and unwrapped. I thought about what she'd look like wearing the new jacket and nothing else.

Fucking-A. There was a thought. *We do it like that, and I'll go raw and rough and deep for hours. This is the only sweet flesh I need, now and for the rest of my life.*

I kissed her deep. Just when I was about to throttle back, she pushed her tongue against mine, gasping a little at the raw passion burbling between us.

Shit, I had to let go. If I didn't, I'd throw her over my shoulder and carry her inside for a pounding right now. Too early for that. This ritual still had another part to it.

"Slide that thing on for me, baby," I ordered. I'd go nuts if I didn't see what it looked like on her sweet body.

She nodded. It was damned good to see her smile again, and she broke into a full grin as I helped her into the jacket.

I hadn't gone for sexy when I had it made, but the fucking thing had that effect anyway. Could it seriously have any other?

I let her walk a little ahead, holding her hand in mine, casting glances at her luscious ass bobbing below the leather every other step.

Hot confusion roared in my brain. Shit, I was half-expecting to lose my mind if she turned me down.

Total fucking opposite! Now I was worried I'd blow or melt from the inside out seeing her like this, seeing her as *mine*. Even with my brand on her, she was driving me loco.

"Boys, I'm not gonna make a big show out of this like some people," I said, approaching my men.

Remembering when Maverick claimed June popped into my mind. He'd done it loudly and boisterously. Not really my style. Until we got married, my circle needed to know, but they didn't need to feel the heat between Saffron and I.

That fire was for us alone, and I was a greedy bastard. I wanted it all to myself.

"Turn around, baby." I gave her a soft squeeze on the ass and she did as I asked.

Bawdy laughter thundered up along with a few cheers as soon as they saw the print on her jacket. The few women with the brothers gasped happily. My hand swept up, resting on her shoulder.

Fuck it. Who am I kidding? It's gonna be loud and wild no matter what I do.

I wrapped one arm around her waist and pulled her into me, giving her a big, long kiss in front of them. Guess doing it the showy way was the only way for us Sturm men, and for guys wearing this patch.

Saffron tensed up. Being a stripper didn't mean she was used to public affection, especially in front of a bunch of big guys who were damned close to being family. I kissed her until she relaxed and started to melt.

When I let her get some air, men started coming over in a line, pounding me on the back. Reb and Roller dolled out stern handshakes, and the girls did neck bending hugs.

"Welcome to the family! You'll be doing more than serving drinks now, honey." Connie, Moose's old lady, tore my girl away from me and I growled jealously.

"Don't mind her, Prez. Seriously, congratulations. This has been a long time coming. Lord knows we can all use a little good news."

I threw my arms around Moose and slapped him on the back. He was a good brother, maybe the best I'd made out here.

Miner hugged me too. The old man winked at me and leaned in close to whisper.

"Not hard to see why you like this one, man." He paused. "Girl makes drinks like you wouldn't believe. Suppose she's an easy looker too."

"Fuck you," I said, laughing the whole time. "You just want somebody else to do all the work at your retirement party."

Laughing, he strolled away, and Stinger took his place.

We stared at each other for several long seconds, man to man. Then he broke into that shitty grin and hugged me tight, giving my neck an aggressive squeeze.

"Congrats. Girl deserves more than a man looking for pussy. I know you're good together."

I nodded firmly. He knew when to bury the hatchet, and I didn't fault him for our little toss up over my girl at the last big party. It took serious and venomous bullshit to make bad blood between brothers.

"Looks like somebody over there's not so happy." Grinning, he pointed.

Anger flashed through me as I turned. It took me a few seconds to see Marianne's sour face pressed up against the window at the back of the bar. The bitch was watching us like a scorned cat, and she wasn't fucking happy about me taking myself off the meat market.

"Fuck her," I growled. "I don't owe her a damned thing, and neither does anybody else who stakes their claim to another girl. Hope she remembers she's just a whore."

"I'll remind her, brother," Stinger said, urging me to turn back around with an arm on my shoulder. "Don't worry about her starting any shit. I'll have her so busy with this dick she won't even think about fucking with you or Saffron."

I looked at him and saw the sincerity in his face. For a few seconds, I hesitated, expecting to feel some little burn, some flash flood of jealousy.

Nothing. No matter how many times I'd fucked her, she didn't come close to one-tenth what Saffron was. The only regret I had was wasting so much time and a lot of good hard-ons with her. No more. From now on, they were all going straight to my old lady, the same way my dick was only going in Saffron for the rest of my life.

"You do that," I told Stinger. "You're a shit sometimes, but you really are a bro."

We hugged again. Damned good feeling. All was right with the MC and with the world when brotherhood trumped bad blood.

If the club had taught me anything, camaraderie and freedom stomped the hell out of everything else. Outlaws didn't go against the civilian world for money or because we wanted to swing our dicks at the world to prove a point.

We did it so we could live and love the way we wanted. Stinger understood that, same as me. Same as every man I called brother here.

Saffron was still chatting with Connie while I pressed hands with the prospects. Those boys weren't bullshitting me either. Soon as this shit with the renegade Grizzlies blew over, they were gonna get their patches, bros as much as the rest of us.

After all the well wishes, I walked over and took her arm. She gave me a hopeful look, like she needed some rescuing.

We walked to the clubhouse, looking for more booze to celebrate.

"You'll get used to Connie," I said. "Everything's gonna seem second nature in good time. You're meant for this, baby. Knew it the first time I laid eyes on you."

"Ha, it'll take a lot of practice to keep up with her motor mouth." She laughed, and I did too.

I sent her behind the bar for ice and a couple bottles of Jack. I was ready to grab the heavy bags out of her hands and make our way to the party when I caught something in the dark corner.

"Hold up," I said, setting the bags down on the counter. "This'll only take a minute."

Tank sat by himself in the shadows with a half-depleted whiskey bottle. He looked up long after I approached and stood at his side.

"Well? You gonna tell me what the fuck's going on and why you aren't at the fire?"

"Nothing, boss. Just a bad run in with the nurse." He shook his head, slamming down what was left in his shot glass. "She was getting too close to me. I know it's not good to mix club business and personal shit."

He looked drunkenly at the bar where Saffron was still gathering stuff and blinked. "Uh, under the wrong circumstances, I mean. Emma's the kind who'd get distracted...and we sure as hell don't need anybody at less than a hundred percent right now. Those fucking Grizzlies are just waiting for us to slip up so they can hit us again. I told her to do her job and keep her ass safe. She didn't take it well."

I nodded. He was thinking like a Sergeant at Arms. Just not much else.

"It'll all work out, Tank. Don't drink in here by yourself like some sorry ass drunk. It's a cool night." I reached for his cane and tapped it on the floor. "How long you need to use this fucking thing?"

"Another couple weeks tops. Fucking embarrassing when I should be on the front lines, just like you."

"I'll be more upset if you don't get your heavy ass out there. Come on."

He followed me to the bar and I grabbed the ice. Saffron walked the whiskey out ahead of us, and he nudged my leg with the cane when he saw her patches.

"Jesus. You two made it official?" Wasn't hard to detect some envy in his voice.

"Sure did. You can congratulate her later before we head in for the night." Tank mouthed a quick congratulations, slurring it a little in his drunken mouth. "Your day's coming, bro. Doesn't seem like it now, but I used to think the same thing. This shit creeps up on you and jumps your back when you least expect it."

He nodded. "I'll take your word for it, boss. Doesn't matter though. I'm not looking for love. Is Marianne working tonight?"

I cocked an eyebrow. "Don't know shit about her schedule anymore. We're keeping it low key tonight so we can all be bright eyed and ready to fuck up bears in the morning. Watch where you stick that bottle and your dick."

He nodded, but I knew a brush off when I saw one.

Whatever. I couldn't imagine making a mistake like that after claiming my woman. Hell, after knowing I *needed* to claim her. When I set my sights on Saffron, I steered away from Marianne like a damned plague. No matter how good the whore would make my cock feel, it wouldn't be half as good as Saffron, and one taste of her meant I'd never settle for lesser pussy again.

Hell no. I'd never, ever get tired of seeing her, smelling her, feeling her, and especially staring at my name on her clothes and inked on her flesh.

Saffron was whole grades higher than any whore ever built for fucking. And speaking of fucking, I was ready. I meant to give it to her so raw and real it would make the last week seem like a bad dream and nothing more.

"Blaze…" I looked down and she was tugging on my arm.

Most of the guys were blasted and sleepy, and the rest were well on their way there. We were about the only ones still reasonably sober. Darkness descended over the mountains, leaving us sitting before the fire like a goddamned tribe ready to face our sworn enemies at dawn.

Saffron looked amazing in the light, the shadows flowing around her curves, newly outlined in the jacket I'd given here. Hell, who was I kidding?

She looked fucking amazing in almost any light. Growling, I put a hand on her hip and jerked her close, not stopping until she was on my lap, face-to-face.

"What's up, baby? You feeling better?"

She nodded, and then leaned in, gently touching her forehead to mine. "I'm sorry for the way I've acted lately. I never should've doubted you. This...this makes a lot crystal clear."

I watched her run one hand over her new leather sleeve. Wasn't meant to be seductive, but damn if my cock didn't jump.

"It's not all clear yet. We need to work hard to get to the truth. I already told you why they call me Blaze. Burning fucks who deserve it isn't the only fire I do. Let me show you. We'll burn until there's no more doubt or confusion about anything in your pretty head."

My hands tightened on her thighs. I held her close, slowly lifting her up, heading for the clubhouse. We'd had our fill of food and company, and it was time to go.

She leaned against me as we headed inside. Lungs rising and falling, I knew she was inhaling my scent. Excitement flickered through my body and pooled in my cock, pulsing now with total need.

Everybody else was outside, leaving the clubhouse to ourselves. Perfect. Nobody to hear her scream when I laid it deep – not that it would've stopped me for a single second.

When I needed to fuck this woman, I needed it down to my molecules. I needed it to survive. I'd go to pieces without her flesh beneath me, her soft moans turning to shrill catcalls in my ears.

I closed the door behind us and went straight for the bed. She didn't resist as I laid her down, finding my way between her legs, quickly tugging at the new jacket. It rolled off her shoulders and fell behind her.

The old fantasy I had right before returned. She started to help me roll off her shirt, but I stopped her when it was halfway up her belly at her gorgeous tits.

"You take it all off, baby. Then put the jacket back on. I want to ride with my old lady tonight."

Must've said something right. She gave me a wide grin and blushed. That made me smile like a fucking fool, knowing she was dirty as the day was long, but she tried to hide it just for me.

Well, no more. No more goddamned secrets. I wanted to own her, real and honest, every sweet side of her. Saffron the slut, Saffron the lover, Saffron the old lady to savor and keep for the rest of my life. From tonight on, everything between us was gonna be as honest as it was when I had my cock between her legs.

So fucking real. Rough, raw, and explosive.

She hadn't finished undressing when I had to kiss her again. Those lips were like molten fire, hot and slippery and perfect under mine. My tongue shot into her mouth, searching for hers to tame.

I found it, sucking at her bottom lip. Her sweet skin twitched in my hands, goosebumps and muscles going wild, all doing the dirty work for me.

That's it, woman. Work it fucking harder. Work it all out on my cock.

Soon as she was naked, I went for my own clothes. Never thought getting naked for her the second time would be as good as the first, but this girl was full of surprises. She reached for me hungrily when I kicked off my boxers, grabbing at my ass.

That set me off. So did having her looking at me like that, keeping her little lips pursed and dangerously close to my cock.

I straddled the bed, grabbing her by the hair. "You got something you wanna do? Don't let me stop you, baby. Suck. Suck it deep and hard as long as you want."

She licked her lips. My whole body tensed, lust exploding dizzying bursts. Shit hit my brain like a damned jackhammer when her pink lips engulfed my tip, and then her tongue went to work, nasty as it was skilled.

"Ah, fuck!" I grunted, jerking her hair hard in my hand.

The roughness didn't deter her one bit. She went deeper, sliding her way down my cock, digging her tongue up into the sweet spot under my head.

Oh, shit. No bones about it: the woman knew what she was doing. Made me wonder where she learned that, though I wished it didn't, because it made me think about her with other guys.

And thinking those thoughts caused my cock to grind angrily against her mouth, hungry to fuck away traces of every lover she'd ever had except me. And that was only the beginning.

I stared at the patches on her back from my perfect viewpoint. PROPERTY OF BLAZE?

Yeah, she fucking was.

Soon she was gonna do more than wear my brand. I'd make her into the Saffron she wanted to be, free as I was to do what I wanted on my terms. I'd fuck the past away, making her scream it out as she spread her legs to be filled, fucking to make room for every future she truly deserved.

Saffron's mouth moved slow, rhythmically, sucking harder each time she went to the edge and then pulled back. I could feel the energy welling up inside her, the desire in her movements. When she cupped my balls and squeezed with several rogue fingers, I nearly shot my load down her throat.

Too much. Time to change the angle.

I pushed my fingers deeper into her hair, really getting her tight. I had full control of everything except her wild ass tongue. Pushing and pulling her head up and down my length in steady strokes, nudging her back when it was too fucking much.

I closed my eyes and let the pleasure strike through me. It cut deep, hot, activating more primal needs. I opened my eyes and took a good, long look at her.

Her nipples were hard and perked out, just pleading to be pinched and sucked. Didn't need to see her pussy from here. I knew it was steaming and dripping wet, the reason she was starting to shake with each new lick.

Fuck! That word ricocheted in my skull over and over like a wild bullet.

I pushed her face completely off me. She looked up, wearing the wicked little smile that was so innocent but so damned naughty.

I reached low and gave her bare ass a good whack on one cheek. She jerked in surprise, and I enveloped her, feeling heat spread through the hot blood pressing against her skin.

"Come on, baby. Get on top. Need to take you for a fucking ride."

Sexy excitement thrashed in her eyes as I lay down. My rough hands grabbed her legs and helped guide her, but they wouldn't stay put for long. I grabbed her breasts hard as she sank down on my cock with a loud gasp.

This was gonna be her ride, just like I said. I'd give it to her, all right, but she could take it at her own pace, a slow motion firecracker meant to explode on top of me again and again.

She leaned forward, grunting and pushing her nipples through my fingertips, perfect vices for pulling, plucking, pinching...

"Oh, God. Feels so fucking good, Blaze. *Deeper.*"

Deeper? Oh, yeah.

I pushed up, grinding against her clit. She started to shake, and I did too when her greedy cunt sucked at my cock, curling lush silk around it.

A man as experienced as me can always control it, but she gave me a run for my fucking money. Had to bare down on my muscles hard as our tempo sped up, and I dug my fingers deep into her ass, watching her tits swing, jerking her up and down on my cock.

The little sounds spilling out her lips were feral and sexy and sweet. One problem.: they were way too fucking tame for my liking.

I lifted one hand and spanked her ass again. Her hips bucked faster, racing along my length, drawing me deep before falling back again.

"You got the idea. Come on, Saffron. Come for your old man. You earned it, girl. You leave me hanging too long and I'll make your ass red. Come like you want to, baby."

My words pushed her to the very brink, but she wasn't going over. Not yet. Her tits rolled and sweat dripped off them. The whole room smelled like raw fucking, enough to make a man trip all over himself if he staggered into it.

Come. The fuck. On!

I slapped her ass, harder this time. She jerked forward, grinding her clit against me, and stopped. I felt the explosion build up above her cunt and race down, before hurtling out in all different directions.

Saffron whipped her beautiful head back and came, growling like a wildcat, losing her ability to make anything but a breathless gasp after a few spasms ripped through her. I held on tighter, and I fucking needed to.

She pinched my cock like a goddamned vice, a perfect ring of pussy locked around my balls, sucking and coming all around my whole length. I thrust up in small, shallow strokes halfway through, making her come even harder, drawing out her orgasm until she cried.

That made me smile.

I wanted it to hurt because it was so damned good. Wanted it to be too much, a full body demo starting in hellfire and ending in pleasure and relief. This was a fuck she'd remember for the rest of her life.

Pretty tall order knowing I'd be giving it to her a lot for now on, but there it was.

I was determined, and I wasn't fucking letting go.

She started to pant coming down from her high. My cue to go all over again, gripping her ass until my knuckles were white, holding her against me as I slammed my cock into her.

"Oh, fuck. Oh, oh! I can't –"

"Let your fucking eyes roll, baby. No more talk. Not 'til you blow for me again."

She spoke with her nails while I had her lips locked up in heaven. Sharp fingernails raked down my chest, right over my club tattoo. Damned if she didn't scratch me like a fucking mountain lion.

Guess sex this intense always hurts and throbs and cuts both ways.

Her nails spurred me to fuck harder. So I did.

Soon, she was coming again, crying out louder before pleasure choked off her screams. Music to my red blooded ears.

I could've kept her riding me forever, fucking and coming until neither of us could walk straight. Could've, if it wasn't for the fire starting to churn in my balls.

Her orgasm was just starting to wane when I lost it. I tossed her sweet ass up high before yanking her close, holding her onto me with a death grip as burning seed shot up my loins.

It hit her deep and we both exploded to a greater high. Coming together was meant to be this, two waves of flesh slapping and mixing, my essence shooting to her womb. Her pussy sucked and twisted at my cock, drawing sperm deep, but she couldn't hold everything I gave her.

I filled her good and it kept going, pouring into her, until I was sure my balls were empty. Our heavy juices slipped out between us.

Even when it was over, I was rock hard. I held myself in her as she collapsed, falling totally exhausted onto my chest. Her muscles seized one more time and she moaned, soft ecstasy breezing out her lips.

I gripped her tight and stroked her hair, loving her lingering warmth.

Yeah, this was right. This was where we both belonged. No matter what happened from here on out, if we melded like this, there wouldn't be any more fears or misunderstandings.

I'd marked her and claimed her in the deepest way I could as my new old lady. There'd be time for a real honeymoon as soon as this shit with the renegades passed. For now, I was satisfied, happy because she was happy. And nothing – no, nothing – was gonna threaten that.

"I've been thinking about Jordan," she whispered later, after we'd finally had our fill.

I'd mounted her and came two more times. Lost track of all the times she shuddered, gasped, and exploded on my dick the last few hours.

Fuck. Thought I'd driven those demons away for good.

I might've thought it, but I knew I was being fucking naive. Good hard fucking was enough to forget, but when it was all over, the same dirty business was staring us in the face. Dirty *and* unfinished.

"What about him? Hope to have a lead on that little shit soon. None of my boys have seen him for a while, but we'll hunt him down. I'll bring you his fucking patch myself." She gave me an intense look. "Our way of proving an enemy's dead and won't be causing no more trouble."

"No, it's not so simple, Blaze." She grabbed my arm and squeezed.

Damn it, I didn't like where this was heading.

"Look, I know what you need to do...I haven't changed my mind. It's just that...well, he's family. The only way I'll ever feel like Mom's resting in peace is if *I* take care of it."

"What the fuck?" I sat up on one elbow and looked at her hard. "You're telling me you want to kill your own brother?"

She nodded. I shook my head. Maybe fucking so rough and long had rattled something loose in her head.

"You're not a killer, Saffron. You had a hell of a time taking out your rapist asshole in the woods. Let the club handle this. Let me."

"It gets easier the more you do it, right?" Cynical words for a pretty lady. "I'm not saying I'll be stupid. I'll do whatever you think is the best way to go about this. You can bring him to me."

"It's not always that easy, baby. Especially if he's brought the whole club along with him. No fucking way am I putting you so close to danger. Already slipped up once not having this place locked down tight and driving you into an attack."

Shit, were we even discussing this? My old lady, my way. I wanted to put my fucking boot down and end it.

"He won't bring his guys," she said, brushing away the warning in my voice. "I've got a plan, Blaze. If it goes like I think, you can lead him straight to us. Squeeze him about the others, I don't care. I need to do this for family. You need it for your club. Won't you hear me out?"

Just my luck. I wanted Saffron deep in the lifestyle, yeah, but I never expected her to turn cold blooded killer and partner in…whatever the fuck we were about to do.

I couldn't believe I listened to her scheme.

VII: Repercussions (Saffron)

There's only one thing in the world harder than killing a human being: killing your own flesh and blood.

I gripped the small gun Blaze had given me, concealing it in a holster behind my new jacket as I stood behind Mom's old apartment. We'd just cleaned up her things shortly after the funeral. The building's management gave us until the end of the month to vacate, pretty standard procedure for the deceased.

There was no guarantee this would work. If it hadn't been for the happy afterglow in his eyes after our sex, he probably wouldn't have listened at all. But special nights do special things.

I was thrilled to be his old lady. Truly. Nothing sounded better than wiping this horror clean so we could get on with our lives.

I told him I wanted to kill Jordan. Truthfully, I was totally prepared to do it the minute the bastard laid a hand on me or confessed a single word about murdering our mother.

But I had to hear it from his lips. I couldn't let Blaze, me, or anybody else kill my brother without knowing he was truly guilty, and if he wasn't...

Crap.

Thinking about that was almost as hard as imagining a bullet in his head. If he hadn't done it, then we had a much bigger problem, and I didn't have a clue how to handle him or keep my love from killing him anyway.

Right now, I waited. Alone, but not really.

Several guys from the club were right around the corner. All the big experienced ones: Tank, Moose, Reb, and Roller. Blaze was up in the apartment, the place where I was supposed to corner him or run to at the first sign of trouble, assuming his guys didn't get to us first.

As expected, Jordan hadn't answered his phone. I left the tearful calls anyway. I set a time and a place and told him to be there if he gave a shit about family at all.

Didn't take much to pour on the sadness these days, even if the intense sorrow I'd felt the week after the funeral was fading like the world's slowest healing sore.

I gave him a time and a place. Now all we could do was hope he showed up. The Devils expected him to come with his friends, and they were standing by to deal with them.

I opened my phone and looked at the time. He was already a couple minutes overdue, but then, my brother had never been punctual. He was used to setting his own schedule, and leaving me to pick up the pieces he refused to handle.

My jaw popped as I bit down and held it tight. This wait was killing me. A few more minutes passed.

I wondered if I hallucinated a motorcycle's rumble a little while later. No, there it was, loud and ominous and way too late to be anybody under Blaze.

My brother pulled in sporting full Grizzlies colors. God, he had balls, showing up in enemy territory like this when he had to have known what had happened…

He saw me standing by the little garden area near the lot and parked. No apartments faced this side of the building and the mostly elderly residents wouldn't be taking any notice while I waited, fingering the handgun one more time. No room for error or going back now. If this ended up like I thought it would, I couldn't hesitate.

I had to be ready. I had to rip it out when he turned away, point it at the back of his head, and blow his brains out.

You hesitate a single second, there won't be a second chance. We need him dead and mopped up before anybody notices. Every fucking second counts.

Blaze's words echoed in my head. I clenched the gun, promising I wouldn't let him down, and then let go. Had to look somewhat normal and relaxed now that big brother was right next to me.

"Shelly? What the hell's going on? You and Mom finally decided to come to your senses after treating me like dog shit?"

I blinked. *Shit* was right. Was it a ploy, a mind game, or was he seriously in the dark?

"What are you looking at?" he asked, growing more irritated. "What? Fucking tell me!"

He reached for my shoulders. I should've grabbed the gun and shot him then, but of course I was too slow, too stunned.

Jesus, my control was slipping. He acted like he didn't know a damned thing.

Reb and Roller were checking on our position from a nearby spot every few seconds, and they had a rifle to shoot from long distances. If they swept their binoculars over us right now, while he was yelling and shaking like a maniac, then he was as good as dead if I wasn't in the way.

I hesitated. They wouldn't.

"What happened?" he demanded.

I opened my mouth and coughed. For the first time in years, I saw serious concern lining his face, the brother I thought I'd lost looking at me with hollow and scared eyes.

"Mom's dead!" I croaked.

For a second, his hands pinched my skin to the bone, and then they were gone. He backed away like a zombie, and going just as pale as one too.

"What're you...this can't be real." Anger added new color to his flesh again. "Mom? You gotta be bullshitting me. What the fuck's happened to our mother –"

He broke and went running. I caught him at the main door, pounding on it with his fists.

Holy shit, this was going sour. If I didn't stop him this instant, he'd wake the whole first floor, and then we'd never kill him, much less hide a body.

But killing was the furthest thing from my mind now. My brother wasn't a good actor. He was a hot-head who ran on pure emotion, and he was doing it now, completely losing his shit as his fists banged raw against metal and glass.

"Shelly? Open this fucking door!"

"Jordan! Stop it!" I pinched his arm until he yelped. "You're not getting in until you tell me if you came here alone. Are there any others? Any of those assholes?"

"No, but I wish I'd brought my brothers!" He sneered. "They wouldn't have let this shit happen. You better be shitting me, sis. If you're not…I won't hold back, and neither will the club. I'll destroy the motherfucker who put her into an early grave."

He was tensing up, so full of rage he wouldn't hesitate to strike, even at me, his own sister. Then, like a fever, it broke. He slumped to his knees, clinging to the door handle, hanging his head.

Okay, things were getting really fucked up. Something was really off.

Jordan didn't look…right.

Not just because he was horrified and wearing those ugly colors either. His hair was slick and greasy, like he hadn't showered for a long time. He had to be on something.

"Let me in...let me see...please, sis. I need to make peace. Won't hurt you. I promise."

Junkie or not, he worked my heartstrings. I gulped, and caught the flicker of a man in leather behind us, walking through the parking lot.

I hadn't totally decided what the hell to believe. I had to know more before I made my decision. But first, the shadows outside moved again.

Crap. Somebody noticed we weren't where we were supposed to be. Reb and Roller would be on us in a second. Had to move.

I unlocked it and flung open the door. Jordan took off, his missing energy suddenly refreshed.

Shit, shit.

Running after him was like chasing a loose dog. I ripped down the halls as fast as my feet would carry me, up the stairs, and only slowed when I saw Mom's old door hanging open.

Oh, God. Blaze, please don't kill my brother. Please don't—

When I got inside, Blaze was knocked flat. My brother was on top of him, beating his fists bloody each time he swung for my old man's face and missed. The men wrestled like two mountain lions, swearing and roaring and spitting in a tornado of muscles and leather.

"Hey! *Hey!*" They didn't even know I was there.

If there was ever a time for that gun...

"Fucking stop it!"

I whipped it out and fired. An accident, done and over in the blink of an eye.

The bullet soared a couple feet over their heads and embedded itself in the wall. The deafening *bang* got their attention. Finally.

Blaze pushed my brother off, snarling. He had his own gun in hand, and he rolled, slamming it across Jordan's jaw and pressing the barrel to my brother's temple as he met my gaze.

"I said stop! Blaze, don't do this!"

"Give me one good fucking reason why not. This wasn't the plan, Saffron!" The nine millimeter wobbled in his hand. I'd never seen him so pissed.

"Plan?" Jordan groaned, as if from another world.

My turn to step forward, while I still could. I raised the gun again, way more careful this time, and carefully trained it past Blaze on my brother.

"I've got him. Back away. We all need to talk."

"There's nothing to discuss!" Jordan roared, seething with more frightful energy. "Nothing except why my fucking mother's dead and my sister's pulling a goddamned gun on me!"

"Quiet, asshole," Blaze growled. "Saffron, you got something to say, you say it now. He's got about thirty seconds, and the countdown already started…"

He wasn't fucking around. I could see him mentally tracking the time, ready to snuff out my brother like a cornered bug. For him, it wasn't hard. He wouldn't hesitate with anyone who was a threat.

"Jordan didn't do this. He's an asshole – a crazy asshole! – but I don't believe he had anything to do with killing our Mom. He didn't know…"

Blaze shook his head, dripping ridicule off his sexy body. "Oh, please. You gotta be shitting me. What'd he say?"

The gun jabbed harder at Jordan's temple. My brother's whole body shook once, as if shocked, and then settled into weaker tremors.

My heart did a painful flip. I saw the boy who used to cry so long ago about middle school drama and his first bad breakup, desperately trying to hide his anguish from Mom and I.

"No way he did it. My brother's fucked up, probably taking drugs, but he didn't kill her. He didn't even know it had happened…"

"Yeah, I've seen this sweaty, manic bullshit before. Fucker's been shooting ice. Isn't that right, you sonofabitch bear?" Blaze's hand twitched on the gun, and I could tell he barely refrained from pistol-whipping him in the jaw again. Then he looked at me.

"Never trust a fucking junkie. The Grizzlies have got plenty of 'em. It's half the reason we always kick their asses. These motherfuckers can't remember what they ate for breakfast, much less what they did a week ago."

"No…he wasn't like this before. Even when he first showed up in town, he was sober. This is new." I looked at Blaze. *Not very convincing,* his expression said.

Crap. Think of something. Think!

"Jordan…" I came closer, as close as Blaze would tolerate. "Where were you? If you don't know about this, you couldn't have been here…couldn't have been with your *club*."

I didn't hold my contempt. He looked up at me like a lost dog. His eyes were glazed and newly bloodshot.

"I'm not telling this Prairie Pussy. Kill me now if that's what you wanna do."

Blaze drew the gun away and gripped it in both hands. "Good call, asshole. I'm much obliged to answer."

"Nooo!" The shrillest, most bloodcurdling scream of my life ripped out my lungs.

It hurt, but it worked. Blaze looked at me with an equal harshness in his eyes, shaking his head. This was my very last chance.

"Jordan, please. If you ever cared about me or Mom you'll tell him. You'll save your stupid fucking life! It's about the last thing you deserve…but it's all you still got."

Please.

There was a long silence. My brother sat up straight, the defiance on his face melting into defeat. He let out a loud sigh.

"Been on a long run out of state," he said slowly, turning to Blaze. "You fucks will find out why soon enough, and so will Saffron if she doesn't stop hanging with you. Brought some new toys back from Idaho to compete with the shit you Devil bastards are playing with."

"Blaze…" I moaned.

"I believe him." Not the words I thought I'd hear. Blaze got up and stepped back, the first step to standing down, though he didn't take the gun off him.

"You're crazy, Jordan. Let me help you." I kneeled in front of my brother and touched his face. He jerked back, as if I was a complete stranger.

"Don't need your damned help, sis. My brothers have got my back."

"You're wrong. Look at me, Jordan." Blaze put one foot forward, warning him to comply.

I waited until he met my eyes. Jesus, he looked like total shit. It was like something had crawled into my brother's body and taken him over.

"Those men you're with are the ones who killed Mom. I saw her myself…the shit they did to her." My turn to choke and cry. "You don't want to know. You need to get out, and then tell us everything you know about them so Blaze can help us get her justice."

"You think you're working for the Grizzlies?" Blaze said. "Guess you don't realize your brothers are a goddamned renegade charter. If we don't blast their asses, Fang will do it for us."

"Bullshit." Jordan's eyes flicked to me, then to Blaze. "Think he's got you brainwashed pretty good, sis. You always were an easy girl to lead around."

Blaze stiffened, gun in hand. "Watch it, asshole."

"This is a fucking trick. I got a real good feeling I'm looking at Mom's killer right now. Devils always were manipulative pricks."

Blaze reached into his pocket and pulled out his phone. I wondered what he was doing, especially as he flipped it open and dialed.

"What the fuck?" Jordan took the words right out of my mouth.

"You don't believe me. Fine. But I think you'll believe it when you hear it from the horse's mouth."

Jordan's face went white.

"Fang? It's Blaze. Missoula. Look, I know this isn't the standard procedure with Throttle and all, but right now I don't give a fuck. I've got a valuable lead on your renegades and I need you to tell this piece of shit with me that his boys aren't real Grizzlies anymore. Yeah? Here you go."

Blaze pushed the phone aggressively to my brother's ear. Jordan's jaw dropped, and I heard a low, sinister sounding voice flowing through the speaker.

"Yeah...yeah...Jesus Christ. I didn't...know. Work with this asshole?" Long pause. "You're sure about this?"

The conversation dragged on. My brother looked like he wanted to puke. Who could blame him?

Jordan iced up and stopped responding. I had to lean in close to find out when the call ended.

"How 'bout that? You believe me now?"

"Fucking monsters...I'll...I'll kill them all myself."

Never thought I'd welcome such evil words. Blaze lowered his gun, this time for good, and stepped to the other side of the room to let his guys know what was going on. Just in time too because Reb and Roller came thundering through the door.

"Welcome home, Jordan. It's not too late. You'll be okay."

I hugged him tight. He was too dazed and sick to hug me back, but I saw pain and promise in his eyes, the same determination I'd shown Blaze a hundred times.

He wanted the men who did this dead as badly as I did. If that gave him a reason to clean up and live, then it was good enough for me.

Jordan never moved. Blaze and his men surrounded us. He had them pick my brother up and carry him into Mom's old room like a piece of wood.

I listened to the intense shouts through the door for the next full hour. Each time my brother got pissy or came close to blubbering, Blaze roared, giving him no mercy until he had everything he needed.

Harsh, but necessary.

Their voices grew quieter toward the end. More guys rolled in, Tank and Moose, giving me quick nods of recognition as they stood like sentinels near the front door.

I jumped when the bedroom door burst open. Blaze and the others filed out. The hellish determination on his face chilled me to the core, but only for a second.

The longer I stared at it, the more I heated. First with desire, and then with shame for thinking wanton thoughts at a time like this. Sometimes, I hated Blaze almost as much as I loved him.

His rough expression proved beyond any doubt that my panties got wet for a monster, even if it was a monster who funneled his rage in the right places.

Blaze was talking to the guys near the edge of the living room in a low, firm tone. I didn't want to interrupt. I got up off the couch and began creeping toward the bedroom when his eyes locked on me.

"Where do you think you're going, baby?" He stepped past his brothers, breaking up the circle that had formed around their leader.

"I need to see Jordan…is he all right?"

"Honestly, I don't trust your fucking brother as far as I can throw him. You leave him to us, baby. We'll figure something out. Gotta check in and verify what he's given us isn't bullshit."

I steadied myself. It took a lot to muster up the energy to meet his wild gaze without flinching.

"He gave you what you wanted, didn't he? I get it. He needs to be in your custody. I can live with that." I swallowed. "But Blaze, I need to try to help him. He's my brother. At least let me do what I can to do get him clean."

Blaze's lips twisted. I watched them pull at his face in frustration, his eyes piercing straight through me with the devastating heat he carried as his trademark.

I should've been used to it by now, but I wasn't. The same chills swept through me, pulsing with defiance, fear, and desire simultaneously.

"Fine. Take this fuck to a pharmacy and get him what he needs." He watched my eyes grow wide. "Don't think

I'm letting you go alone. You and your bro aren't getting out of my sight for a single second."

He snapped his fingers and slowly turned to his guys. "Moose, Reb, Roller. Follow Saffron to the pharmacy and make sure they both get to the clubhouse after that. Tank and I'll meet you back there tonight for church. Call in all the brothers. We've got to move fast before his buddies know he rolled on them."

Blaze turned away. I smiled and nodded in his direction, and then walked toward the dark bedroom.

"Wait!" he said at the last second, crossing the room to me. "Give me that gun. Gotta get you some shooting lessons, babe. Until then, the guys with you are gonna be the only ones packing heat so you don't take somebody's fucking head off."

I smiled sheepishly. Only took me a second to hand him the weapon and unhook the holster. Then he nodded, freeing me to continue on my way.

God, it still smelled just like Mom in the old room still, even when it was stripped bare. All the years she'd suffered and hurt in here left its stench like angry phantoms.

My heart cracked when I saw Jordan sitting on the dusty spot where her bed used to be. His head was pressed tight into his hands. It hurt to see a big man in a near fetal position – especially when he was my own flesh and blood.

I rested one hand gently on his shoulder. He didn't move, even when I crouched, sinking next to him.

"Hey…it's going to be okay. The worst is over now. Let's go get you some food and plenty of water, Jordan. I'll see about getting you off this crap tomorrow. I'm here."

I reached for his hands and squeezed. Slowly, he lowered them, and I held my shock when I saw how bad he really looked.

He'd been tortured. Not by the Devils, but by his own mind and body, traitors who'd sent him straight for hell while he was alive.

"I fucked up," he said, voice like rustling leaves. "Best thing you can do is let me die in peace, sis. I'm never gonna live this down…never gonna feel a working brain in my fucking head ever again."

"Not true." I squeezed his fingers harder. "It's going to be hard, no BS. But we can get you whole again, brother. Let's try."

He looked at me for a long time with his dead, sad eyes. Then he jerked away, shaking his head.

"I'm poison. Mom saw it before anybody else. Why can't you? Stay the fuck away from me before something horrible happens, sis."

My heart nosedived. I wanted to throw my hands around his neck and hug and cry, but we were way passed that.

If he had a chance, I needed to rehabilitate him gradually. He wasn't kidding. Jordan had brought me a lot of pain and his club destroyed our family. But I wasn't giving up.

This wasn't unforgivable or irreversible, not the way it had seemed at first. As long as he was breathing, he'd always be my big brother, no matter how fucked in the head he was. If I could un-fuck him, just a little, then there was hope.

Maybe I was being stupid, crazy, naive. But when your junkie brother is shivering beneath you like a sick animal, lost and helpless, you'd be a bitch to turn away. Mom's murder ripped through my heart, killing distant parts even Blaze or Jordan would never bring back to life, but it wasn't all gone.

I had my family and my future. Becoming Blaze's old lady was a stark reminder. As long as I was breathing, I wasn't giving up, no matter how dark or hopeless or impossible it seemed.

"Come on," I whispered, taking one of his hands in both mine and pulling. He stood on shaky legs. "Let's get the hell out of this miserable place. We'll remember the good times with her. We don't need to remember this, and you know it."

I waved in a half-circle, taking one more deep breath of the stagnant, sickly air in the old apartment. It was the last time I'd smell my family's pain in this hellhole, and I didn't miss it one bit.

"Let's get this done. Blaze doesn't want us away from the clubhouse too long with *him* hanging around." Moose pointed at my brother.

"Gotcha." I smiled politely.

I tried to move fast, practically dragging Jordan along with me by the hand. Whatever had broken in his head caused him to revert to a child-like state since we'd climbed into the car.

The pharmacy was weirdly empty and it wasn't that late. I saw a long line of people waiting at the register with nobody behind it.

I started to throw things in my little basket while our bodyguards hit the bathroom and went for snacks. Didn't help that I was totally ignorant about *how* to help my brother. I needed to call Emma for some real advice.

I went down the aisles, adding aspirin, food, and plenty of tissues and toilet paper to the basket. Jordan took several big gallons of distilled water in his arms when I pushed them into his hands.

Before we'd left, Blaze said something about him being burned out. Crystal, weed, and God knows what else circulated in his system, frying his nerves.

Crap. Will this be enough to do anything?

I took one last inventory of the stuff in my cart. No clue, but it was better than nothing.

The line had only grown longer when we got to the front to checkout. We stood next to the guys, and Reb was the first to turn and look at me, his brow furrowed.

"This is bullshit."

Moose overheard him. "Everybody wants to stand here like goddamned cattle. There's gotta be somebody in this drugstore to ring us up."

The guys took off looking for an employee. I followed behind them, making sure Jordan stayed close. We couldn't have gone more than thirty steps to the other side of the store where the little pharmacy window waited.

When I looked back, my eyes nearly popped out of my head.

My brother was gone.

"Shit!" I froze, and the guys whipped around to find out why I was cursing. They joined me with much stronger words when they saw him missing.

"Fan out. We need to find wherever the fuck he went," Moose growled, casting a hungry eye at the beef jerky he had in one fist. "Don't have time for this shit."

None of us did.

I stayed by the pharmacy with Roller, gripping my stuff. He grabbed me by the shoulder when I started to move toward the Employee's Only door. I didn't think Jordan would wander back there, but who the hell knew?

"I'm just trying to find him!" I whined.

Roller smiled and shook his head. "Not alone, you're not. Let me take the lead."

Okay, I could live with that. I followed the tall man through the thick doors. I was so sick with worry and distracted I just let the grinning devil on his cut lead me along.

In a split second, the horned character on his patch wasn't smiling anymore. It wilted and went down, along with the rest of him. Roller collapsed.

I spun, and ran right into a hard chest. The stink of bad tobacco and unsavory stuff I couldn't identify hit me.

"Come on, little girl. Don't make me hit you with the same shit we gave him." His rough hand covered my mouth. I still tried to scream as I looked at the dirty man towering over me in his leather.

My eyes went to the ground. A skinny dart was firmly planted in Roller's thigh, right through his jeans.

I struggled for breath, trying to scream a second time. Big mistake. The man's hand pressed tighter, and my face went over the shoulder.

Several people were in the corner, their hands behind their backs, gags in their mouths. A couple pharmacists in white coats plus the cashiers were slumped against the wall, knocked out and breathing as shallow as Roller.

Oh, God. Jordan, if this is you…

My heart started to pound. Bile churned. Betrayal stung worse than the fear of what was going to happen next. But betrayal didn't make sense. There's no way my brother could've had contact with them since he came to us.

"Hold her, Twitch. Bitch is hyperventilating all over you. We need to keep this thing swift and silent. I'm gonna give her the shit…"

His grip relaxed. I jerked around. The same bald, cruel looking man who'd stabbed Tank outside the clubhouse was coming toward us.

He stepped over Roller's limp body. When he got to me, he looked me up and down, and then snorted.

"Fuck. I don't see any resemblance. Your mother must've whored herself out plenty to end up with two fuckups who look so different."

I shook my head. Couldn't comprehend what he was talking about, and it didn't matter either.

Jordan was slumped in a puddle of water behind him. One of the jugs had fallen and broken open when they hit him with a dart.

No, he hadn't betrayed us. He'd been taken too.

Small consolation. A second later, the bald man shook his head, signaling to more rough looking men near my brother.

"Believe me, honey, I don't like doing it this way neither. Too bad. Least I'll hear you scream plenty later tonight…"

He cut me off just before I tried to make another sound. Brutally.

A thing that looked like a gun went up, and he didn't hesitate. It made a gentle popping sound after he aimed it at my stomach.

I screamed, thinking I'd been shot. But a bullet would've burned worse, right?

Sharp pain turned to numbness in less than a second around my tattoo, and everything began to blur.

I went limp in the brute's arms and felt myself being passed to the bald man, clearly the leader. Then the black tidal wave roaring up in my brain snuffed out all the light. I couldn't feel anything but a great nothing eating my whole universe.

"Wake up, baby doll. Wake up, cunt."

The first time he said it, I hallucinated it was Blaze. I registered the last word slowly, and all my hopes melted.

Blaze wouldn't ever call me that. Jesus, no.

My eyes refused to open until something cool and sharp pressed against my neck. The adrenaline my heart pumping to my brain almost caused me to pass out all over again.

He'd pushed me against a wall in what looked like a dank old cellar. No surprise to see these assholes setting up shop in a bona fide dungeon. Of course, that meant torture was a given, and my brain ran through all the scary possibilities.

His hand squeezed my neck hard. A little above it, his other hand held a knife to my throat. Pain welled up around the strip of flesh where it was poised so viciously. He could've easily killed me in a single swipe. He stopped just short of cutting into anything vital, deciding to choke me instead.

"The game's simple, bitch. You answer every question me and Ursa have about the Devils' clubhouse, and we let you walk out of here alive. Damaged goods, for sure, but alive anyway. You get to decide how bad we beat you up, baby doll. Understand?"

I refused to answer. He started to squeeze tighter. I shook my head, and his bald face turned red, rage and surprise flickering beneath his skin.

"Irons…don't," an older voice said behind him. "We need her alive."

The bald man – Irons – let me go, falling backward in a huff. He stepped back and I saw the VP patch on his cut. The older man came up to me. He was wearing a PRESIDENT tag on his breast, the same as Blaze.

"You'd best cooperate. I can't keep his thirst for blood under control forever." Ursa coughed, cleared his throat, and looked at me with mad, mad eyes, lowering his face to mine. "Here's an easy one: how many men they got? We've counted about six or seven. Is that accurate?"

I stared dully. The undamaged skin on my neck tingled as blood ran down it in little drips, pooling on my shoulders. I watched and bled, reaching deep inside myself to switch off the fear.

Unlike Irons, I didn't hesitate. I killed my terror. I thought about Blaze. I thought about Mom. Hell, I even thought about Jordan, wherever he was.

They can hurt you, but they can't kill you. Only when you give up what they want.

"Fifty guys," I spat. "And every one of their cocks is a lot bigger than yours."

Several guys on the other side of the room chuckled. Ursa blinked. I expected him to hit me, cut me, or maybe push his old hips between legs.

Instead, he just stared, a long vacant stare that lasted at least a full minute before he shook his head and turned away.

"Soften her up," he told Irons. "This is going to be a long night. Brass is too fucked to crack, so we need to break her wide open."

Irons stepped up. The knife was on my throat, pressing with just enough precision to feel its sharpness along the cut it made earlier.

"You're a brave little bitch," he said. "I'll give you that. Right now, I'm gonna do you a solid and give you one last chance to answer the Prez like a good girl. Here, maybe this'll help loosen up your tongue…"

The knife pulled away from my neck. I licked my lips, swallowing more anxiety, and stared right at him as he turned his back.

Over in the corner, I heard Jordan groan. I saw his boots sticking out at the edge of a table where they'd laid him out.

Jesus. Did they hurt him, or is he just fucked up from earlier?

Not a clue. All I knew was that I wasn't giving these fucking bastards anything.

""Never," I whispered hoarsely.

When Irons finished his circle and faced me again, he was holding something else. Now, he looked really pissed. It was a thick glass whiskey bottle, the same kind I'd held dozens of times tending the bar at the Devils' clubhouse.

God help me, I flinched when he thrust it in my face. I thought he was ready to smash my skull with it, but he pushed the uncapped bottle to my mouth, shoving the glass behind my tongue.

"I get it." Irons snorted. "A nasty cunt like you needs to be loosened up to scream and moan. Here! Drink, bitch!"

The bottle tipped, and just kept going. Bitter whiskey ripped down my throat in waves.

Too much. Too fucking much!

I started to choke, feeling the stuff blasting my throat like sandpaper and burning in my stomach.

Jesus Christ. I can't breathe!

I snorted with all my might, struggling for precious air. Feeling the sharp whiskey blast out my nostrils and sinuses almost made me pass out.

"Jesus, brother! That's enough." Ursa growled, slapping Irons' shoulder.

Vicious reluctance flashed in his eyes as he finally pushed my head level. The glass retreated, and I coughed violently, spitting pure liquid fire in all directions.

"Whore!" He struck me across the face, sending my choking lungs into overdrive. "You spit that shit on me again and you'll do it with a busted lip and half your tongue gone. This is your last chance."

I looked up, dripping and moaning pathetically. As bad as I sounded, I wasn't beaten. This monster pouring poison down my throat just pissed me off more.

"Just give us what we need," the old man said behind him. "You can walk out of here alive."

I was too sick, too far past fucked up to speak. The whiskey kicked in like lightning on an empty stomach. I already felt it rumbling in my veins and turning everything hazy as it throttled my system.

I shook my head one way. *No.*

"Give the girl a damned break," Ursa said. "We got other ways to do this without killing her…"

Irons chuckled. He reached into his pocket and I watched him light a thick cigar with an old silver lighter. He stepped aside and threw his arm around me.

Bastard. I instantly recoiled at his touch and tried to shake him off, but it was no use.

"See your brother over there? He's about to get the special treatment. This is what we do to little cocksuckers who turn tail on our patch and snitch."

My heart started to pound. Even through the drunken haze, I cleared my throat, tensing up as Ursa moved around him.

"Don't! Don't hurt him. He's been through so damned much…"

"Sure has." Irons laughed. "Don't worry, baby doll. You can't hurt a man if you're sending him straight to heaven."

What the hell was he talking about? Ursa reappeared in the light a second later, holding something long and plastic he'd produced from a little black box. When it caught the dim lamp perfectly, I saw the huge needle on the tip.

"This is for both of you," Ursa growled at me. "For the next five minutes you refuse to talk, Brass here gets a little deeper into a trip that's truly out of this world. We gotta do it for him, see. This fucknut doesn't have the balls to shoot a dose that would stop an elephant's heart."

Ursa gripped the syringe savagely and stabbed it right into my brother's chest. My mind blanked with horror and whirling whiskey. His thumb pressed down, sending the cloudy shit into his veins.

Jordan's arms and legs moved, suddenly energized. He groaned, as if entering a deep ecstasy, like someone had just given him the best blowjob of his life.

"Holy fuck. Holy fucking *shit!* It's too…sweet." My brother slumped, moving his mouth like a fish, suddenly speechless.

Irons' dirty fingers tightened on my shoulder. I was too numb to turn away in horror as Ursa produced a second shot from the black box. Only my throat still worked, and it swallowed a small boulder.

"Heh. Look at him go. Knew a guy who used to shoot up junkie fuckheads for fun and watch 'em self-combust. Vulture, I think. He was a hell of a guy." Irons turned to me darkly. "Until your asshole boyfriend and his pussies blew him sky high."

The second dose went into Jordan's arm. His delirious groaning lessened, and his breathing grew slower. His head rolled on his table and he stared in my direction, looking right through me.

He was too fucked up to beg me for help.

I'm sorry, I thought, looking away from the gruesome scene as much as I could.

Who was I kidding? Sorry didn't begin to cut it. But even with my brother dying in front of me, I wouldn't talk.

As long as I kept them away from Blaze and the club, they'd get what they deserved. I knew it. If I let fear take over and I spilled everything, then they wouldn't just kill me or Jordan.

They'd kill Blaze, his brothers, and how many more? How many innocents who've never been in an MC at all?

Men like this didn't stop. I had a flash of the future where the Grizzlies were back on the rampage, owning Missoula like they used to, piling their victims higher and higher in a mass grave.

On the third shot, Jordan stopped breathing. His whole body seized up thirty seconds later and started to convulse. I watched him twitch and foam and jerk, sniffing back tears.

Oh my God…

Blaze, where the hell are you?

He was lifeless by the time Ursa injected the fourth hit into his neck. The old man was starting to turn red, pissed as all hell that I hadn't reacted to the nightmare the way he wanted.

"Fuck number five," he growled. "Bastard's gonna be dead anyhow. And this bitch still won't talk to save her brother. Looks like we're not the only ones who hate this little cocksucker."

Without warning, Irons grabbed me with both hands, picked me up, and slammed me against the wall. The knife returned, pressing so hard I swore he'd nick an artery and I'd bleed out right there.

"I see you've made your choice, baby doll. If you're not gonna cough up what we need about your boyfriend and his Prairie Pussy buddies, then I guess we'll do things the hard way." His dirty smile appeared. "Lucky for you I like it hard."

"Kill me now. You're a dead man either way," I snarled. "Just wait until they find you."

Moving like a beast, Irons lived up to the club's name. I imagined being mauled by a grizzly as he tore at my pants, fumbling with my belt. The jeans dropped as he mumbled something about how he was going to take his sweet time before killing me later.

When he found my tattoos, my heart stopped. Calloused fingers passed over my roses, and I jerked until he flattened me harder, steamrolling me with his weight.

No! The only fingers that should be there are Blaze's. Not there. Please. God.

"My, my. Pretty flowers for a pretty lady. It's nice to have something I can ruin. Hold still, doll. Those flowers can't do much screaming, but you sure as hell can…"

My jeans hit the floor. Dirty cigar smoke rolled up my nose and I pinched my eyes shut, just as the heat began teasing my inked skin.

"Stupid fucking cunt. It didn't have to be this way…"

The tip went deep. Somehow, I held in my screams and my sobs. A little wince and a feral growl was all he got each time he stamped the cigar to my flesh, burning away my life's trail. The blank spot near my thigh hit me the hardest, the place where I was going to get *PROPERTY OF BLAZE* tattooed between two new flowers.

I cleared my mind and let the fire burn.

Maybe it was the whiskey or just the surrealness of being taken and tortured, watching my brother get killed in front of me. Whatever it was, I didn't think about the agony. All I thought about was Blaze.

Beautiful, powerful, insatiable Blaze.

If I died here tonight, I'd go thinking only about him.

Irons laughed each time my body jerked away from the flaming tip branding my flesh. He had to re-light the cigar several times to keep the torment going.

Do I regret this? The same question echoed in my head, over and over as each flaming imprint destroyed my tattoos, annihilating my flowers.

No. Hell no.

I wouldn't change a single thing. If these brutes were meant to end my world, then so be it.

Irons' cruel stabs over and over on the same spots must've left second degree burns. I literally couldn't feel a damned thing on my skin anymore except for a dull heat. Knowing I was being tortured to death burned, sure.

Just not as bright as my love for Blaze each time I thought about him. These bastards keeping me from seeing him alive again was the real hell.

The whiskey's stark numbness hit my brain in deeper, darker waves. Even Blaze's memory became a blur and I totally shut down. A rush of cool air bristled on my skin as

Irons stepped aside, letting me slump to my knees. It was only then I realized he'd torn my panties down and planted several thick burns on my bare ass.

His next words came like a demon speaking from another world.

"Well, doll? Are you gonna talk? Or do I need to start in on that pretty pink pussy next?"

VIII: Inferno (Blaze)

I swore I'd kill every last asshole when I found them. Hell, that was coming before they took Saffron and her bro away from me, before Moose caught the last glimpse of her limp body disappearing into a truck at the fucking drugstore…

Now? It was a goddamned certainty.

Nobody with their patch was leaving Montana alive.

Church went fast. We didn't bother using the meeting room. My boys met me in the big garages instead, everybody except Roller, who was still shaking off that shit they pumped into his system.

"All right. The good news is the little shit gave up their clubhouse before he disappeared. We know where they are. We know how to hit 'em. That doesn't mean it's gonna be easy."

All my brothers nodded at me solemnly. Tank, Moose, Reb, Stone, and Smokey. Miner didn't have to worry about riding into battle, but even he looked ready for war. Stinger was especially strange without his big smile.

"Let's wipe their asses out," he said, pushing his hands together so his muscles bulged.

Good. Everybody was hungry for blood.

They knew the shit the renegade Grizzlies did cut me the deepest. But fucking us over like this, stealing our informant and an old lady was a crime against the club. Saving Saffron became every brothers' business as soon as I claimed her and laid my brand on her.

"All ready to go, boss. What's one more wound? What's the plan?" Tank shifted his weight. The big bastard was supposed to be using his cane, but he refused, afraid I'd make him stay behind if he looked too screwed up to serve as Sergeant at Arms.

"Head on. It's the only way. We bring along the new toys we got from mother charter. Their place is far enough from town to keep a firefight concealed. This is a kill job. Nothing else."

"You're sure?" Moose stroked his beard. "These fuckers are pretty dumb. We wait another day or two and they'll show up here and rush the clubhouse. We could mow them down then."

"Laying traps is Maverick's style," I growled. "Not mine. Besides, we wait ten more hours and our people might end up dead. The fucks are laying into them this minute, probably torturing my old lady to find our weaknesses. We need to vote and get going. *Now.*"

Fuck, thinking about those dirty bastards hurting Saffron boiled my blood. I promised I wouldn't suffer them breathing a minute longer than necessary, and I wouldn't take any surrender either. Soon as I saw she was safe and they were in our open sights, they were dead men.

This wasn't just a war between MCs. This was a fucking extermination campaign waged on vermin, and there would be the same mercy they'd given to Saffron and her luckless family in all this.

None.

"We vote. Miner goes first because he's proxying for Roller."

There was no hesitation for anyone. All the votes were unanimous 'ayes,' giving me all the approval I needed. Yeah, Moose had a preference for something more cunning, but it didn't stop him from voting for Satan's Scythe.

These were the times when being President came naturally. I was out to protect my woman and my club, to savage and destroy anyone or anything who got in the way. This was clear cut, without politics or mind games.

My boys knew what was going down. I knew it too. And if anybody forgot, all they had to do was look at the PRESIDENT tag on my chest.

It took a frenzied moment to grab all the new gear and load it into the truck. Tank drove that vehicle since he knew how to use the new shit best. The rest of us were on our bikes.

I fixed my helmet tight, waiting at the head of the line as the gate opened. We rode out in formation, and I sped down the little mountain roads, into the darkness.

Hunting for Grizzlies made everybody's balls crawl up their guts with anticipation. I felt it too, but for me it was all different.

This was about more than putting some really nasty fuckers into the ground. I was going after Saffron, and I *had* to bring her back in one piece.

No ifs, ands, or fuckups about it.

Hold on, baby, I thought, gripping my bike until my hands hurt. *I'm coming.*

We slowed when we approached the shitty little building. It was way out in the boonies, an old trading post barely bigger than the abandoned rat's nest we'd searched in town a few weeks ago.

Would've been easy to blow right past it on the map if we didn't have the coordinates marked. As soon as we pulled up several feet away, I signaled to kill the engines. We all paused for a second, listening to the still mountain darkness.

I raised my binoculars. The dim lights in the cracked windows told me we'd come to the right place. So did the small gaggle of beat up old Harleys parked near the back.

The Grizzlies were in there, and so was Saffron and her brother.

My boys went to work like panthers in the night, surrounding the place in the shadows, shotguns and side arms drawn. Tank set up in front of their main door, training a rifle on the place so big he had to keep it mounted on a fucking tripod.

"I'll approach. Need to find out where the fuck they're being kept," I whispered over the walkie-talkie and quickly cut it.

I dove into the dirt and crawled toward the window where the glow was brightest. The closer I got, the easier I could see silhouettes moving inside, guys with cuts moving around.

I pressed my face to the dirty glass to get a good look. Fuck, I'd know those curves anywhere.

Saffron was slumped in a corner, her arms twisted at her side. Heartbeats so fierce they rattled my fucking bones started thumping in my chest. It looked just like she'd been shot and was applying pressure to the wound.

A few feet away, a body lay on a table. Had to be dead, and I guessed it was Jordan.

Sick, sick motherfuckers. You boys are done. Should've killed all your asses yesterday.

My finger pressed to my walkie-talkie. "Found her. Probably the brother too. They're both in a shitty little cellar. Have Tank blast the door and give these fucks a wake-up call on my mark. I'll go in to get her out."

"Roger."

I raised my hand, ready to swing low and shout over the radio again. I barely heard the distant rumble in time, a sound like thunder rolling in from the road.

Holy fuck. Nobody as experienced as me would mistake the growl of Harleys, and certainly not so many.

"Boss? Company's coming. You want to turn all these guns around?"

"Fuck!" I didn't switch on the radio at first.

I slapped the old brick wall with my fists, staring through the hazy glass. We had the firepower to take them down even if they were about to double their numbers.

Still, I didn't think these bastards had so many in their ranks. There was no mistaking what was about to happen with their friends arriving. We were gonna be pinned down in two different directions, and some brothers were bound to die.

Think about Saffron, asshole. Focus on her. Long as she's safe, everything else is second.

I nodded to myself, stuffing panic down into the deep dark pit in my gut. One hand tightened on my gun, and the other on the walkie-talkie.

"Tank, Moose. You two take the guys on the road. Tell everybody else to shoot anything that comes out through the doors or windows."

The bikes were on top of us now. Harleys passed our rides and turned onto the little dirt drive, rolling up, just a few feet from Tank's position.

I took a deep breath, ready for all hell to break loose.

Adrenaline pulsed, hot and rough, when I heard the single gunshot. Then there was a long silence, and several loud…voices?

"What the fuck is going on?" I growled into the radio.

No answer for a solid minute. I was about to ask again when it crackled.

"Not the Grizzlies we expected, boss. Man here needs to talk to you."

Damn it! I slapped the brick one last time with my fist and walked away. I went running toward Tank's position, and swerved just in time to avoid a nasty hole in the ground.

A bullet exploded past my head. The radio screamed to life.

"Shit! We've been spotted. Everybody down!" Tank's roar may have saved my life.

I got down and kept crawling toward him, stopping a few feet away to fire some shots at the clubhouse. Bullets whipped past and hit the ground. The Grizzlies fired long and aimlessly into the darkness. Doubted they hit a damned thing, but then neither did we.

"Well? What the fuck is this?" I climbed next to Tank, heart racing.

Another man lay on the ground next to him. No, three more men, and one big brute I'd seen once before.

"Fang? You're the last fucker in the world I expected to see here."

"Came to finish the job you boys couldn't. Thanks for leading us right to them." He grinned. "Pack your shit up and go. We'll take care of our own. Our right as the MC getting pissed on by these cocksuckers."

I was fucking seething. "No. They got our people. You're the ones who weren't fucking invited. Let us do this."

Fang got up and stepped over me. Crazy bastard. Several bullets exploded around us, and another right next to my shoulder, kicking up dirt onto my jacket.

Several Grizzlies – real Grizzlies – ran up to cover their leader. They approached the door and the shooting slowed.

"Hold your fire! We're all wearing the same patch, you dumb bastards!" he roared.

I stood and started to approach. The main door Tank had been aiming at swung open. A pack of the dirtiest, nastiest fuckers I'd ever seen came piling out. They were wide eyed and totally high, fingers twitching in surprise.

"Who the hell are you? Is that...Fang? No fucking way!" The men grunted and chattered among themselves.

"Everybody come on out. Line up." Fang's voice was wickedly calm. "You boys out here are right about one thing: we've been neglecting you too long. I'm finally here. Just like I promised. We'll sort this all out."

The renegades had flashlights and guns trained on Fang and his three men. I stepped up behind them, and recognized two of the fuckers. One was Ursa, the same bastard President we'd devastated in Missoula before. The other was the bald headed piece of shit who attacked us, the VP named Irons. Jordan told us about him.

The renegades behind their leaders began to push forward, down the short rickety staircase. Then Irons swaggered down and raised one hand.

"Hold up. What the fuck's that Prairie Pussy doing with you? Brothers, stop!"

The renegades froze. I stepped deeper into the light. I could feel the rage and annoyance rolling off Fang, and he eyeballed me a furious warning.

"We're here to get our hostages. We know you fucks have them in there, and we're not leaving until they come out safe." My eyes narrowed. "Bring her out and let's get this done."

No fucking requests. Just a demand. I was past giving a damn who it pissed off – Ursa, Irons, Fang – fuck them all. I wanted my old lady, and I wasn't gonna walk away with anything else.

"Doesn't seem right," Irons leaned in and whispered to Ursa. The old President nodded, squinting at me like he was ready to put a bullet in my head himself.

Fang's lips twitched in surprise when they drew their guns and aimed them at us. The renegades nearby were a lot more cautious. They had their hands in their pockets, but they didn't move.

"Looks like a goddamned trap," Ursa said. "Bring out your weapons, boys. Whoever's there, they're gonna get filled with lead if they come a step closer."

Our turn. Fang's crew drew their weapons and I heard my guys readying their guns behind me. Locked and loaded. Between our two crews, the renegades were fucked, assuming Devils and Grizzlies didn't start shooting each other first.

"Prez? They're national." A skinny young man with a tattered cut and greasy hair looked like he was about to start hyperventilating.

Ursa didn't acknowledge he'd heard him. Skinny boy broke. He went running toward us, and so did several other greasy motherfuckers. I watched Ursa's face twist into a monstrous grin.

He fired first. Never knew if he was aiming at his own man for going coward or trying to surprise our asses.

The bullet cracked right past me and nailed Fang in the stomach. The Grizzlies President dropped, spitting blood, growling a muddled "shoot back, dammit!"

Everybody opened up at once. I hit the floor and began to crawl. Several guys screamed as bullets found their mark. Nothing left to do at this point but hope and pray they weren't my boys.

My place wasn't in this fucking crossfire. I had to use the distraction to get to Saffron.

Heading right for the window, I grabbed my gun by the barrel and bashed it against the glass when I was close. A stray piece cut the back of my hand, but it did the job. Kicked the rest out with my boots, and then I was sliding through, straight to Saffron.

"Jesus. Fuck." I ran over, ready to help stem the damage.

She looked unconscious. For a second, I feared the absolute worst, ready to watch my word imploding into pure despair. Then I scooped her up and she groaned.

Shit! She was alive, and I didn't see the blood that wouldn't been spilling all around her if she'd been shot and bleeding.

It was a relief just having her in my arms. My relief was short lived.

As soon as I saw what those fucking animals did, I screamed like demon. She was naked from the waist down, and I winced in rage and horror when I felt the burns.

It was too late to protect her. Too fucking late! All I could do was soothe the pain, and make sure I gave it to every last fuck who'd been involved with this, until their lifeless carcasses were at my feet.

"Saffron? Talk to me, baby!" I shook her lightly.

She opened her eyes and let out another weak moan. Thank fuck.

She was hurt like hell, but they hadn't killed her or put her into a coma. That was something.

Her breath stank like…Jack? What the fuck?

I searched the floor for her jeans. Didn't bother with the burn marked panties wadded up beneath the place where she'd been sitting. I helped her into her pants and threw her over my shoulder, taking a quick look at Jordan in the corner.

I reached out to touch him. Her big bro was warm, but almost certainly dead. Fucking weird, especially when I didn't see a gunshot or any other trauma.

Saffron groaned again. She retched, and I held on tight, steadying her over the ground as she went into dry heaves.

Shit! It was like she'd binged and drank herself stupid. I didn't understand what the hell happened here, but now I stopped worrying about the burns and started to freak about too much crap in her system.

"It's gonna be okay, baby. We'll get you home. I'm so fucking sorry I couldn't get here sooner. So sorry, love. The fuckers who did this are *dead.*"

I listened close to what was happening outside. The gun fire had died down, but shots were still going off in staggered bursts. Loud manly screams and a thousand sailor's curses filled the night.

"Blaze..." she coughed. "What about Jordan?"

My fucking heart constricted. Poor, poor baby, always putting everybody else first. Didn't have a good answer for her, so I didn't answer at all. I just waited until her stomach stopped going into spasms and then threw her over my shoulder, ready to haul her the fuck out of here.

The asshole sliding in through the window didn't let me get that far. Ursa rolled onto the floor, gripping a gun and bleeding from one leg. The filthy grin he gave me pulsed pain and hatred.

"You! This is your fucking fault, Devil." He raised his gun, pointing it at Saffron instead. "That worthless, tight-lipped whore...I should've killed her an hour ago."

Fuck. I had to take my chances, even with her between us.

I fired first. He jumped.

Ursa let out a horrific scream as my bullet found its mark somewhere in his side, but somehow the old bastard didn't go down. He staggered up, fell halfway across the table against her brother's body, and pulled the trigger.

The bullet missed us by a long shot. I wasn't taking anymore chances.

Sonofabitch grunted and bled, and violent satisfaction jolted through me for a second. I was about to aim for his head when something jerked up behind him.

"Fucking-A," I muttered, holding my fire.

Saffron's big bro wasn't so dead after all. He wrapped his hands around Ursa's neck and slammed his head into the corner of the table, thrashing like a ghoul. The boy might as well have come back from the dead.

He choked the renegade President and bashed his head into the chipped wood again and again. Took all my strength to lower my gun and let him have his fucking fun.

I wanted to kill Ursa myself. On the other hand, this poor bastard deserved something after what they'd done to him. I let Jordan do the dirty work, watching as he continued ramming Ursa's face into the table, long after the shithead was dead.

Saffron collapsed into a half-conscious stupor. I held her tight and reached for my radio.

"Tank? What the fuck's happening out there? Is it clear yet?"

"Safe enough," he chattered back. "Where you at? Fang and his guys got the last few Grizzlies cornered and disarmed. Only one got away, and we're hunting him down now."

"Bring the truck around. We're near the side window."

One got away...

I was never a believer in psychic bullshit, but I had a good feeling who was it was, waiting for me to finish him. Bloodthirsty excitement stormed in my blood.

There was still a chance to make this right, to make them pay for torturing my woman...

I stayed near the window, cradling Saffron. The kiss I planted on her forehead wouldn't do much to heal her awful fucking pain. Too bad. We both needed it.

Hold tight, baby. They're all gonna be dead. Just one more fuck to go...

Jordan slumped back onto the table after his wild murder frenzy. He wasn't out, though. The boy looked at me with bright, angry eyes, his skinny chest rising and falling.

"Stay there. Don't move." I wasn't taking any chances, even if he'd done me a big favor.

He was definitely hopped up on some vile shit. Junkies were always unpredictable, especially when they'd nearly been fucked into an early grave.

The truck pulled up, along with several bikes. I quickly passed Saffron through the window to Moose. Tank helped me climb out.

My eyes lit up when I came face-to-face with Fang, noticing the Harleys weren't ours. Fucking Grizzlies. This shit wasn't their business.

"You're still standing?" I said, genuinely surprised.

"Yeah. I've had worse than this." Someone had tied a shitty tourniquet around his stomach. "Not leaving this place until they're all dead. How many more down there?"

"Just one. He's our guy. Pretty fucked up on smack or crystal, I'm not sure which." I gave him a sour look. "You're not gonna kill him, are you?"

Fang refused to answer. Not this shit again.

I held my gun tight and watched as he bent near the window, ordering Jordan to come out. The kid had just enough strength to walk up to the window. He let one of Fang's guys reach in and pull him up.

"Shit. Wanted to do Ursa in myself. Guess that's worth something, though." Fang slapped one hand on Jordan's shoulder and then ran his fingers down his Grizzlies MC patch. "You're the bastard who rolled on these motherfuckers, aren't you? Come on, boy. You're coming home with us."

He climbed stupidly onto one of the Grizzlies' bikes behind the driver, a mean looking bastard with a bandana tied tight around his frizzy hair. I looked at the truck and saw Saffron slumped against the window.

Her eyes were open and she was alert. It looked like she was saying *no, no, no*, begging her fool brother to turn around. No such luck.

Dammit. Maybe I should've put a bullet in his head when I had the chance. Brother or not, he was just one more fuck screwing with her head, causing more pain.

Whatever. There was no stopping it. The Grizzlies were doing us a favor by getting his stupid ass out of our sight.

"That's it?" I growled to Fang. "What about the rest? I know you took some prisoners."

He turned to me, face twisting in pain as he pushed a hand against his stomach wound. "They'll burn. We're just waiting to find the last asshole. Then we load them inside this shithole and light it up. You don't got a problem with that, do you?"

I thought hard. Long as they weren't putting Saffron's bro in there with the others, I really didn't care.

None of these men were innocent. They were vipers, renegades, junkies, and killers. Exactly the kind of assholes who just need killing.

My boys were tired and lucky to be alive from the firefight too. We were in no position to tangle with the Grizzlies and prevent a massacre of fucks who actually deserved it.

I looked at Fang coldly and nodded. He shrugged.

"Go home, Blaze. We'll find the last turncoat here and raze this place to the ground. Better get your girl patched up."

"You handle your business and we'll handle ours. I'm not done here yet."

Tank raised an eyebrow as I pushed past. Fang and his men went on their way, riding past us, toward the dark brush behind the battered building.

"Boss?"

"Take her home right now," I growled. "We need to find the asshole who took flight before they do. Moose, you're with me."

We piled into the truck and rode back to our bikes. I gave Saffron one last squeeze until she opened her eyes and looked me.

"Blaze. Don't leave me alone." Her voice was a faint whisper.

Fuck me. It was mighty tempting to turn back then and there, but if I did, the possibility existed the same shithead who'd hurt her would find us again. I'd taken too many chances tonight, and I sure as hell wasn't taking one more.

"Easy, woman. I'll be with you before you know it. Try to get some sleep. Emma will have you all fixed up by morning. I promised to keep you safe, and I fucked it up. Nothing's gonna stop me from salvaging the last way I can live by my word." I looked past her at Tank. "Drive! Don't worry about us. Make sure you get her to the clubhouse safe."

Tank questioned me with his eyes. I saw what he was thinking. If everybody but Moose and I took off, we were out here alone with Fang's crew, pretty much at their mercy.

I didn't fucking hesitate. The demon inside me was too unstoppable now, howling his thirst for blood, his need to annihilate the rotten shit who burned my girl.

"Go," I said one more time, and slapped the truck's side angrily.

Fuck him for caring. Fuck the Grizzlies. Fuck everyone who got in the way of this.

Moose and I mounted our bikes and took off down the dirt road. We chose a different gravel fork than the one Fang and his guys had followed. If they'd found Irons by now, I would've heard the gunshot or the roar of their bikes coming back to put him with the men they were going to roast.

No more chances. No more games.

I needed to keep Saffron safe. Just as much as I needed vengeance too. I wouldn't rest ever again if a bear killed that motherfucker before I did. Or worse, if he escaped.

Moose and I found the overturned bike near a shitty overgrown path leading into the dark forest. Bastard must've wiped out in some brush. We parked and got off, using our flashlights to follow the bloody trail.

It didn't take long.

Irons was in a shallow ditch, his gun resting in one hand. At first I thought he was dead because he didn't raise it to defend himself. No, he was too busy keeping pressure on the bullet someone planted in his leg, probably the thing that caused him to wreck.

"Oh, fuck!" He lifted his head. "Not you assholes. Oh, fuck!"

"Keep saying it," I smiled. "You've lost a lot of blood, but if you were gonna pass out, you wouldn't be talking."

"This asshole's all yours, Prez." Moose grinned and leaned back against a thick tree. With his big beard and huge teeth shining in the night, he looked like a monster.

Fine by me. Because out here in the dark, I was going to show this bald sonofabitch that monsters weren't just in fairy tales. They were right here, breathing down his neck, gatekeepers between the Montana wilderness and the hell he was heading to.

Irons looked up and yelled as I grabbed his hand. Didn't take much effort to bend it back and make him drop the gun. Of course, I kept going, not stopping until his fingers snapped one by one.

His screams were constant. Good thing we had plenty of space between us and Fang's search crews. Out here, nobody would hear him but us, and we'd just gotten started.

"Why? Why the fuck did you pick on her? The girl and her family weren't even part of my club when you bastards showed up." I had to ask.

Irons winced, looked at me, and opened his lips. "Because she was easy pickings. Needed to make you fuckers so mad with rage you'd charge in and do something stupid. Didn't exactly work out. We were close…so fucking close…"

He elbowed him in the side. Had to shut his fucking yap. I'd gotten my answer – the same bullshit I'd expected – and now the time for talk was over.

"You know those burns you gave my girl?" I said, reaching near my belt and unsheathing my hunting knife.

He whimpered like a bitch. Music to my ears.

"I'm gonna do you one better. See, the great thing about getting sliced and diced is the nerves don't die 'til it gets real deep. You'll be feeling this until your body's got no more blood to keep your ass alive."

Irons howled like a beast caught in a trap. Then he turned, wilting when I kneed him in the stomach, twisting his head in agony.

Fucker looked right at me. I saw the cold acceptance of a man who was about to die there.

"Fuck you, Prairie Pussy. Least I ruined her inks. Just wish I'd torn up her rotten little pussy the same as momma's before I —"

I grabbed his chin and forced his mouth open. Honorable men deserved last words. This piece of shit didn't.

My knife started on his tongue so I wouldn't have to hear a single filthy syllable more. Then I flipped him over, cut through his leather and shirt, and went to work on his vertebrae. One by one, I made him pay double for Saffron's suffering.

Behind me, Moose grunted with satisfaction.

Fang and his guys were pissed off, lounging around and smoking when we rode up to the front of the shitty pseudo-clubhouse. If the dumb bastard had any sense, he would've been getting his gut wound patched up by now.

Whatever. I wouldn't keep him waiting.

"What the fuck took you so –"

I snapped my fingers. Moose pulled up and dumped the mutilated body off the back of his bike. Fang staggered over with several guys and looked down in surprise.

"We're done with him. He's yours now. Not the same as doing him in yourselves, I know, but you can burn the body just the same. Didn't even take his patches as trophies."

Fang looked at me with a smirk. I had my gun ready for trouble. He shook his head and almost laughed.

"We're done here. You…you're all right, Blaze. Even if you are a goddamned Prairie Pussy." He clapped his hands. "Let's go! I'm starting to feel a little sick with this fucking hole in my side."

I looked at Moose and nodded. We hit the road, and were almost all the way to the highway before we even heard the muffled screams. There was no avoiding the bright light in the distance.

Whatever the Grizzlies used to the fire, it moved fast, consuming the old building and all the men they'd locked inside, plus one very dead body. I watched the fire dance in my mirrors for several long Montana miles.

The road was finally open, and not just the one Moose and I were taking to Missoula.

With this shit settled, Saffron was mine, and nothing was keeping me from making her the happiest old lady who'd ever lived.

"How is she?"

Emma was just leaving the infirmary when I arrived. Fuck, how many times had I seen the same catty, melancholy look on the nurse's face? If Saffron's condition was making her wear it, I swore I'd find my way back into the boonies to desecrate that motherfucker's bones.

"Well enough," Emma said, adjusting her scrubs. "The man who did this must've been drunk or something. The burns are bad, but they would've been a whole lot worse if he'd gone at her with any precision."

"Why the hell was she so out of it?"

"Somebody gave her liquor, and lots of it. She'll feel like shit in the morning, but we're getting all the fluids into her we can." She watched me raise an eyebrow. "It's okay. No risk of poisoning or anything."

I clenched my jaw and turned away. It wasn't just the dead Grizzlies crew responsible for this shit. I wanted to rip my own guts out for being so late, for letting them hurt her and nearly kill her stupid bro.

Her bro. Best not to think about Jordan, I told myself. *If that shit gave a damn about her, he'd be here right now.*

Fuckup or not, you're all she's got. You're her everything.

"I need to see her." I started to push past.

Emma got in my way, blocking the door with her short, curvy body. "She needs rest, Blaze. The more she gets, the better. It's the only way to heal burns like that."

I wasn't listening to another word. Went right past her and jerked the door open, letting her jump aside at the last minute.

My girl looked so damned innocent and beautiful laying there in the little bed. One of those thin aqua-green medical sheets covered her, shielding the damage her tormenters had done. Good thing too, because seeing those burns would've made me break shit for sure.

"Blaze, I don't think…" Emma started weakly behind me, standing in the doorway. She swallowed her words the instant I scooped Saffron up by the shoulders.

Held her tighter than I'd ever held anyone in my life. I watched as she slowly opened her eyes, two gems waiting just for me, diamonds no fuck would ever dull again.

"Hey, beautiful. I'm here for good. Not gonna let you go. Ever."

She gave me a long, soft stare, and then her lips pulled up in a thin smile. Thank God.

Saffron gripped me back. I held on tighter and cradled her in my arms. My bones were giving me hell after hardly any rest and a lot of kicking ass, but I didn't care for a fucking second.

All that mattered was right here in my arms, the only thing that would ever matter to me again.

"You're never getting out of my sight, babe, you understand?" I told her, feeling that heavy rock starting in my throat. "I fucked up, Saffron. Never should've put your safety in another man's hands, even my brothers'. Well, make no mistake. Those days are absolutely fucking over. From now on, you're mine. Morning, noon, and night. If I'm not holding you or kissing you or just watching you do your thing, you slap me right across my goddamned face. Scratch my fucking eyes out. If they aren't on you, baby, then they're somewhere they shouldn't be."

She opened her lips slightly. I was all ready to catch the tears pooling near the corners of her eyes. Jesus, I was afraid what would happen when they came. Nothing worse than an MC President cracking up and blubbering like a damned baby in front of his old lady.

"What're you talking about?" She looked seriously confused. "You got there just in time. The shit they did…it was about to get worse. The bald bastard would've made sure we never had kids. He ran off as soon as the shooting started. You saved me from something a lot worse than some scorched up tats."

I stood, considering her words. Was she serious, or just making excuses for my overdue ass? Before I could speak, she reached up and grabbed my shirt, urging me low. I went.

"Just shut up, Blaze. Shut up and kiss me. Make me forget about them…I only want to see you, me, and the future. Past is past. You did your job, and I'll love you forever for it."

The rock in my throat shrank small enough to swallow. I leaned in, smiling the whole time, rubbing my stubble across her soft cheek just the way she liked.

"Baby, I can do that. I can do that for the rest of my life," I whispered in her ear, feeling her body tremble tenderly against my chest when she sensed the heat.

We kissed. Through all the pain and bullshit, we kissed like it was our last, just as hot as our very first. We kissed until Nurse Emma had to turn away in disgust, until my lips were numb, and I still held on, knowing I'd never get enough of her.

"Easy, girl. Make a little room…"

I lifted her gently, careful to avoid the injured patch around her hip, and slid in the bed next to her. Fucking thing wasn't really meant for two people and it creaked under our weight, but that didn't stop me.

I held her tight, nuzzling her neck. If I was finally gonna get some rest, then I'd do it with Saffron at my side. Right here, right now. No other way.

"Blaze…this is way outside standard procedure," Emma said meekly at our side.

Both Saffron and I gave her stink eyes. Emma shifted uncomfortably.

"It's okay. There's not any real danger, is there? You said my chances of getting an infection were real low." Obviously, my girl wanted me there, and I smiled like a fool.

"No…you're good…it's just that…"

"This is our infirmary. Not a goddamned hospital, Emma. Take your business somewhere else and let me hold my girl if it's not doing any harm. Go kiss and make up with Tank so we can get some shut eye."

Her face darkened, but my words did the trick. After she left the room and closed the door behind us, Saffron laughed.

Sweet, sweet music to my ears.

"What?" I said, running my pointer finger up chin. God damn I loved that little nook where her jaw met her ear.

"You're an asshole," she said, still laughing. "Poor Emma."

"Yeah, but you love me anyway. Nothing's gonna change that, no matter how many fucks I have to beat or how many times I taste your sweet lips."

She settled happily into the pillows, spooning herself perfectly against me. It was gonna be a long road to recovery, but I'd be right there at her side. Had a feeling everything would work out all right.

It better. Asshole or not, you always get your way — especially now that your way's merged into hers forever.

IX: So Bright It Hurts (Saffron)

The third night started in fire, and ended there too.

I never, ever forgot the way they burned me. But the memory that truly stands out is Blaze. Deadly, rock hard, beautiful Blaze, laying with me all night like a tiger protecting his mate.

I laid awake in a pleasant half-dreamy state long after Blaze began to snore and he thought I was out. No, it wasn't just all the crap they were pumping into my system to kill the pain, along with a small lake through the IV to help me fight the inevitable whiskey hangover.

I'd finally found my man tonight. I knew it before, but now I truly understood because Blaze shielded me. When he couldn't completely save my body from that bastard Irons, he saved my psyche, my heart, my soul.

He truly loved me, and I loved him.

Back in the ratty cellar, before my mind shut down from the torture, I accepted it. Pain was a real risk in this life, but I wouldn't have given it up for anything. I found myself as much as I discovered my one true love, my destiny as Saffron, and I swore if I got out alive, I'd be the best old lady a badass ever had.

And now I'd gotten my chance. Wishes came true.

Before I passed out into a deep, dark sleep, I squeezed Blaze's hand. My other, I ran down my unburned side, all the way to the hip, feeling the pure, perfect flesh.

The bastards hadn't burned everything. Not even close. Emma said the tissue they'd damaged would heal in time. It would definitely scar, probably so bad I'd never have good ink there again.

I didn't care.

I had a perfectly good man and a whole lot of pure skin. Soon as I was on the mend, I promised I'd scrawl the rest of my life on this flesh, starting with my love for the bad boy pressed up to me.

"You sure you're ready for this?" Tank hovered above me, his face tight.

"Emma says I'm good to go. Might be a little phantom pain and the usual discomfort…but it's not like I haven't been inked up a dozen times before. Let's do it."

Tank went to work. He was the best man for the job and one I could trust to keep things under wraps. I found out at the bar he'd learned how to do some wicked tattoos from his army days. Some guy named Freak back in North Dakota taught him a few things too.

Three months passed in a blur. The window in the little workout room was open, and a cool mountain breeze blew in, carrying all autumn's icy caresses.

The needle hit my skin. I squeezed the bar above my head to deaden the pain. Crap, Emma hadn't been kidding about phantom pain.

The burns had settled, smoothing away a little more of their red, rough exterior by the day. Now, they stung with damage, pulsing as the huge man navigated the needle gun over virgin skin.

Pain? Totally worth it.

The last three months had given me the calm everybody in the club needed. I healed, rested, and wiped away bitter memories in between serving up drinks to the boys.

Blaze was as good as his word. He cared for me the same way he did the first night I ever saw him, gentle and patient, even when the pain caused me to get pissy. Healing like this reminded me how Mom used to feel.

As far as I knew, my bastard brother hadn't visited her grave. I'd only done it a couple times, going with Blaze to lay flowers we picked out in the wild.

A few weeks into my recovery, I got a letter forwarded from Mom's old address.

The damned thing was short, but it sure wasn't sweet.

Jordan thanked me, said he was sorry, but he had to stick with his club. He'd disappeared out West, somewhere he said he 'belonged.' Thinking about Jordan diving back into the same shitty lifestyle that nearly got us both killed enraged me so much I tried not to think about it.

Guess you can lead a stubborn ass brother to safety, but you can't make him think...

On the bench, I grunted. Tank edged the needle gun off me for a second and looked up, concern showing in his eyes.

"You okay?"

"Yeah. Just keep going. I'll work through it." I saw him raise a skeptical eyebrow. "Trust me, I wouldn't be doing this if I weren't ready. Check with Emma yourself if you don't believe me."

He growled a low reply and continued. Nobody knew exactly what the hell was up with those two. All through my treatment, Emma made sure to skedaddle the minute she saw him, heading straight home when her work with me was done and none of the brothers needed anything.

I waited until the tattoo was all done before I said anything else. Didn't want to screw up my ink at the last second by saying something that would jolt him. Tank lifted the needle gun away and told me to stay still. He held up a mirror in his big paws.

The man was quite a beast, but nothing compared to Blaze. I caught the smile on my face in the reflection as he passed it lower.

"Wow," I hissed.

Wow didn't begin to describe it. For a hulking quiet guy who was used to inking up skulls, fire, and demons, he did flowers pretty well. And the letters? Well, those were killer.

PROPERTY OF BLAZE, it read, flanked between two dark roses with twisting stems going down my hip.

Beautiful. Perfect. Overwhelming.

Giddy excitement shot straight to my head. Jesus, it was going to be hell making it through the day. I couldn't wait to show him tonight.

"Well?" Tank said.

"Oh, sorry. I was too busy gawking to answer. It's awesome!" I reached for his big arm and gave it a crazy squeeze with both hands. "Thank you so much! I know exactly who I'm coming to next time I need some ink."

He smiled, got up, and stepped away to clean up.

"Seriously, Tank...you should check up on Emma," I said, biting my lip.

He looked up. No anger there. More like a fiery longing, the look I saw on Blaze when we were alone together and we couldn't rush away to dive between the sheets.

"I already checked on her, Saffron." His voice was stern. "She's not like you. Girl's here to do a job and get out. Doesn't want anything to do with me or the club."

"That's what I thought too at first. Then Blaze changed my mind, and you guys helped. I consider this place and everybody here family, even if it took me awhile to figure it out after I took his patch."

"You've chosen this life and you're cut out for it. Wouldn't have expected anything less for the boss. He got himself one badass bitch…"

He trailed off and I folded my arms. He mumbled an apology. I just laughed.

"Thing is, Emma ain't like you," he repeated. "I've been torn up too many times and watched lots of other guys get burned. I know how fucking dangerous this lifestyle is, and people like you and me are a rare breed. I'm okay with that."

"If you say so." I stood, turning my back and sliding my pants back on. "What doesn't kill you only makes you stronger. You know that old cliché? Well, it's not bullshit, Tank. Some of us need to find out what's best the hard way. You mean well, I know, but you can't stop a girl from finding herself, or the guy she's meant to be with, no matter how much it hurts along the way."

"No," he agreed. "But I can sure as hell stop anybody who's not fit for this shit from taking the wrong turn. This isn't just about her. It's about protecting everybody."

I cocked my head, wondering what he meant.

"If anybody hurt her the way those fuckers did to you, I wouldn't have been as easy as Blaze. I'd kill every motherfucker wearing that patch, and probably get the whole club killed too. Boss is right. I'm a loose cannon. Need to keep a lid on it if I don't want the whole fucking world going to kingdom come."

The last words ended in a growl. His eyes pierced right through me, a frustrated intensity that sent chills up my spine.

"Got it. Hope I'll see you at Miner's party tonight. Thanks again for the tattoos."

He nodded and I closed the door gently behind him. Should've known better than to stick my nose where it doesn't belong. But then, wasn't that how I ended up here in the first place with my knight in boots and leather?

Poor Tank. Poor Emma. I shook my head softly. They both needed to be smacked upside the head and realize life was too damned short for these games.

Good thing I had a happier thought on the brain.

Poor Blaze. When he sees the new ink tonight, he's a goner. I'm gonna fuck him silly and remind him where I belong, and who I belong to.

"Alaska? You're gonna freeze your fucking balls off, man." Moose slapped Miner on the shoulder.

"Good rides and awesome fishing. I'm only gonna be up there in the sunny months, soon as I get my shit set up this Fall. I figure taking one Alaskan winter's just paying my dues. Shit, maybe I can be the first Prairie Devil up there in the tundra." He grinned, a split second before Moose gave him another manly handshake.

If the old man wasn't sore in the morning from all the congratulations flowing his way tonight, then I'd be really surprised.

Blaze and I had already given him our best.

It was sad to see him go. But he'd be back, welcome to meetings and events for the MC.

Your Soul Belongs Forever was inked on Blaze and lots of other brothers. This catchphrase was one more reminder that the club never let go. Once a brother, always one, and Miner was welcome here whenever he came home.

And the doors weren't just open to old brothers either. The club expected more men rolling in to visit from North Dakota for business before winter made their routes far more treacherous.

Blaze didn't talk to me direct about club business, but I overheard plenty. The Devils were outlaws with good hearts, and at the end of the day, I was okay with that.

"Hey, go easy," I whispered, watching as Blaze tipped a bottle of Jack to his lips. "You want to feel more than just whiskey kicking in your veins, don't you?"

I reached behind, unseen, and gently squeezed the erection straining against my ass. He'd had it there for at least the last five minutes.

The six weeks we had away from sex while I healed was pure hell. We were still making up for lost time, but tonight was extra special.

I squeezed him again until he grunted in my ear. The guys laughed, drowning out our desire. Not that it was anything unusual in the clubhouse tonight.

One look around the room told me as much.

Reb and Roller were firmly planted at the bar with new whores on their knees. The prospects were circling each other for their first shot at the skanky blonde slut, Marianne, who used to share everybody's bed. I still watched her like a hawk at the bar, though she'd been nothing but friendly.

She missed Blaze, and it wasn't hard to tell. I feared for the way I'd lay into her if she ever got too close.

He rubbed his hard-on against me through my jeans. God, he was so long, so ready, so eager to claim my flesh.

No, I didn't have much to fear from whores and skanks. His interest was focused on me like a laser beam, and tonight was no exception. Whenever I began to doubt it, he reminded me, hot and forceful and totally irresistible.

"Let's go, baby. I've been nursing this shit all night just so I don't have to wait to drive. I'd rather have you riding me warm than Jack any fucking night." His hand slid around to my thigh, clenched, and then moved up.

I gasped, sharper than usual. The fresh tattoo still tingled, but it was nothing I couldn't handle.

We got up and started our slow trek to the garages, pushing through brothers, associates, and party girls who shared the evening cheer. Tank sat by himself on the outskirts, a bottle of whiskey at his side.

His loneliness made me wince, but so did seeing the poison. After what happened on that horrible night, I'd drink anything except whiskey. Wasn't sure I'd ever taste the stuff without retching up my dinner.

Blaze jerked the door to the garage open and we nearly ran smack into Stinger. The VP had his back to us near the door. He stood on the single step leading down as some girl below him had a mouthful of…

"Oh my God!" I started to laugh.

Stinger turned, red faced, frowning as big as he usually smiled. I never knew a man could zip up so quickly without getting it caught. The whore on the ground wiped her mouth and stood up, brushing dirt off her skirt like she'd been doing nothing crazier than sweeping up a spill.

"Hey, Prez. Goin' home?"

Blaze looked at him coolly. After an awkward minute, he threw one arm around Stinger's neck and pulled him in close.

"We'll all pretend we didn't fucking see that. It's too nice a night to dress you down for fucking around in the garages. Just get a fucking room, brother."

"You're the boss. Come on, Sangria." He tugged the girl up and pushed the door open, urging her ahead of him with a slap on the ass.

He paused just before going inside. "Damned good to see you two happy again. I just hope you can drag yourselves in tomorrow to greet Throttle's crew. Those boys are gonna be thirsty after a long ride, Saffron."

"Hey, fuck off, asshole," Blaze growled. "I know how to hold my booze and my dick. I can go all night and still put on a tie in the morning."

"Yeah, brother, maybe around your dick. We're all pretty fucking lucky there's not much to throwing on leather and jeans after a long night."

The men enjoyed a loud, raucous laugh before the VP disappeared inside, chasing down his girl. When we were finally alone, I burst out laughing. The rough way bikers razzed each other was like two bears wrestling, and it made me giggle every time.

Blaze looked at me with questioning eyes. I caught his gaze and held it. "Did you really mean that? Think you can handle me tonight without limping in tomorrow?"

He smiled at the challenge. I squealed as he swept me off the ground, throwing me high over his shoulder and carrying me to his bike.

"I'd fucking better, baby. Everybody sleeps better after they come, right? Gonna be doing a lot of that tonight. If we're not sleeping like babies for a few hours before sunup, then I know I'm getting old." He brought a palm to my ass and I jerked in his arms, delighted.

No matter how many times Blaze sat me on his backseat and fixed my helmet, I never stopped feeling all tingly. It was one more subtle way he loved me. Hell of an appetizer for what we had waiting for us at home too.

"You keep your hands above the waist while I'm driving," he warned. "You can have this all to yourself when we get home. Don't need my dick to blow up in my pants while I'm on the open road."

I laughed. He started the engine and hit the automatic switch behind him.

I held my hard, sexy, crude man as we roared onto the winding mountain roads. God help me, I didn't have a clue how I could hold any more love for him.

Then we got home and he had a surprise that knocked me stupid.

Blaze ravaged me.

No sooner than I stepped out of the bathroom after changing into fishnets, I propped myself against the door, running my splayed fingers along the fresh ink.

His muscles jerked and he sat up on our bed. "Holy fucking shit. Is that what I think it is?"

"Careful," I purred to him as he crossed the room. "It's a little tender. But it's all yours, *baby*."

I smiled, stealing his pet name for once. His hand caught me near the knee and slowly inched its way up, taking in the old lady's brand with his name on it.

"Property of Blaze," he said in a low whisper. "No shit. Hope you remember how well I treat everything I own."

"Show me," I said, pushing against his broad chest.

He pulled me in close and kissed me like a man possessed. My fingers tightened on his bare chest, running my nails down his ink as my hands glided over him. I reached into his boxers, the only thing he had on, and tugged at his magnificent cock.

It was hard, giving me a salute no other man could hope to match. I moaned into his mouth, never taking my fingers off his length, rubbing slowly up and down as we kissed.

His tongue pushed in, tasting me deeper, fucking past my lips. I must've been fooling myself if I thought I had a prayer of lasting in this heat.

I melted closer to him. When he felt my nipples against his skin, he cupped my ass in both hands, pulling me off my feet. My cue to hold onto his neck.

In an instant, we were across the room, and he rolled on top of me. Blaze kissed and sucked and ran his wicked mouth down to my breasts, making me whimper. My nipples plumped to lush fullness in his mouth, trained to dance so well against his tongue.

His flesh was getting hotter by the second. When he pushed one hand between my legs and found my clit, I jerked like he'd shot lightning through me. His laps moved faster, winding me up with heat and wetness, readying me for the inevitable.

He brought me to the very shaky, breathless edge. Orgasm teased my brain, a fire building in my cunt with evil need, tightening around his fingers each time he stroked me deep. Around and around and around like rampant clockwork.

He only stopped when he sensed me coming close, pausing to pull back and rip away his boxers.

"Not yet, baby," he growled. "Get on this dick and ride. I wanna see my new brand up close."

I smiled. No way to say no to that.

We rolled, and I straddled him, planting my hands perfectly around the devil on his chest. Their fierce expressions almost matched as I lowered myself onto his cock, cursing when he shifted deep inside me, finding his place.

"Oh, fuck," I hissed.

"No. You say that when we're going eighty miles an hour over the cliff, baby. We're not even doing fifty yet..."

His hips began to rock. This time wasn't slow and sensual, a gradual glide to release.

He fucked up into me like a fast moving storm, holding my ass and jerking it back and forth to match his thrusts. His eyes flicked from my swaying tits to the fresh tattoo, and it excited him a little more each time he saw it.

"Oh, fuck, oh, fuck, oh, fu–!"

Rude spasms cut me off. I convulsed on his cock, whipping my head back and locking my legs around him. I couldn't move another muscle because everything below my waist turned to stone, but he kept me going, shifting me hard onto his length when he buried himself deep.

Fire, fire, nothing but endless fire.

I was barely finished coming when he kicked into a higher gear, bouncing me so high on his cock the old mattress beneath us shook and shrieked. A wilder ecstasy flooded my veins, energizing me again.

An old lady gives as well as she receives...

Through the sweet madness, I focused on him. I rolled my hips forward, fucking him the same way I used to dance, jerking him off in my wet, hot, hungry heat. I wanted to milk every last drop from his balls and feel his muscles stiffen in passion.

I pushed my fingers into his and rode harder. Must've been doing something right, because soon his fingers were locked on mine like a vice. Our romp was becoming more like some strange dance than two people in bed fucking.

I sweated, I screamed, I ground my hips into him. I saw his eyes roll and lose their focus just one second before I exploded a second time. Blaze took one last look at my rippling tattoos and came with me.

Savage little growls and sharp gasps snorted out our lips. Every muscle from my head to the ends of his toes seized up, burned, and pulsed in a shower of sparks. Our release moved in a wave, all pure fire, ending in the thick ropes he hurled into my womb.

I choked a little when it finally stopped. It was like my body had tried to digest a slice of something too good, too pure for this world.

"Come here, pretty woman. Rest your head on old scratch. Need you to catch your breath before we do anything else..."

He slid out of me and pulled me in, nestling me perfectly on his chest. I listened to the steady thump in his chest slowly calming, recovering its normal beat.

We lay like that together for a solid minute before he reached to the nightstand.

"Been saving this for a special night. It's my call, and I've decided it's this one."

I blinked and lifted my head. He helped me sit up and shoved a small object with smooth edges into my hand.

When I saw it was a ring box, my heart almost stopped. I would've dropped the damned thing if Blaze didn't wrap my little hands in his and give them a good squeeze.

"I've never been much for tradition, but this one's important. I already claimed you, baby. Now let's make it official." He fished the box from my hands and popped it open with his thumb, holding the ring out to me. "Will you marry me in Reno next year?"

Holy, holy shit. I tensed up. Never expected a man to propose to me naked and sweaty after sex, but somehow this was distinctly Blaze, and that meant it was totally perfect.

"Really need a yes," he said, a hint of nervousness creeping into his deep voice. "We can take a few weeks, go down to Reno, have the brothers take care of everything…"

"Oh, Michael. Oh, Blaze…it's not a yes. It's a *hell yes.*" I threw my arms around his huge neck, holding him so tight he forgot to breathe.

Smiling, he kissed me deep. He took the box, plucked the ring from its holder, and tossed the empty container across the room.

I laughed. That was all Blaze too. Typical, savage, and sweet.

The laughter faded when the ring was actually on my finger. It glowed beautifully in the dim lamplight. Couldn't wait to see how it looked out in the October sun tomorrow.

"Now kiss me again," he growled. "Those lips taste fucking awesome as my old lady. Always had a feeling they'd taste even sweeter as my wife."

Oh, I kissed him, all right.

I gave him a deep, wet, succulent kiss. It lasted so long the gold band on my finger heated with our passion, and soon was I underneath him, clawing at his back all over again.

Love like this is never for the faint of heart. I smiled, overflowing with love and pleasure, and it wasn't all the ring or the expert way he sent my flesh to heaven.

I knew I'd truly started the rest of my life, lost forever in this bad boy's raging love.

Thanks!

Want more Nicole Snow? Sign up for my newsletter to hear about new releases, subscriber only goodies, and other fun stuff!

JOIN THE NICOLE SNOW NEWSLETTER! - http://eepurl.com/HwFW1

Thank you so much for buying this book. I hope my romances will brighten your mornings and darken your evenings with total pleasure. Sensuality makes everything more vivid, doesn't it?

If you liked this book, please consider leaving a review and checking out my other erotic romance tales.

Got a comment on my work? Email me at nicolesnowerotica@gmail.com. I love hearing from my fans!

Kisses,
Nicole Snow

More Erotic Romance by Nicole Snow

SEXY SAMPLES: NOMAD KIND OF LOVE

He looked me up and down. My panties drowned with wet heat, forced out as his eyes crawled over my flushed skin.

I was losing control, and it felt good. Damned good.

Where the hell had the shrieking bitch gone? Was she really put down so easy by a few shots?

"You know, I've seen hundreds of guys watching me shake my thing. But nobody watched me the way you did that night."

"Yeah?"

The air between us swarmed with heat and pheromones. Maverick recognized the animal glint in my eyes and threw his arms around me at once, jerking me onto his lap.

Holy shit. What's happening? Why can't I stop?

The mutinous nub between my legs pulsed, sending rough, filthy fire straight up my core. It was like two years of pent up frustration boiled over at once.

I shouldn't have been surprised. A young girl can only hold her body under the big, sexy gun without going further for so long. I just never expected I'd throw myself at a biker – not a man like the brutes who'd wrecked my life.

Was I that f*cked up?

It sure didn't feel like it with his hot breath on me. Maverick leaned in, one little touch away from fusing his lips to mine. I wondered if he'd taste as good as he smelled.

"You like being watched, babe?" He was only an inch away, running the very tip of his tongue over his bottom lip.

Hearing him call me 'babe' didn't upset me anymore. It had a nice ring to it in his deep, slightly smoky, and very manly voice.

"I like touching more." Crap. I almost said *f*cking*, but then I would've sounded like a complete and total slut.

His hands tightened around me. *Good,* I thought.

Let him think I'm a wounded little birdie if it gives me this heat, this sweet distraction. Hell, maybe I need to let go a little. I need something new to take away the memories.

I wasn't a tiny girl, but Maverick was huge. His hands traveled lower down my back, stopping on my hips to squeeze and throw me forward.

My legs went around his waist, and I sensed the very edge of a raging hard-on below his jeans. My hips bucked instantly, grinding against him.

"F*ck!" he whispered, pressing one hand behind my head.

No more screwing around. He pulled me into him, and his lips were on mine. It was a world shattering a kiss, a kiss so wicked and intense it caused me to short circuit.

I moaned into his sweet lips, running my tongue across them...

Don't Miss Maverick and June's story in the second Outlaw Love book!

Look for Nomad Kind of Love at your favorite retailer!

73046966R00161

Made in the USA
Columbia, SC
01 September 2019